ORDINARY MAN

By R.J. Cadmus

ISBN: 9781522093640

For Dave – thanks for saving the life of my friend and your neighbor

***

"The mass of men lead lives of quiet desperation." – Henry David Thoreau

Chapter 1
Mid-April, Saturday

Bill Ward drove down the on-ramp and merged onto the highway. Not that much "merging" was required on a Saturday morning. During the week, this was part of his regular commute and the highway would frequently turn into a parking lot. But this morning traffic was light, and he quickly brought his Toyota Camry up to road speed.

It was just as well, since this was a typical Saturday for him and he had a lot to do. As usual, he'd gotten up around 7, made a quick breakfast and then took his yellow Lab, Buddy, out for a long walk. Buddy was 11-years-old now, and hadn't been quite right lately – ambling around a bit more slowly, sleeping a lot more, moving with some discomfort. But he still enjoyed his Saturday walks. Bill made a mental note to call the vet for an appointment.

Now he was headed for Home Depot to get weed killer and nylon line for his string trimmer. And 65-watt outdoor spotlight bulbs – one of the lights over the driveway was burned out. He didn't know why the builder had mounted it up near the eaves, but it meant he'd have to use the extension ladder to get to it.

After Home Depot, he had to stop off at the auto parts store – the cars needed oil changes this month. That would be a project for next Saturday morning, but he had to get oil, filters and other supplies so he'd be all set. He also had a couple gallons of used motor oil to drop off for recycling from last time he worked on the cars.

After the auto parts store, it would be back home to mow the lawn – with trimming and clean-up, it would take him a couple hours. It was almost impossible to keep ahead of it this time of year -- you could practically hear it growing. He could cut it every five days and still not keep up. It had been a week since last time he mowed and with all the rain since then it would be heavy and succulent – a real pain to deal with. He'd be lucky if it only took two hours.

Focused on his thoughts, Bill barely noticed the tractor-trailer about a half-mile ahead of him. The truck was hauling a flatbed trailer loaded with large spools of metal cable, each roughly six feet in diameter and weighing several thousand pounds apiece. The truck had just started climbing a slight incline when it hit a bump in the road. For some reason, that was enough to jolt loose a tie-down holding one of the spools onto the trailer.

The truck driver instantly felt the load shift and slammed on the brakes, nearly jackknifing the rig. In his side-view mirror he saw the spool of cable roll off the back of the trailer and begin spinning and wobbling wildly across the roadway.

It smashed a small Honda sedan before rolling off the highway into the woods. A minivan following close behind veered sharply to avoid the Honda, went out of control and ran off the road on the right side, straight into a concrete overpass.

Bill saw the whole thing happen ahead of him as if in slow motion. He braked his car and pulled off the road, stopping about 30 feet from the minivan. He could hear other cars on the highway slowing to move past the wreckage of the Honda and steer around the truck, but no one else stopped. As he exited his car, he saw the truck driver descend from the cab of his truck and yelled to him to call 911.

He approached the minivan and saw the front end was smashed nearly flat against the concrete abutment. He could smell gasoline and hear the pinging and popping of the hot engine. The fuel line had ruptured in the crash, and gasoline was pouring out onto the engine block and pooling under the van.

In the driver's seat, he could see a woman slumped over, unconscious. The airbag had deployed and knocked her out. The door was locked and he couldn't open it, so he thought for a second about how to get her out.

He reached into his back pocket and removed a knife. It was the liner-lock with a black aluminum skeleton frame and three-and-a-half-inch blade that he normally carried on the weekend for use around the house and in the yard. He grasped the closed knife in his right hand, fingers wrapped around it and thumb over the top, with about an inch of the frame sticking out at the bottom of his fist.

Turning his head away from the window, he swung his arm down in an arc so that the butt of the knife struck the glass. It shattered immediately, and he was able to reach in and open the door.

The woman was held into the seat by her safety belt, and he couldn't reach the buckle, so he flicked the thumb stud on the blade to open it and quickly sliced through the fabric of the belt. Without thinking, he refolded the knife and stuck it back in his pocket, then started pulling the woman from the wreckage.

He heard her groan, even though he was lifting her out as gently as he could. After she was free of the vehicle, he half-dragged, half-carried her over to where his car was parked. As he set her on the ground, she came around and spoke in a groggy voice.

"What happened?"

"You were in a car accident."

"Is my baby okay?"

Bill heard the infant crying in the van. He didn't know why he hadn't heard it before – it probably had been crying the whole time.

He went back to the vehicle and saw a baby wearing a pink jacket and a bow in her hair, strapped into a safety seat in the back of the van, screaming but apparently unhurt. He reached around through the broken front window, unlocked the rear door and slid it open.

The gasoline odor was stronger now, and he also could smell smoke and see it rising from the under the crumpled hood. He unbuckled the baby from her car seat, gently lifted her out, carried her over to his car, and laid her on top of her mother. The woman, still semi-conscious, said nothing but instinctively clutched the baby. Bill opened the trunk of his car, pulled out an old blanket he kept there, and placed it over them both.

He then heard a loud "woof" and turned to see the front end of the minivan burst into flames. The fire quickly spread to the gasoline that had spilled on the ground and made its way back to the fuel tank. Soon the entire vehicle was engulfed in fire. The heat from the fire was intense, even from 30 feet away, and he wondered if he should move the mother and daughter farther from it. But he suddenly was too tired.

He slowly sat down on the ground and sat there a bit stunned.

Fire trucks, ambulances and police cars had begun to arrive. The firefighters focused their attention on putting out the fire and attending to the Honda, which was squashed nearly flat.

A local police patrolman approached Bill, and asked him what happened.

Bill absently recounted the last few moments … was it 30 seconds or five minutes? Time ceased to matter and it was almost as if someone else was saying the words. He briefly described the accident and what he did afterward. A pair of emergency medical technicians began attending to the woman and her baby. A television news truck pulled up and started filming the scene.

The patrolman continued his query of Bill.

"You okay?"

"Yeah, I think so. A little lightheaded, I guess."

"You're probably in shock. And your hand is bleeding."

"Oh."

Bill looked down absently at his right hand, where blood was running out a long gash on the heel.

"I guess I did it when I broke the glass."
The patrolman asked one of the EMTs to take a look at Bill. After the EMT bandaged his hand, Bill spoke to him and tried to get up.

"I think I'm okay."

The patrolman put out a hand, gesturing him to stay put.

"Why don't you just sit there for a minute? I think maybe we ought to take you to the hospital, get you checked out."

"No, I'm all right. I can't just leave my car here."

"Don't worry about it – it will be fine. We should get you checked over, and we'll need to get a statement from you for the accident report."

"Okay."

***

Television reporter Dave Streader and his cameraman climbed out of their remote truck and quickly got to work. They were lucky to have been nearby when they heard the emergency call on the scanner in their truck and arrived at the accident scene almost before the first-responders did.

He spoke to the cameraman as they exited the van.

"Jerry, get B-roll of that fire first – firemen are gonna put that out pretty quick. Then get that Honda, the tractor trailer, the fire trucks and cop cars and anything else that looks interesting. We can sort it out later in editing. I'll go find out what happened."

The newest reporter at local NBC affiliate WEST, Dave usually drew weekend duty, but he didn't mind too much, particularly when something like this was going on. "If it bleeds, it leads," the old news business expression goes, and it's true. He was young and he still dug the rush he'd get when he was sitting in the van and the police scanner went wild. It beat the heck out of covering city council meetings anyway.

He walked over to one of the police officers.

"Hey, Bobby, what's up? Boy, what a mess."

"Yeah. That tractor trailer up there dumped part of its load – one of those bobbins of steel cable. Crushed that Honda pretty quick – guy inside didn't know what hit him, never had a chance."

"Anybody else hurt?"

"Woman and her baby were in that minivan over there."

The patrolman gestured over to where they were lying.

"EMTs are checking them out now."

"Who's that guy sitting next to them?"

"Dunno – some guy. Pulled the lady and her kid out of the van before it blew up."

"No kidding. Who is he?"

"I said I don't know – just some guy driving by."

"He okay?"

"I think so, but I think they're going to take him in to the hospital with the lady and the baby."

"You think I could go over and talk to him?"

"Hmm, better not – he seems a bit spaced, and we haven't gotten his statement yet."

Dave didn't really need permission, but he also knew that ignoring the patrolman's request could mean getting the cold shoulder from him and the other officers in the future. It might even get him frozen out of another story down the road, so better to play it cool and do as he'd been asked.

"Okay … I understand. Where are they taking them?"

"Probably Stanhope Memorial."

"All right, I'll see if I can catch up with him there. You think someone can give me a stand-up on what happened here?"

"Sure, lemme go find the chief for you."

"Thanks, Bobby."

Dave then turned and yelled to his cameraman.

"Jerry get some footage of that guy over there, and that lady and her baby."

The reporter and cameraman shot their standup with Chief Forgas, who did a good job of succinctly describing what happened. He'd been in office for about 10 years and knew what he was doing when it came to talking to a TV reporter. Keep it tight, stick to the facts, try to say something in a nice bite-sized quote.

"Tragic accident. It was a gutsy move for that guy to pull that lady and her baby from a burning car."

Good story, Dave thought. And they had good visuals to with it. Local hero saves woman and baby – people love stuff like that. The network might pick it up and go national with it.

Dave and Jerry finished their interview with the chief and stuck around until Bill, the woman and her daughter were loaded into an ambulance. Then they climbed back in their van and headed for the hospital.

***

A bald man in a lab coat stepped inside the curtain in the emergency room cubicle and spoke to Bill Ward.

"Hello, I'm Dr. Gupta. How are you feeling, Mr. Ward?"

"I'm okay. I was a little dizzy before, but I feel okay now."

"Yes, well, you've had quite a morning. The lightheadedness was probably just the adrenaline crash after what you experienced. But let me check you over anyway, just in case. Who is your primary physician?"

"Um, Doctor Bynes, at Southwest Regional Family Practice."

"Oh, good. They're in our network, so I can pull up your medical records."

Dr. Gupta accessed Bill's files on a tablet.

"Says here you're up to date on tetanus, so we shouldn't have to worry about that. Let me just check a few things, and then I want to take a look at the hand."

Dr. Gupta checked Bill's heart rate, blood pressure, eyes for dilation, and breathing. Everything appeared normal. He removed the bandage on Bill's right hand and carefully inspected the gash.

"I want to poke around in this a little bit – make sure there's no dirt or glass stuck in it, and then put in a few stitches. This could be a little uncomfortable, so I want to give you a local anesthetic."

Dr. Gupta gave him a shot, cleaned the wound, and stitched it up.

"Try to keep it dry. Use a waterproof bandage on your hand when you shower. Take ibuprofen if it hurts. And you'll need to get the stitches out in about two weeks. Your regular doctor can do it. Other than that, I think you're fine. One of the nurses will be in to have you sign some paperwork and then you can be on your way."

"Do you know how that lady and her baby are doing?"

"They've been admitted for some minor injuries, but nothing too serious I don't think. My guess is they'll be discharged in a day or two."

"Oh good. Geez, what time is it?"

"It's about 1 p.m., Mr. Ward."

"Oh man! I better call my wife. I was planning to be home hours ago. She's going to be pretty mad."

He reached for his cell phone, and then realized he'd left it in his car.

"You saved two lives today, Mr. Ward. Under the circumstances, I think she'll understand."

"Is there a phone here I can use?"

Chapter 2

If they were being honest, everyone who knew Bill – personally, professionally or socially – would use the same word to describe him: average. Average height, average build, average looks. Reasonably smart. Even tempered. Modest, friendly, polite. Not a funny guy, but knew a funny joke when he heard it. Pretty good health – a little back trouble, knees getting a bit tender, some eczema during the winter, fighting the spread around his middle.

An average man with an average background. Good parents, two siblings, modest home, middle-class neighborhood, nice town. In high school, a two-sport varsity letterman and honor student, but neither the best athlete nor the brightest student – what he lacked in natural gifts he made up for with effort.

After high school, he attended one of the more selective public universities, but it was still a state school. He majored in business, studied hard, made dean's list. He met a girl he liked. He participated in social activities, but not too much. He graduated, got married, began a career. He started a family, bought a home. He worked hard, started to move up through the ranks at work – associate, team leader, manager, director. He participated in activities at his church and in his community. He lived a quiet, content, normal life.

As he entered his 40s, things began to slow down a bit. His progress at work cooled and his career trajectory began to flatten. His wife withdrew as the years passed – perhaps a bit bored with their life, their home, with him. As they progressed through their teens, his son and daughter became a bit distant, developing into their adult selves and finding it harder to relate to him.

His experience was one shared by many men his age. The way they react to that reality varies widely.

Some make a radical change – they quit their jobs and find new ones or start ventures of their own, with varying degrees of success and failure. Others dive into hobbies, from model trains to restoring classic cars. Some strike out to reclaim their health and vigor – exercising, losing weight, competing in marathons and triathlons. Or they pour themselves into service activities – church, Kiwanis, Little League, local politics.

And some go full-blown middle-age crazy – buying a motorcycle, a convertible or a boat. Getting liposuction, a face lift, a tummy tuck. Dumping the wife and taking up with a woman half their age, whose attention they'd hold only until the money ran out.

Bill chose none of these – none of them suited him, and would have felt silly and wrong if he tried them on for size. He accepted his middle years, the plateau of his prospects and his growing isolation with resignation and resolve. His values and his responsibilities were more important to him than any satisfaction he might derive from any of the usual diversions.

Average. And probably a little boring.

Nothing in his temperament, his behavior or his experience would have led anyone to predict that he'd do what he did that Saturday morning out on the highway.

***

Maggie paced through the kitchen, picked up the cordless phone and called Bill's cell a third time. After several rings it went straight through to voicemail. Again. As the morning progressed into early afternoon and he hadn't returned or called, her emotions progressed from impatience to annoyance, to anger, to anxiety. This was not like him.

Their daughter Olive called from the family room.

"Mom. Come in here and look at this. Daddy's on TV!"

"What?"

Maggie walked into the family room and looked at the screen. Channel 8 was broadcasting a news bulletin about a bad accident on the highway that morning. Bill would have gone by there.

The camera showed the firemen dousing the flaming minivan, the crushed Honda, the big semi idle in the road.

And then she saw him – Bill sitting on the ground, bandage on his hand, two EMTs nearby tending to a couple figures lying under a blanket. The blanket from Bill's trunk.

The reporter described the scene, then interviewed a policeman who said the man sitting nearby – Bill – had rescued a woman and a baby from the burning wreck.

Maggie felt the blood drain from her head, and sat down on the couch next to Buddy, who looked up at her curiously.

The phone in the kitchen rang.

***

Maggie looked at the caller ID on the phone – it said Stanhope Memorial Hospital -- and she picked up the receiver to answer.

"Hello?"

"Hi, Maggie. It's Bill."

"Where are you?"

"At the hospital. Almost done here. There was an accident, and …"

"I know – it's on TV. Are you okay?"

"Yeah, I'm okay."

"Do you need me to come get you?"

"No. I have to give the police a statement about what happened, and then they said they'd take me back to my car."

"How long will that take?"

"I don't know – maybe an hour or so."

"Why didn't you answer my calls? I've been worried."

"Sorry – I left my phone in my car. It's been kind of crazy. This is the first chance I had to call you."

"Well, call me when you are headed home."

"Okay."

There was a flat quality to the conversation, an almost business-like dryness, lacking any feeling. They rarely shared emotions with each other, even strong ones. Certainly not on the phone, and when necessary only in the most private moments. Typically it was when she was expressing displeasure and dissatisfaction in general, or with him.

***

As Bill hung up the phone in the reception area, he saw the patrolman from the accident scene walking over to him.

"Mr. Ward, I'd like to take your statement now if you don't mind. We can sit in the lobby – it shouldn't take long. Then I'll take you back to your car."

"Oh, okay officer. You can call me Bill."

"I'm Patrolman Bob Sturgis."

They sat for about 15 minutes, went over his personal details and what he remembered about the accident. Bill told him everything he could recall.

"Okay, I think that about does it, Mr. Ward. We'll be in touch if there's anything else we need. You'll probably be contacted by the insurance companies as well, and probably some lawyers."

"Lawyers?"

"Yes. I wouldn't be surprised if there weren't lawsuits after an accident like this, and you saw the whole thing. Why don't we head out to my patrol car?

"Okay."

"I should warn you – there's a bunch of reporters waiting for you outside."

"Reporters?"

"Yeah –what you did today is pretty big news. They have most of the details from the police chief, but I'm sure they'll want a statement from you. You don't have to talk to them if you don't want to."

"I don't really know what to tell them."

The patrolman sympathized with Bill. Law enforcement professionals saw tragedies like this all the time and learned to cope with it. But something like this could be a bit overwhelming for the average citizen. And Bill seemed like a good guy – he certainly went out of his way to do the right thing that morning.

"Well, we'll move along pretty quickly then."

There were about a half dozen reporters and a couple TV cameramen waiting for them when they emerged from the emergency department. One of them spotted Bill and the police officer and began shouting.

"Mr. Ward? Are you Bill Ward?"

"Yes."

The reporters took turns peppering him with questions while the video crews recorded the scene.

"Can you tell us what happened this morning?"

"Well, I think you know all about the accident."

"Can you tell us what you saw and what you did?"

"Well, after the big reel of wire fell off the truck and smashed that one car, I saw a minivan run off the road and hit the overpass. So I pulled over, and helped get a woman and her baby out of it."

"Was the car on fire when you got to it?"

"No, but I could smell gas. It started to burn right after I got the baby out."

"What happened to your hand?"

"Oh."

Bill looked down at his hand self-consciously.

“I cut it breaking the window. I couldn’t get the door open so I had to smash the glass.”

“What did you smash the glass with?”

“I used the handle of my pocket knife.”

“Why were you carrying a knife?”

“I always carry one.”

“Why?”

“You never know when you might need one.”

“Like today?”

“I suppose so, yes.”

“Can you show it to us?”

Bill pulled the knife out of his pocket and held it up for the reporters and cameramen.

The questions continued and Bill recounted his own actions plainly, with no bravado or embellishment. He started to look uncomfortable and shot a glance to the patrolman that said “Get me out of here.” Before they could depart, a reporter shot one more question at him.

“Why did you do it? What made you stop and pull that lady and her kid out of that car?”

Bill looked puzzled by the question, and after pausing to ponder a response he shrugged and answered matter-of-factly.

“They looked like they needed help.”

The patrolman then intervened, saying “Okay, guys we have to go.” He led Bill to the patrol car, as a couple of reporters shouted questions after them.

***

Bill slid into the passenger side of the police car and spoke to the patrolman.

“Thanks for getting me out of there.”

“You looked like you’d had enough.”

“You ever talk to reporters like that before.”

"No."

"You know anyone who has?"

"My neighbor's in public relations. I don't know much about what he does, but I'm pretty sure he deals with the media."

"You might want to call him. This may not be the last of it."

***

When the patrolman returned Bill to his car, he checked his phone and saw there were six messages – three from Maggie, which reminded him to let her know he was headed home He started the car and pulled onto the highway.

Within 15 minutes he was a few blocks from the house. A car rolled through a stop sign and cut him off, but he saw it in time to avoid an accident. He didn't even bother to honk the horn.

As he pulled the car into the driveway, he hit the button on the garage door remote to open the door, paused while it rose, and then pulled the car in. He turned off the ignition, hit the garage door remote again to close the door, and sat for a minute.

Maggie and Olive both heard the garage door go up and then down, and went into the kitchen to wait for Bill. He came through the door from the garage and stopped when he saw them standing there.

"Hi."

Olive greeted him

"Hi, Daddy. We saw you on TV."

"Oh."

Maggie spoke to Olive.

"Olive can you go into the family room and let Daddy and me talk for a minute?"

"Okay.

Olive walked over, gave her father a hug and left the room.

Maggie spoke to Bill, her voice tense.

"Are you okay?"

"Yeah."

"What happened to your hand?"

"Just a couple stitches. It's okay."

"Is it? What were you thinking?

"I don't know. Are you mad at me?"

"No … no. I was just … worried, and scared. You could have been killed."

"It really wasn't that bad, Maggie."

"I saw the TV! The man in that car was killed. And that fire!"

"He was killed before I got there. And the van didn't catch on fire until after I … after I got the lady and her daughter out."

"Are they okay?"

"Doctor at the hospital said they'd be alright."

"Do you need anything?"

"I don't think so. Oh … doctor says I can't get this wet. Do we have any waterproof bandages?"

"I'll have to check in the linen closet."

"I can do it. I need a couple Advil too. I know where they are."

With nothing else to say, Bill left the room. He went upstairs, checked the linen closet – no bandages. He'd have to get some later. Or tomorrow. He took a couple Ibuprofen tablets, changed into his work clothes and then headed back downstairs.

He walked through the kitchen, headed for the garage. Maggie looked up from the counter, puzzled, and spoke to him.

"Where are you going?"

"Mow the lawn."

"Now? After … today?"

"It won't mow itself. Supposed to rain tomorrow."

Maggie started to object, and then stopped herself.

"Okay. Dinner is around 6. Olive's going out tonight, with TJ."

"Oh. Okay."

He didn't like TJ.

He walked out into the garage, pulled out the lawnmower, gassed it up, hit the primer three times, depressed the dead man's switch, pulled the lanyard to start the motor, and pushed the mower out to the lawn.

Chapter 3

After he finished mowing the lawn, Bill went inside. Maggie was about to put dinner on the table, so he washed his hands and sat down to eat.

The television wasn't on, so they didn't see it, but the evening news had just started.

While the news program was in commercial, anchors Bart Gardetto and Liz Ross chatted with reporter Dave Streader, who was doing a live remote from the scene of the accident earlier in the day. Most of his report was recorded and edited, but he would open the report live and offered them suggestions on questions they could ask him to close the segment.

"Okay, that's pretty much how the story goes – whole thing runs under two minutes. At the end you could ask me about the knife he used to break the window and cut the seatbelts, and you could ask me about the condition of the woman and her baby."

Bart responded.

"He had a knife with him?"

"Yeah, says he usually carries one."

"Okay, I think we're all set. Thanks Dave."

The program returned from commercial and, Bart looked at the camera and read from the teleprompter.

"Welcome back. Next fall's elections are beginning to heat up, with the local public employees union in Bridgeton announcing that they are endorsing Democratic candidate Mario Vallone in his run for mayor. Vallone has served as the city's controller for the past six years, and said he was gratified and encouraged by the endorsement."

Liz commented.

"So I guess you could say the city workers are pro Vallone."

"Yes. But they're also on the record as being anti-pasto."

They both chuckled, and then Liz addressed the camera.

“Tragedy on the highway this morning, as a terrifying accident left one man dead and sent three more people to the hospital. But the devastation could have been far worse, if not for the quick action of a local man. WEST reporter Dave Streader was at the scene.”

The screen cut to the scene of the accident, showing Streader with the burned out hulk of the minivan behind him, and he spoke to the camera.

“It happened in an instant, when a giant spool of steel cable broke loose from a flatbed trailer this morning at about 9:30, rolling across the highway and leaving a trail of death and destruction in its wake.”

The screen cut to a series of shots recorded earlier, showing the tractor trailer, the crushed Honda, and the burning minivan with firefighters extinguishing the blaze. Streader’s voiceover continued as the images flashed.

“Thirty-one-year-old Roberto Gonzales of Stonefield Center was killed instantly when the reel of heavy wire crushed his car. A second vehicle, the minivan you see here engulfed in flames managed to avoid the oncoming wheel of cable, but the driver lost control, slamming into the overpass abutment.

“Trapped inside the vehicle were 28-year-old Shannon Gales and her infant daughter, Lucy. The woman was knocked unconscious by the crash, and both she and her child would have likely been incinerated by the fire resulting from a ruptured fuel line. Fortunately for them, Derbeville resident Bill Ward stopped when he saw the wreck and quickly came to their aid.”

The screen cut to a shot of Ward sitting on the ground near his car, with the Shannon and Lucy nearby being treated by the EMTs.

“Ward ran to the vehicle, and finding the doors locked, smashed a window with the handle of a pocket knife, cut the seatbelts and dragged the woman and her daughter to safety just seconds before the minivan erupted in flames. Emergency responders were quickly on the scene, extinguishing the fire and tending to the accident victims.”

The screen cut to Police Chief Forgas, who quickly summarized what happened.

"The preliminary results of our investigation indicate a chain holding the spool of cable broke, releasing it onto the roadway and causing the accident. We're still investigating the incident, but there's no indication that the truck driver was speeding or driving recklessly – just one of those things. Of course, the death of the young man is tragic, but under the circumstances it could have been far worse. Horrible accident. It was a gutsy move for that guy to rescue that woman and her baby from a burning car."

The screen cut to the scene outside of the hospital when Bill Ward and the patrolman exited, and Dave's report continued.

"The young woman and her baby were taken to Stanhope Memorial Hospital for treatment of their injuries. Mr. Ward was also examined and treated at the hospital for a minor wound he received on his hand when he broke the glass. We caught up with him there."

The screen cut to Bill Ward and Patrolman Sturgis exiting the hospital, and then Bill addressing the reporters.

"When I got to the van, I could smell gasoline and could see the woman was unconscious. The door was locked, so I smashed the window, like this (demonstrating his downward stroke), opened the door from the inside. Then I cut the seatbelt and pulled her out. When I put her down, she said something about her baby, so I ran back to the van and got the girl out."

The scene switched to one of Bill and the patrolman leaving to exiting, and a reporter off camera could be heard shouting one final question.

"Why did you do it?"

"They looked like they needed help."

The screen split between the reporter at the scene of the accident and the anchors at the studio. Bart engaged Dave to wrap up the segment.

"What a dramatic rescue."

"Yes, I would imagine Mr. Ward had no idea his day would turn out this way. But there's no question that this man is a hero tonight."

Liz addressed Dave.

"Why did he have a knife?"

"He said he always carries one. Looks like it was a good idea he had it with him today."

"I'll say. And how are the mother and daughter doing?"

"Hospital officials say they're both doing fine, with only minor injuries. They're being kept overnight for observation and treatment, and will most likely be released tomorrow."

Bart closed the segment.

"Well, thank you, Dave, for that incredible report. And we'll return in a moment with more news and the weather forecast for tomorrow, after this commercial break."

Earlier that afternoon, the Associated Press had put out a story on the accident from one of the local newspapers in its network, drawing interest from national media. By later that evening all the major television networks and cable news outlets had picked up the report from WEST.

***

Bryce Ward was lying on the top bunk in his dorm room at Northern Connecticut State University, thinking about his options for the evening. It was about 8:30, and he and his roommate, Donnie Walbridge, had returned from dinner in the cafeteria about an hour before.

That cute girl, Eve, from Bryce's economics class had told him there would be a party in her dorm just across the quad that evening. The two of them had been flirting for a few weeks now, and he figured it was about time he made a move. Dorm parties were usually boring affairs, but he thought maybe he could convince her to leave for a drink at one of the bars off campus.

Donnie was at his desk looking at his laptop when he called up to Bryce.

"Hey Bryce, I think your Dad is on the news."

“For what?”

“Some accident. Pulled a woman and her baby out of a burning car.”

“No way – can’t be him,”

“Sure looks like him.”

Bryce jumped down from the bunk and looked over Donnie’s shoulder at the computer, a tab open to CNN’s Web site. Accompanying the story was a photo of Bill Ward sitting near the woman and her baby, with the burning van in the background. Bryce nudged Donnie and asked him to play the video accompanying the article. Donnie spoke first after the video ended.

“Well that was something.”

“Yeah. Wow. Huh. Never would have guessed he could do something like that.”

Bryce reached for his phone and called home.

***

TJ dropped Olive off at home at 11:30 p.m. She ran in the house after exiting the car, looking back once as she ran up the steps and in through the front door. He backed the car out of the driveway, and took off down the darkened street, frustrated.

The evening hadn’t really gone as he’d hoped. He and Olive had been going out for a couple months now, and his plan had been to close the deal tonight. He’d even cleaned all the Red Bull cans and Whopper packages out of the back seat for the occasion.

He’d been building up to it for a while, adding a little pressure every time they went out, taking things just a little further. Olive was a “nice” girl, and he knew you couldn’t rush her type. Frankly, he was surprised she even talked to him when he approached her at a party a few months back.

He wasn't the kind of guy he thought she'd normally hang out with – not exactly honor-roll and debate-team material. But he was smart and quick, and ran with the wilder crowd at school, popular in his own circle. He'd been doing some parties as a DJ and rapper under the name TJ Cool, and was starting to attract a following.

He was also the guy to see at school if you wanted to buy a little weed, coke or oxy. Nothing big time – he didn't want to do anything that might attract the attention of the cops. But enough to keep his car running, buy him the clothes he wanted, let him do whatever he liked, and start building up a pile of cash for after high school.

Graduation was just a couple months away, and he figured he go a little bigger with one last push – take advantage of all the kids celebrating, cash in on all those checks from relatives they'd be receiving. Then, he'd move out to LA, work his way into the music business. Maybe do a little dealing there to tide him over until he broke in.

There was no room in that plan for Olive, but she didn't need to know that. In the meantime, tonight was going to be the night for her. He'd put in the time and had been moving her along. And if she wasn't quite ready to go along, TJ didn't usually take "no" for answer.

But after she told him about what happened with her father that day, he figured he better hold off. He'd previously written off her dad as one of the usual clueless middle-aged loser parents of the girls he went out with. But now he figured there might be more to this guy than he originally had thought. The last thing he wanted to have to deal with was some psycho dad pissed off because someone had messed with his daughter.

***

Olive came in the front door and walked into the kitchen to say good night to her mother. Buddy raised his head, but didn't get up from his bed over by the back door. She gave him a pat, talked with her mother for a few minutes, gave her a kiss and went upstairs to bed.

Maggie sat for a minute longer, then got up, rinsed out her tea cup, put it in the dishwasher, turned off the kitchen light and headed upstairs. Bill was in bed asleep, the lights and TV still on. He must be exhausted, she thought.

She clicked the TV and lights off, and went in the bathroom to prepare for bed. About 15 minutes later, she crawled into bed next to her husband, being careful not to wake him.

She thought about what had happened that day and tried to sort through it. She was upset, annoyed, frightened and more than a little surprised. At this point in their relationship, Bill was nothing if not predictable – sometimes frustratingly so. But what he'd done that morning had shaken her complacency and shattered all her assumptions about him.

She lay awake for a long time, wondering who the man lying next to her really was.

***

Sunday

Bill was the first one up on Sunday morning, around 7. He showered quickly while Maggie dozed, then dressed and went downstairs. He put on a pot of coffee, and heard Maggie start the shower upstairs.

Buddy lifted his head as he watched Bill fill a bowl with dog food and place it on the floor, then rose slowly and lumbered across the kitchen to eat his breakfast. After finishing, he took a long drink from his water bowl and then sauntered over to the back door, his tail wagging slowly. Bill let Buddy out the back door to do his business, following him out and grabbing a small shovel from the back deck to clean up after him.

A few minutes later, they returned to the kitchen. Bill poured a cup of coffee, added some milk from the fridge and sat at the kitchen table, while Buddy returned to his bed.

***

"Hoo boy, here we go."

Howard Jones stood at the front window of his house looking across the street at the Ward's home. It was only 7:30 a.m. and it was already getting busy. Several television satellite trucks were parked along the curb, and a small crowd of reporters, photographers and TV cameramen had started to mass on the sidewalk and front lawn.

Howard had heard about the accident from his wife the previous evening, and had checked the coverage online and on television before calling over to talk to Bill. Maggie had said Bill was already in bed, and she'd have him call back in the morning.

He had hoped to have time to speak with Bill before it got busy with the media this morning, but unfortunately hadn't had the opportunity yet. He and Bill had grown pretty close over the past couple years, but the relationship hadn't taken hold instantly.

The Joneses had moved in about five years before. Howard wasn't crazy about being one of the few black families in the neighborhood, but his wife, Judy, loved the house and they both liked the schools for their kids. Maggie had been especially nice to Judy, quickly settling her into the community. But he and Bill just didn't seem to have much in common – just another boring suburban white guy spending way too much time on his lawn.

They got along well enough – small talk at the occasional neighborhood barbecue, but that was about it. And he didn't see any reason for it to go any further.

But things had changed a couple years later. Howard had injured his back that fall – two ruptured discs in his lower spine, requiring surgery and a long recovery. Winter came early, dropping snow about once a week from about mid-November through February. The first time it happened, he realized he hadn't made any arrangements for getting the driveway and sidewalks cleared, and he was expressly forbidden by his doctors to do it himself. He made an effort to head outside anyway, but was stopped cold when Judy just about threw a fit.

He watched helplessly as she and his two daughters, Jasmine and Jade, bundled up to go outside and start shoveling, when he saw Bill steaming across the street with his snow blower. Bill quickly cleared the driveway and then grabbed a shovel to clean up the walks and front steps. Judy brought him coffee and thanked him, and Howard waved from the window. Bill then went home and went to work on his on driveway and sidewalks.

The next week, another snowstorm, and once again Bill took care of the Jones' driveway, this time bringing his teenage son, Bryce, along to help. When they finished, Howard went outside and thanked them. Bill smiled and waved before heading home.

The third time it happened, Howard grabbed a couple cups of coffee, threw on a jacket and some boots and headed outside as Bill finished up.

"Here, thought you could use a cup of coffee."

"Thanks."

"Thank YOU, for taking care of my driveway and stuff. I wish I could do it myself, but …"

"I know. It's no big deal. Glad to help out."

"Well, it's a heck of an inconvenience. You haven't done your own yet. I wish there was something I could do in return."

"That's not necessary. Like I said, it's no big deal. You'd do the same for me, right?"

"Sure."

Although he answered affirmatively, Howard really wasn't sure he would have been as generous to Bill. The situation puzzled him, and he continued.

"Can I ask you a question?"

"Sure."

"Why are you doing this?"

Bill looked a bit puzzled by the question, hesitating for a second before responding.

“You’re my neighbor. You need the help.”

“Really? It’s as simple as that?”

“Yeah.”

Spurred by the simple guilelessness of the response, Howard became more candid in return.

“You know, to be honest, I don’t even like you that much.”

“I know.”

“You do?”

“Look, we live across the street from each other. Our wives like each other, our daughters are friends, and our kids all go to the same schools. And there are plenty of families just like us in this neighborhood.”

“I suppose so.”

“It doesn’t mean we all have to be best friends. But if we can just try to get along, look out for each other a little bit, help each other out when we can, it just makes it better for everyone in the long run. Right?”

“Right. I guess so. Yeah.”

“In fact, in some ways it’s probably better if we’re *not* best friends. Otherwise we could end up like Doug Heffernan and Deacon Palmer on ‘The King of Queens’ – always getting into each other’s business. And who needs that?”

“Doug and Deacon, huh? And which one would I be in that scenario?”

“You’d be Deacon.”

“Riiiiiight …”

“Because you’re taller.”

“Oh … uh, right.”

“So, right now you need help with your driveway. It’s no big deal. It’s just what neighbors do for each other. Anyway, thanks for the coffee.”

After that, their relationship warmed. Howard realized there was more to Bill than he'd originally thought. There was a simple decency about him that Howard found very compelling. And there were worse things in the world than having a dependable neighbor with a lawn fetish.

Now Bill was the one who needed some neighborly help, and Howard was going to take care of it.

"Judy, I'm going across the street to the Ward's"

Judy started to respond and then looked out the window.

"So early? ... Holy Moses! Yeah, you better get over there."

"Be back in a while."

"Tell Maggie to call me."

***

Howard walked quickly across the street, and a couple of the members of the assembled press corps recognized him right away. He had gotten there in time, just before one of the reporters knocked on the front door. He moved around to the front of the crowd, positioning himself between them and the house. At six-foot-five and 230 pounds, he could be a bit imposing, and he used his size and height to full advantage in letting them know who was in charge.

"Good morning, ladies and gentleman, for those you who don't know me, I'm Howard Jones, senior vice president at Bonham Kramer Powell Communications. I'll be representing the Wards today. If you could please provide your business cards, and if you don't mind please try to watch the lawn. The man is very meticulous about his grass, so if you could please stay on the sidewalk and driveway, I'm sure he would appreciate it. Then I'll go have a quick word with my clients and see how they want to proceed this morning."

Howard greeted the reporters as they filed up to hand over their business cards.

"Hello, Deniece, nice to see you. Oh, you're with NBC now. Movin' on up! Congratulations. Hi, Bob, good to see you back in action. How's the knee? Good, good ..."

One of the national TV reporters out of New York who didn't know Howard spoke up.

"So are you saying the Wards have hired a press agent to represent them?"

"No. They just have the good fortune to live across the street from one. Now, your business card, please?"

***

Maggie and Bill were in the kitchen when they doorbell rang, Bill sitting at the table while Maggie made breakfast. Bill looked at Maggie, slightly puzzled at who could be stopping by so early.

"I wonder who that could be."

She just shrugged and continued making a pan of scrambled eggs, and Bill got up and walked through the hallway to the front door. He opened it, finding Howard there and starting to greet him, when saw the growing crowd in the front yard.

"Good morning, Howar... Holy cow!"

"Hi Bill. Mind if I come in?"

"Sure, but what about ...?"

"We can deal with them in a minute, but maybe we should talk first."

"Um, yeah, okay."

Howard followed Bill into the kitchen, where Maggie looked up and smiled.

"Hi, Howard. What are you doing here so early?"

Bill replied first.

"Take a look out the front."

Maggie walked into the living room, looked out the window, and rushed back to the kitchen.

"Oh my goodness, Howard!"

Howard smiled.

"It's okay, Maggie. That's why I'm here."

"Thank you!"

"It's not a problem."

"Would you like some coffee?"

"Yes, please."

Howard and Bill sat at the table, while Maggie brought Howard a mug of coffee and a small pitcher of milk, placing them on the table.

"Thank you, Maggie. Well, that's quite a zoo out there. I called to talk to you last night, Bill, but Maggie said you were in bed. I had a feeling this might happen, so when I started to see the crowd gather I thought I better come over."

"What do they want?"

"Well, I'm sure they want to talk to you. What you did yesterday is pretty big news. I tracked the coverage last night, and all the wire services have covered it and the story has been picked up by all in all the major print and broadcast media – the Associated Press, Reuters, Wall Street Journal, New York Times, CNN, NBC, ABC, CBS, Fox News."

"Really?"

"Uh huh. Blowing up pretty big on social media too. You're a trending topic on Twitter, with a couple different hashtags, like #knifeguy and #bladehero. There's also a lot of talk on Facebook."

"Good grief. What should we do?"

"My guess is this will probably blow over in a couple days. Something else will come along to capture everyone's attention and they'll move on. In the meantime, there's going to be a bit of a frenzy – these guys can be a bit insatiable when it comes to a hot story, and they're going to look for a 'day two' angle. Dig into your background, try to figure out who you are, see if there are any skeletons in your closet. You know, get the 'real story.'"

"There is no 'real story.' I don't have any skeletons."

"I know, but that won't stop them from poking around, talking to your neighbors, following you around, asking you questions."

"So what do we do?"

"Well, the best thing to do is give them what they want – to a degree. We'll feed them enough detail to satisfy them and give them a reason to stop digging. Call it laziness or deadline pressures, but they usually stop poking once they find something they can use. So we'll feed them the narrative we want them to go with and that should take care of it. Like I said, I think in a day or two this will blow over – most of it, anyway. For now, the goal is to manage this as best we can."

"How do we do that?"

"Well, I think in a little while we should have you, Maggie and Olive go outside and talk to them for a bit – answer any general questions they have about the three of you, four including Bryce."

"What then?"

"What were you planning to do this morning?

"Go to church."

"Then go do that – maintain your normal routine as best you can. What time are you leaving?"

"Service is at 9, so we usually leave around 8:30."

"What time will you be home?"

"Probably around 11, 11:30."

"Okay. After that, just do what you normally do, although I'd stick close to home. I'll vet requests for more in-depth interviews and pick a few for you to consider doing. I'm thinking maybe the AP, maybe CNN and a few other major outlets if they ask, which they probably will. Those stories will get reprinted and rebroadcast to a lot of other outlets. That will keep the story consistent, and relieve you from having to answer the same questions over and over. Probably should give some of the local press equal time so they don't feel slighted."

"What else?"

"Well, if I were to guess, you'll probably get a few requests for tomorrow – maybe some of the morning shows. Can you take the day off?"

"Do I need to?"

"Well, like I said, best thing to do is feed the beast just enough it until it decides it wants something else."

"Are you sure about this?"

"It's what I do. There's not much else going on this weekend, so for the moment you're the 'big story.' They're not going to go away until they get what they want."

"Okay, whatever you say, Howard. I trust you. And thanks."

"Hey, you'd do the same for me, right?"

Olive came downstairs and into the kitchen.

"Mom, Daddy, do you know what's going on outside? Oh, hi Mr. Jones."

Howard smiled and responded.

"Hi, sweetie. Yeah, we know. That's why I'm here."

Howard spent the next 10 minutes walking them through some of the questions reporters might ask, and helping them shape their responses.

***

Howard and the Wards were just wrapping up their conversation, when there was a knock at the front door. Howard leaned back in his chair to get a peek at the window near the door, seeing a reporter peering in.

"Okay, here we go folks. I'll go tell them you'll be out in a few minutes. Then when I bring you out, I'll introduce you and start taking questions. Remember, stick to the truth and to what you know. If they ask you something you don't know, say so, and move on – don't ramble. If they ask about something you don't want to answer, just say 'I'm uncomfortable talking about that,' and move on. Don't say 'No comment' – that's for amateurs."

Bill responded.

"We ARE amateurs."

"Nevertheless, don't do it. Just say what I told you to say and move on. If they ask the same thing again – and some of them might – stay with your answer. If they become real persistent, I'll step in and redirect them. Okay, why don't you take a few minutes to compose yourselves, and then I'll go outside and get things started. Just wait in the house until I come for you."

Maggie looked a bit self-conscious.

"Do I need to change my clothes, fix up my makeup?"

"Maggie, you look lovely. You too, Olive. I know you're nervous, but try to relax – I'll be there the whole time to help you out."

Chapter 4

Howard stepped out of the front door, and the reporters, photographers and TV crews immediately started moving forward.

"Take it easy folks. I'll be bringing the Wards out to talk with you briefly in just a few minutes. As I'm sure you can understand, yesterday's events were a little traumatic for them and they're still trying to process it all. We'll do our best to address your questions, but I'll ask that you try to show a little restraint, ask your questions one at a time and wait for me to call on you. Try to remember, they're ordinary folks and not used to this, so take it easy."

A reporter Howard hadn't met before spoke up.

"Are telling us we can only ask softball questions or you'll cut us off?"

"No, I'm just saying they've never experienced anything like this before – try to keep in mind, they're not celebrities or serial killers. Okay? And watch the grass! Please?"

Howard ducked back in the front door and a few seconds later reemerged, leading the Wards out – Bill first, then Maggie and Olive.

"Good morning again, everyone. I'd like to introduce the Wards – this is Bill, his wife Maggie and their daughter Olive. They only have a few minutes, so let's we'll try to be respectful of everyone's time and so we can get to as many questions as possible. Who's first? Deniece?

The NBC reporter started, and more questions quickly followed.

"Mr. Ward, how do you feel today?"

"Um, okay I guess. My hand hurts a little."

"No, I mean how do you feel about what happened yesterday?"

"I don't know. I guess I'm still really figuring it out."

"What were you thinking when you rescued that woman and her baby daughter."

"I don't really know what I was thinking. I just saw that they were in trouble and I reacted."

"Did anything prepare you for this incident? Do you have any military or emergency response training?"

"No, not really."

"Can you describe what happened?"

"Well, I saw the minivan crash into the bridge, so I pulled over and ran to the driver's door of the van. I could see a woman inside. But she was unconscious, and I couldn't get the door open, so I broke the glass. Then I was able to unlock the door and pull her out."

"What about the baby?"

"I didn't really notice the baby until the lady said something."

"So you almost left the baby in the car?"

"Yeah, I suppose so. After she told me her daughter was in the van, I ran back over and got her out."

"What happened then?"

"I got a blanket out of my trunk and put it over the two of them. Then I sat down."

"What happened to the minivan?"

"It caught on fire."

"Were you scared?"

"I don't know. Like I said, I didn't really have time to think about it."

"What about the other car?"

"I only looked at that one real quick. It was completely crushed, so I don't think I could have done anything to help."

"Can you tell us a little about yourself – who you are, what you do?"

"My name is Bill Ward. I'm 47 years old. We've lived in this neighborhood for about 15 years now."

"What do you do for a living?"

"I work at OpenSwitch Technologies over in Stilton."

"What do you do there?"

"I'm a team leader in our Business Compliance and Process Controls organization."

"So, you're an accountant."

"No. Our group is responsible for ensuring that all of OST's operations comply with our internal process controls, covering everything from product quality to human resource policies to government regulations. I help develop the business processes for managing all that."

"So you're a lawyer?"

"No. It's kind of hard to explain."

"What about your family?"

"Well, this is my wife Maggie. She has a jewelry design business. And this is our daughter Olive. She's a junior at Derbeville Senior High School. And we have a son, Bryce, who's a sophomore at Northern Connecticut State University."

"Mrs. Ward, what about you – how do you feel about what happened? Are you proud of your husband?"

Maggie looked almost stunned by the question, and paused painfully for a moment before responding.

"... Yes, I, um, I'm very proud of him. And grateful he was able to help those people and didn't get seriously hurt."

"Ms. Ward, what about you – what do you think about what your father did?"

"My Dad is a real good man. He always helps people. I'm very proud of him too."

"Mr. Ward, can you add anything else?"

"I don't know, guys, it's all a bit overwhelming. I guess ... I guess I'd like to think anyone would have done the same thing in those circumstances."

Howard stepped in at this point.

"I'm sorry, folks, but I think we better wrap this up now. The Wards have to get going.

"Where are you going?"

Bill responded.

"To church."

Howard inserted himself again.

"If anyone has additional requests or inquiries, you're welcome to reach out to me. I live right across the street and I'll be around all morning. Thank you for all your questions."

***

Bill pulled the car into the parking lot of Grace By Faith Community Church, swung over to the front door to let Maggie and Olive out, and then went in search of a parking spot. They were running late because of the impromptu press conference so he had to explore the back lot to find a spot. Usually, they were early and parking wasn't a problem. Bill hated being late.

After hiking back to the front door, he entered the lobby to find Maggie waiting for him. Olive had already gone upstairs to join the youth program. They walked over to the worship center, made their way in and started searching for seats. Heads swiveled as they walked around the room and a few people closest to them as they passed smiled and greeted them. Most of the auditorium was full, as was their usual spot halfway down the center aisle, and they had to cross the back of the room to find a place to sit.

The worship band – bass, guitars, drums, keyboards, piano and three vocalists -- were well into their second song and quickly transitioned to a third before stopping to allow one of the assistant pastors to take the platform, greet the congregants and offer an opening prayer.

The service progressed, but Bill had a hard time focusing on it. Normally, he paid close attention during the sermon, but found his mind wandering, sorting through the events of the past 24 hours. He snapped back to attention when he heard Senior Pastor Claude Cleaver say his name. Looking up, he saw that Pastor Cleaver was on the third point of his sermon, the words "Service and Self-Sacrifice" projected on the large screens on either side of the platform at the front of the sanctuary.

"Most examples of this kind of unselfish behavior, of thinking of others, of loving and serving our neighbors, aren't quite so dramatic. But yesterday we saw an extraordinary act of selflessness by one of our own community members, Bill Ward. Bill, would you and Maggie please stand up?"

Looking somewhat stunned, Bill and Maggie rose to their feet, and Pastor Cleaver continued.

"Most of you have seen the news reports, so I don't need to go into too much detail. But just to highlight what occurred, when Bill saw a horrific accident out on the highway and noticed two people were in mortal danger, he ran to their rescue at great personal risk. In saving their lives, he quite literally risked his own without any regard to his own safety. He didn't pause. He didn't hesitate. He acted. Swiftly. Saving the lives of a young woman and her infant daughter as the vehicle they were trapped in became a raging inferno.

"Those of us who know him know Bill to be a quiet man, a good man, a devoted father and husband, a faithful servant in this church through a number of ministries. While no one could have anticipated what happened yesterday or how they would react in similar circumstances, Bill's own selflessness in this case is a model for serving our neighbors and community to the point of self-sacrifice."

At that point, applause broke out in the congregation and grew louder, accompanied by shouts of praise for Bill. Those sitting nearest to Bill and Maggie stood up, and soon all the congregants were on their feet, continuing to applaud. After this went on for nearly a minute, Bill raised a hand and nodded toward Pastor Cleaver, who quieted the congregation and resumed his sermon.

Bill and Maggie regained their seats, with Bill sitting in stunned silence, while Maggie blushed and beamed next to him.

The service continued with Pastor Cleaver concluding his sermon. The worship band remounted the platform and led the congregation in a final song, and Pastor Cleaver closed the service with a few reminders of upcoming events and activities, a benediction and an invitation for congregants to come forward for prayer.

Bill and Maggie rose from their seats and made their way toward the exit with difficulty, as they were frequently stopped by friends and acquaintances. They finally reached the lobby and waited near the café and bookstore for Olive, chatting with people as they stopped by to say “hello.” Olive finally emerged from the upstairs Youth Center and they exited the building and headed toward their car.

There were well out of the parking lot and on the way home before anyone said anything. Bill was the first to speak.

“Okay, that was weird.”

Maggie looked up.

“What?”

“All that commotion at church, Pastor Cleaver bringing it up in his sermon, asking us to stand up, all that.”

“I thought it was nice.”

Olive added from the back seat.

“All the kids were talking about it upstairs – they think it’s pretty cool.”

Bill shook his head.

“Well, I don’t know. I’m not really used to all this attention. I can’t really understand all the fuss.”

Maggie responded, somewhat exasperated.

“You mean you really don’t think what happened yesterday – what you did – is a big deal?”

“Well, I don’t know. I mean I guess I understand that part. I just don’t understand why everyone is acting so weird about it? Are you mad at me?”

Olive spoke from the backseat.

“Guys! Don’t fight!”

Maggie responded.

“We’re not fighting, sweetie.”

Maggie turned her attention back to her husband.

“No … no … I’m not mad. It’s just that, well, honey, I have to tell you, you’re probably the only person on earth who doesn’t think what you did is amazing. Does it really bother you?”

“A little. Anyway, I hope Howard is right and this all blows over in a day or two so we can get back to normal.”

When they pulled into the driveway at the house at around 11:30, there were still a couple TV trucks parked along the street. Howard was waiting for the Wards on the front porch and walked over to the driver’s side window while they waited for the garage door to open. Bill lowered the car window to speak with Howard.

“Hi, Howard.”

“Hi Bill. Why don’t you leave it in the driveway, and we’ll want to back Maggie’s car out too.”

“What for?’

“A couple television networks want to do some brief interviews with you this afternoon. I thought maybe we’d set them up in the garage.”

“In the garage?”

"Well, better than having them drag lights and cable into your living room."

"But, in the garage?"

"Trust me, Bill, your garage looks nicer than some people's living rooms."

It was true. Bill's garage was spotless. The floor was painted with a grey, oil-resistant paint, the walls with a flat, off-white latex – two coats. In the left back corner was a work bench with tools neatly arranged on a pegboard over it. At the top of the pegboard was a sign that said "Dad's Workshop. Don't touch my stuff – I know where everything is." A large vise was bolted to the left end of bench and a light-duty electric grinder was on a small shelf hanging from the right side.

All around the normal contents of the garage was neatly hung, stacked and shelved by category – lawn chairs and yard games on the left, shovels, rakes and other gardening tools on the right. It looked like something out of a handyman's magazine.

Bill looked resignedly at Howard.

"Okay, Howard, what else?"

"There's also a couple print reporters who'd like to speak with you. And a couple majors would like to speak to you by phone."

"Majors?"

"New York Times, Wall Street Journal, USA Today."

"Seriously, Howard? Is there any end to this?"

"There's more – 'The Today Show' would like for you to come into Manhattan tomorrow morning and appear on the show with Shannon Gales and her daughter. Matt Lauer will do the interview."

"The Gales? Are they out of the hospital?"

"Released this morning."

"Are they going to do it?"

"I believe so – the producer said so."

"You think I should do it?"

"Like I said this morning, best thing is to manage the story as best we can until they lose interest. At least so far, we're doing it on our terms. This afternoon should go pretty quick – I'm not giving anyone more than 30 minutes with you. With any luck, 'The Today Show' should be the last of it. Unless ..."

"Unless what?"

"Unless someone decides to dig into your background and see if they can find anything scandalous. 'Hero turned villain' is a great second-day narrative."

"Howard, I already told you. You know our family. No scandals."

"I know. But that may not stop them from poking around. So if you've got a drunken uncle or a cousin who used to be a stripper, they could find out."

"Seriously, Howard?"

"Hey, I'm not saying it's right – I'm just saying it's the way it is."

Bill sighed.

"Okay. What time do we start?"

"First interview is at 12:30 p.m. With a few breaks, we should be done by 5 or so. Then you can rest up for tomorrow morning? Can you get the day off."

"Yeah, shouldn't be a problem. I'll email my manager when I get in the house, tell her I've got some personal business to take care of tomorrow."

"You don't think she'll connect the dots?"

"You think she knows?"

"Bill – *everybody* knows."

"Oh. Right. Will you come with me tomorrow?"

"Of course I will. Well, why don't the three of you head into the house, have a bite to eat and relax for a little bit before the first interview. I'll take care of everything."

***

Bill spent most of the afternoon alternating interviews with print and television journalists. The television networks agreed to share some equipment in the garage to save time. Bill moved back and forth between recording broadcast interviews in the garage and discussions with print reporters in the living room, along with a couple phone interviews with national media. Maggie and Olive generally stayed out of sight and Howard kept things on schedule, letting the interviewers know when it was time to wrap up.

In essence, Bill answered the same questions over and over again from interview to interview, describing the events as he remembered, what he was thinking, how he felt, etc. Occasionally, a reporter would think of something new to ask, but for the most part they all stayed to the same script of inquiries. As a result, the accounts were relatively uniform from interview to interview, with very little differentiating the broadcast accounts and print articles from one another.

In all, Bill did TV interviews with CNN, Fox News, CBS, ABC and NBC, phone interviews with National Public Radio, USA Today, the Times and the Journal, and met with print journalists from the Associated Press and Hearst Newspapers, which owned the local daily newspaper and a string of others across the state. It was more than Howard had expected, but it was a slow news weekend and people seemed intrigued with the story.

It was nearly 6 p.m. before all the reporters, TV crews and photographers had left. Bill was drained and Howard suggested they take some time to relax and have something to eat. He ordered in some Chinese food, and his wife and younger daughter came across the street to join him and the Wards for a meal.

Afterward Howard and Bill talked in the living room about how things went during the interviews and what to expect in the morning. Maggie and Judy cleaned up dinner and chatted in the kitchen, while Olive and Jade talked and watched TV in the family room. The day had been stressful and fatiguing for Bill, and he found the rhythms of normalcy that evening soothing.

At around 8:30 p.m., the Jones said goodbye and headed home. Howard told Bill a car service would pick them up at 4:30 a.m. and deliver them to NBC Studios at Rockefeller Center before 6, so he'd better try to get to bed early and get a good night's sleep.

After the Joneses left, Bill went upstairs, showered and got ready for bed. It wasn't even 9 p.m. when he got in bed. He tried to read but felt himself fading fast, so he put down his book and turned off the light. He was just starting to doze when Maggie crawled in next to him. After a moment, she rolled on top of him and kissed him gently and sweetly.

"What's this?"

"Well … we missed last night."

"True."

"So …"

"… Well, okay. But go easy on me – I have to be up early."

Maggie giggled and kissed him again.

Chapter 5

Monday

"The Today Show" transitioned back from commercial break to host Matt Lauer sitting at the news desk flanked by co-host Savannah Guthrie and weatherman Al Roker. Matt addressed the camera.

"It's nine minutes after 8 a.m. Two days ago on one of our nation's highways, a story of tragedy, heroism and rescue. A terrible accident took the life of one young man and nearly claimed the lives of a young mother and her infant daughter, but for the quick action of a local man. We have that woman, her baby and their savior here in the studio to talk about what happened. But first, some background on these dramatic events."

The program segued to an edited version of WEST affiliate Dave Streader's on-the-scene report.

"It happened in an instant, when a giant spool of steel cable broke loose from a flatbed trailer this morning at about 9:30, rolling across the highway leaving a trail of death and destruction in its wake."

The screen cut to a series of shots, showing the tractor trailer, the crushed Honda, and burning minivan, with firemen fighting the fire. The reporter's voiceover continued as the images flashed past.

"Thirty-one-year-old Roberto Gonzales of Stonefield Center was killed instantly when the reel of heavy wire crushed his car. A second vehicle, the minivan you see here engulfed in flames managed to avoid oncoming the wheel of cable, but the driver lost control, slamming into the overpass abutment.

"Trapped inside the vehicle were 28-year-old Shannon Gales and her infant daughter, Lucy Gales. The woman was knocked unconscious by the crash, and both would have likely been killed by the fire caused by a ruptured fuel line. Fortunately for them, Derbeville resident Bill Ward stopped when he saw the wreck and quickly came to their aid."

The screen cut to a shot of Ward sitting on the ground near his car, with Shannon and Lucy nearby being treated by the EMTs.

"Ward ran to the vehicle, and finding the doors locked, smashed a window with the handle of a pocket knife, cut the seatbelts and dragged the woman and her daughter to safety just moments before the minivan erupted in flames. Emergency responders were quickly on the scene, extinguishing the fire and tending to the accident victims."

The camera cut back to the reporter for his signoff.

"This is Dave Streader reporting for NBC affiliate WEST."

The camera transitioned back to the NBC studio in New York, where Matt was shown sitting across from Shannon Gales, who was holding her daughter on her lap. Bill Ward was seated to the left of Shannon.

Shannon looked relaxed, Lucy sitting contentedly on her lap. Bill looked uncomfortable and a bit tired.

"Mrs. Gales, Mr. Ward, thank you both for being here."

Both nodded and spoke quiet acknowledgements. Lucy gurgled happily on her mother's lap.

"Mrs. Gales, let me start with you. Can you tell me what you remember about the accident."

"I was driving south on I-687, about a quarter mile from Exit 8. There was a big truck ahead of me and a smaller car between the truck and me. I saw something big fall off the back of the truck, bounce and roll, and land right on the car. It was terrible. It was headed straight for us. I turned the steering wheel as hard as I can, and it missed us, but then I couldn't control the car and I guess we ran into the bridge."

"What happened next?"

"Well, I'm not sure. They told me the air bag must have knocked me out. The next thing I remember was being in the car, and my head hurt and it smelled like something was burning. I was still pretty out of it. I heard glass breaking and the door opening. I felt the seatbelt slide off me and someone lifting me out of the car. I guess he must have carried me, I don't think I could have walked. He set me down, and then I realized Lucy was still in the van.

"I saw a man – Mr. Ward – standing over me, and asking me if I was alright. I told him my daughter was in the car, and I watched him run back to the van. He slid the door open and got her out of her car seat. As he ran toward me carrying Lucy, the car just exploded in flames behind him. It was terrifying."

"Then what?"

"He laid Lucy on my chest, and then put a blanket over us. After that, it's all kind of a blur. The paramedics came and took care of Lucy and me. The firemen came and put out the fire. They put us in an ambulance and took us to the hospital."

Shannon paused, and Matt spoke.

"That's an incredible story, Mrs. Gales. Mr. Ward, what can you tell us about what happened?"

"I was about a quarter mile behind Mrs. Gales' minivan, and I saw pretty much what she saw. By the time I caught up, the cylinder of wire had rolled off the highway and down an embankment, and the semi had stopped. I pulled over and yelled to the truck driver to call 911. I saw the other car – it was crushed beyond recognition. I couldn't see anyone in it and didn't think anyone could have survived that crash.

"I ran over to Mrs. Gales' car – she was slumped over in the driver's seat. I couldn't get the door open so I smashed the window."

Matt interrupted.

"With your knife."

"Yes."

"And that's how you injured your hand."

Bill held up his hand self-consciously.

"Oh. Yeah. I guess. Anyway, I cut the seatbelt and lifted Mrs. Gales out of the car as carefully as I could. I guess I half carried, half dragged her over to my car."

"And that's when she told you about her daughter?"

"Yes. I didn't even realize the baby was in the car until she told me. I ran back, pulled the sliding door open, cut the straps on the car seat, and took the baby out. Then I carried her over to her mother. That's pretty much it."

"You cut the straps on the car seat?"

"Yeah, I, uh, couldn't figure out how to undo the buckle thing."

Bill paused, and Matt continued.

"Mr. Ward, what were you thinking when all this was happening?"

"To be honest, I really didn't have time to think. I just ... did it."

"Were you frightened?"

"I don't recall. I don't think I had time to be afraid, really."

"And how do you feel about it now, now that you've had time to think about it. What are your feelings now?"

"Oh, a number of things, I guess. I'm very grateful I was able to help Mrs. Gales and her daughter. I'm glad they're okay. I'm sorry I couldn't help that young man who was killed, but I don't think there was anything I could do for him. And I'm grateful no one else got hurt. Overall, it could have been a lot worse."

"You, yourself, could have been seriously injured, or even killed."

"I suppose so."

Bill didn't embellish, and Matt turned his attention back to Shannon.

"Ms. Gales, is there anything you'd like to add, to say to Mr. Ward?"

Shannon paused, took a deep breath and responded near tears.

"I just want to thank Mr. Ward for saving us. If it hadn't been for him, I can only imagine what would have happened."

Matt addressed them both.

"Mrs. Gales, Mr. Ward, thank you both for being here and sharing your stories."

Bill and Shannon nodded.

"Let's pause for a commercial break. In the next hour, Savannah will talk with Bachman and Turner, producers of the new hit children's animated series featuring robotic skunks who live in New York City's Central Park and fight crime – 'Smelldroids.'"

***

Mort Mortefolio was in his office at NBC early that day. He usually didn't come in until around 9, but Mort had a problem this morning. Mort was a producer for "The Tonight Show with Jimmy Fallon," and was primarily responsible for booking the show's guests. That evening the show was supposed to feature pop singer Swallow Craft and R&B singer Shaniquah performing their crossover duet, "Respect This."

But Sunday evening he'd gotten a call from Swallow's agent saying she was ill and would not be able to appear on the show. Now he to find another guest for that evening, and he didn't have much time.

For the past half hour, he and one of his assistants, Chris Burger, had been going down a list of potential guests.

"What about Dwayne Johnson? He's got that new movie out -- something about a giant forest fire, or a tornado, or something. He's supposed to be on later this week any way, and Jim likes him."

“Right, yeah – ‘Firestorm.’ No, he can’t. We actually wanted him for tonight but we bumped him for Swallow and Shaniquah, and now he’s got another thing.”

“… What about …”

Mort paused for a minute to look at the television on the wall across from his deck. The TV was tuned to “The Today Show.”

“Holy crap!”

“What, Mort?”

“That guy with Matt Lauer. That’s my college roommate, Bill Ward. What’s he doing on the ‘Today Show’?”

“I dunno. Let me turn it up.”

“Yeah, and scroll it back so I can hear the whole thing.”

Chris hit a button on the remote to rewind to the beginning of the segment, then hit play and turned up the volume. He and Mort watched the interview, then Chris hit pause when it came to the commercial break.

“Son of a … I can’t be believe it. Bill’s a hero.”

“Yeah, that’s something.”

“Chris, get down to ‘The Today Show’ set right now, find him and don’t let him leave until I get there.”

“What should I tell him?”

“Just tell him I’m here and I want to see him.”

“You guys close?”

“We were – still stay in touch. He’ll stay if you tell him it’s me.”

“What are you going to do?”

“I have to make a call.”

Chris left the office, and Mort picked up his phone. He and Bill had been paired as roommates their freshman year of college and hit it off right away. Mort was kind of the fun-loving party guy – in fact, "Mort" wasn't even Mort's name. It was Michael. "Mort" was a nickname he assigned to himself because he thought it sounded more funny and fun. Somehow it stuck.

Bill, on the other hand, was the rock-steady pal who went along with Mort's fooling around, but never let it get too far out of hand. They were a good pair, and lived together the entire four years of college – the first two in the dorm, and the final two in an off-campus apartment.

Mort picked up his phone, searched the directory and hit one of the contacts.

"Hi, Jim? It's Mort."

"Hi, Mort – and it's Jimmy, not Jim. What's up?"

"Well, I'm just going over the guest list for tonight and I think we solved our problem."

"Oh right, Swallow can't make it. What's wrong with her?"

"I dunno, flu, laryngitis, frostbite, something or other."

"Okay. Well what have we got?"

"Did you hear about that real bad accident this weekend? Guy got killed, but another guy pulled a lady and her baby out of a burning car?"

"Oh yeah, up in Connecticut, right? I saw something about that."

"I can get that guy."

"I dunno, Mort. You really think that's a good guest for the show?"

"Look, Jimmy, you know you've got the hippest late night show on TV right now. Problem is it might be a little too hip. You saw the latest ratings. People are getting bored with the pop divas and wild-man celebrities. Bringing on a guy like this will give it a little substance. And you've still got our other guest for tonight."

“Oh yeah, Javier Fernandez, from the new ‘Gay Bachelor’ reality show.”

“Yep. So it will even out real nice.”

“You sure you can get this other guy? What’s his name?”

“Bill Ward. Yeah, I can get him. He’s downstairs right now doing ‘The Today Show.’ And you know how much the network likes it when we double up on guests like that. Plus, I know him personally.”

“Okay, Mort. You know what you’re doing. I trust you. Go set it up.”

“Thanks, Jim. You won’t be disappointed.”

“It’s Jimmy. Later, Mort.”

***

Bill Ward and Shannon Gales were escorted backstage at ‘The Today Show’ during the commercial break after their segment. Shannon’s husband, Tommy, and Howard Jones were waiting for them. An intern asked if they would wait for a moment while she used her phone to shoot a couple photos for “The Today Show’s” website. Shannon turned to Bill and spoke.

“Mr. Ward, this is my husband, Tommy.”

“Pleasure to meet you. And please – it’s Bill. This is my neighbor, Howard.”

Howard, Shannon and Tommy acknowledged each other with nods, and Tommy spoke to Bill.

“Mr. … Bill, I want to thank you for saving my wife and daughter. If you hadn’t been there and done what you did, I don’t know what …”

Shannon interrupted.

“What you don’t know, Bill, is that you didn’t just save our lives – you gave Tommy and me a second chance. The reason I was driving to my mother’s was to talk to her about leaving Tommy.”

Bill wasn’t sure how to respond.

"Oh my. I don't really understand …"

"I love my husband, but he never seemed to have time for Lucy and me – he works all the time. I mean, he works hard, and I know he thinks he's doing it for us. But he's never home, and when he IS home he's tired and irritable. I was just so … lonely. But when were we in the hospital and he came running into our room, I knew by the look on his face … I knew ..."

Tommy picked up the conversation there.

"I drove to the hospital as soon as I got the call from the police. Shannon and I talked for a long time as we held Lucy and each other. Sometimes you … you forget what's really important until you nearly lose it."

Bill felt very self-conscious and uncomfortable and looked to Howard for help. Howard just shrugged.

"Well, that's really very … nice. I mean, I'm glad I could help out. But I really don't think I can take credit for the rest."

Shannon responded.

"The way we see it, we can't really separate the two events."

The intern asked Shannon and Bill to pose with Lucy. Bill looked at the baby.

"Your daughter is beautiful, and such a sweet baby. I love babies."

"Oh, would you like to hold her?"

"Well … sure."

Shannon handed Lucy to Bill and the three posed for the camera – Bill holding the baby, with an arm around Shannon's shoulder, Shannon and Lucy looking at Bill.

***

After the photo session, Bill and the Gales said their goodbyes. As they started to leave, Shannon paused, turned back to Bill, gave him a hug and a kiss on the cheek.

On their way back to the green room, Bill and Howard were intercepted by Chris Burger.

"Excuse me, Mr. Ward. I'm Chris Burger and I work on the production staff for the 'Tonight Show.' One of our executives, Mort Mortefolio, would like to have a word with you. Would you mind waiting here for just a moment until he gets here?

Bill looked at Howard, and Howard responded to Chris.

"'The Tonight Show?' What does he want to talk to Bill about?"

"I'm sorry, I can't really give you any more details, but it will only be a minute or two if you could just …"

Bill responded to Howard.

"He was my college roommate."

"Seriously?"

"Probably just wants to say 'hello.'"

Mort walked in.

"Bill Ward! What's it been, 10 years?"

"Hello, Mort. I guess so – what's new?"

"Oh you know, hair getting a little thinner, waist getting a little thicker."

"Aw, you don't look so bad?"

"Me? I was talking about you."

They both laughed, and then Bill introduced Howard to Mort.

"Mort, this is my neighbor, Howard Jones."

Howard nodded, and Mort responded.

"Pleasure. I know who Mr. Jones is – partner at BKP Communications, right?

Howard responded.

"That's right. You know BKP?

"Yep, small but pretty influential specialty PR firm – mostly B-to-B and B-to-C clients, including some pretty large consumer brands. Some political consulting."

"That's right."

"I assume you've been helping Bill manage things with the media for past couple days."

"Well, like he said, we're neighbors, so …"

"Well, I'm sure he appreciates it. He's a great guy."

"I agree."

Mort turned his attention back to Bill.

"So, listen, Bill, I don't want to take up too much of your time but this is more than just a social visit – although I am glad to see you. I'm producing 'The Tonight Show' and was wondering if you'd be interested in being a guest this evening? Jim's heard all about you and what happened this weekend, and he's very excited about it. That was some pretty incredible stuff you pulled. What are you, Superman now?"

"Jim? Jimmy Fallon?"

"Yes."

"Gee, I don't know, Mort. We had to be here pretty early for 'The Today Show' and I'm already kind of beat from everything that's gone on over the last couple days. I'm not sure I'll be up to it by 11:30 tonight."

Mort smiled.

"No Bill, that's just when the show airs. We record it at 5 p.m. Look, we'll get you a hotel suite here in Midtown where you can go and relax, get something to eat, and freshen up. You need a clean shirt, underwear, whatever – we'll take care of it. Then you don't have to be back here until about 4 p.m. and you should be all done by around 7 or so. And we'll even arrange for a car service to take you home. We'll take care of everything. What do you say? It'll be great."

Bill looked at Howard, and Howard shrugged as if to say "up to you."

"Well … I don't know, 'The Tonight Show.' I mean, I'm not an entertainer or an astronaut or anything."

"That's okay. Jimmy likes to have all kinds of people on the show, not just celebrities – politicians, academics, heroes like you."

“Well, I’m not really a hero.”

“Bill – you’re a hero. Trust me. This is going to be great. Do it for an old friend?”

Bill thought about it again, looked at Howard, and then looked at Mort.

“Well, if you put it that way. Okay.”

“Great! That’s great! Chris will make all the arrangements and have you taken over to the hotel. Thanks for doing it, Bill. I think you’re going to enjoy it, and I know Jim will.”

“Okay if we make a quick stop on the way?”

Chapter 6

Bill stood backstage at "The Tonight Show" studio with Howard and Mort, watching the show on a TV monitor. After talking with Mort after "The Today Show" earlier, a town car had taken Howard and Bill to the Waldorf Astoria, where a suite had been reserved for them.

At around noon, lunch was sent up via room service, and afterward Bill went into one of the bedrooms and put his feet up for an hour. Howard checked his email for work on his phone and made a few calls.

After his nap, Bill watched TV for a bit, skipping the news channels to avoid any coverage on what had happened over the weekend. He peeked regularly at his smartphone. Despite the fact that he was on vacation, his boss had been peppering him with emails periodically throughout the day, requesting updates on projects and revisions to documents. Some of these he handled directly, others he delegated to members of his team.

At about 3:15, a car picked them up for the return trip to the studio, then it was into makeup and waiting in the green room before production started at 5 p.m. While they were waiting, Jimmy Fallon came in to introduce himself to Bill and the show's other guest for the evening, Javier Fernandez, from "The Gay Bachelor. " Bill, Howard and Javier chatted nicely before the show began, and then Mort came to retrieve Bill for his appearance on the show.

As they watched on a monitor backstage, the show was returning from a commercial break, with house band The Roots playing Al Green's "Take Me To The River" for the bumpers. As the band finished the song and the audience applauded, Jimmy Fallon addressed the camera.

"All right! Thanks to Questlove and the Roots for bringin' it. Love that song. We're back. I want to thank my good friend, singer Jason Tenderland for joining me before the commercial for our slow jams – that's always a great time.

"Now, I know a lot of you saw on the promos that we were supposed to have Swallow Craft and Shaniquah with us tonight. Unfortunately, Swallow's feeling a little ill …"

The audience interrupted him with groans and awes.

"No, no, it's okay. She's doing fine and we'll have her on again real soon. But instead we have someone else here I think you're gonna really like. How many people saw the news this weekend?"

There were quiet stirrings in the audience.

"I know, right. There's a big accident up in Connecticut – real bad. This guy is driving down the road, see's what's happening, and saves a lady and her baby from a burning car. How about that? He's here tonight – ladies and gentlemen please welcome Bill Ward."

The audience applauded and cheered, and The Roots played the opening bars of Kool and the Gang's "Hollywood Swinging" as Bill walked onstage and took a seat next to Jimmy Fallon. The applause continued after the band finished and Jimmy had to calm the audience.

"I know, I know. Right? Bill, welcome to 'The Tonight Show.'"

"Thanks, it's a pleasure to be here."

"Are you sure? You look a little nervous."

The audience laughed.

"Oh … well, I'm not really used to this kind of thing, and I'm a little tired. It's been a long couple days."

"I'm sure. So, you're what, driving down the highway, and you see this huge crash, and you pull over, run to a burning car and pull a woman and a child out. Just like that?"

"Pretty much, I guess."

"And I heard the way you got them out was by breaking a window with a knife. Like MacGyver or something?"

"Yeah. I suppose."

"So is there anything in your background – any kind of training – that prepared you for this? Volunteer fireman? The Army? Something like that?"

"Not that I can think of."

"And you had this knife with you – like Rambo or Crocodile Dundee or something?"

"Well, no exactly, it's just a three-and-a-half-inch linerlock, with a skeleton metal frame. I used the handle to smash the glass, and then cut the seat belts with the blade."

"And why were you carrying a knife?"

"Well, when I was younger I ran with a crowd that encouraged its members to always carry a knife and know how to use it?

"Street gang?"

"Boy Scouts."

"Ohhhh …"

The audience laughed, and Jimmy continued.

"So, Boy Scouts. Maybe that was it – 'Be Prepared,' all that stuff."

"Maybe, I guess."

"And do you have your knife with you now."

"Not the one I used Saturday – just my everyday carry."

Bill pulled out a small lockback with a black Zytel plastic handle.

"Comes in handy – you need to open a letter or package, trim something, cut a piece of string or tape …"

"Or save someone from a burning wreck."

"Yeah, I suppose. My other one would probably be better for that – bigger, heavier handle, tactical blade."

The audience laughed again. Bill reached into his jacket pocket and pulled out a small gift box, and handed it to Jimmy.

"Here. I brought one for you."

The audience erupted in applause and Jimmy looked genuinely surprised.

"Oh my, you brought me … I can't believe this. That's so nice."

Jimmy removed a small, slim penknife with a brushed stainless steel handle from the box and held it up for audience to see.

"Well. Thank you. I don't really know what to say."

"You're welcome. I hope you like it."

"It's not every day a hero gives me a present."

"Oh, I'm no hero. I'm just a regular person who had an opportunity to do some good. That's all."

"And modest too. So what else don't we know about Bill Ward?"

"Nothing really to know. Married to my college sweetheart for 25 years. Two great kids – a son in college, a daughter in high school. I'm a lead supervisor for Business Compliance and Process Controls at OpenSwitch Technologies."

"Any hobbies, interests?"

"Well, some people say I pay a little too much attention to my lawn."

The audience laughed.

"But I like to read a lot. Right now I'm working through 'The History of United States Naval Operations in World War II.'"

"That sounds heavy."

"Well, it's 15 volumes, so…"

"Fifteen volumes!"

The audience laughed, and Bill looked a little confused.

"Why do they keep doing that?

"Well, you're the first guest we've ever had with such a deep reading list. Except perhaps Stephen Hawking."

The audience laughed.

"So what else is there to Bill Ward? Any other interests? Movies, TV, music."

“Oh, I love music. I was a drummer in bands throughout high school and college. I don’t have much time for TV – mostly just your show occasionally and ‘That Metal Show’ on VH1 Classic.”

“’That Metal Show’ – what’s that?”

“It’s hosted by legendary DJ and rock historian Eddie Trunk, with co-hosts Jim Florentine and Don Jamieson. And as the name indicates the show focuses on hard rock and heavy metal. Last week, the guests were singers David Lee Roth from Van Halen and Vince Neil from Motley Crue. They usually have a guest musician to play on the segues for commercials. It’s kind of a heavy metal version of your show.”

The audience laughed, and Jimmy continued.

“Wow, I don’t mean to insult you, but I would never have made you for a headbanger.”

“Well really more hard rock than heavy metal. I cut my teeth on stuff like Led Zeppelin, Deep Purple, Aerosmith, Rush, Uriah Heep, Def Leppard, Triumph, Alice Cooper, bands like that.”

“Oh, Alice Cooper – ‘School’s Out.’”

“Right, although ‘Billion Dollar Babies’ is my favorite record by him.”

“Well, for a regular guy you sure are full of surprises, Bill – national hero and heavy metal Boy Scout.”

“Really more hard rock, actua…”

Jimmy addressed the camera.

“We have to go to commercial, and when we come back we’ll have Javier Fernandez from ‘The Gay Bachelor’ join us.”

Questlove cued The Roots and the band dropped into “Bitch” by the Rolling Stones as the show broke for commercial.

***

While they were on commercial break, Bill started to exit his chair like Mort had instructed him to do after his segment when Jimmy turned to him.

"Hey, thanks again for the pocket knife, Bill. That was really very thoughtful of you."

"Oh. Glad you like it."

"Listen, I heard you and Javier kind of hit it off back stage. Why don't you stick around for his segment?"

"You sure?"

"Sure – could be fun."

Bill looked over at Mort off stage, who shrugged and nodded.

"Okay."

***

The Roots finished up the bumper as "The Tonight Show" transitioned back from commercial, and as the audience applauded, Jimmy Fallon addressed the camera.

"Welcome back. Let's bring out our next guest. For more than a decade, we've watched men and women search for their perfect mate on television – first on 'The Bachelor' and then 'The Bachelorette.' This year, the producers of those shows decided to open things up a bit more, with the first show dedicated to same-gender couples, the 'Gay Bachelor.' The show debuts next week in prime time, and tonight we have as our guest the first bachelor of the show. Please welcome Javier Fernandez."

The audience applauded as the band played a few bars of theme music from "The Bachelor" series, and Javier emerged onstage, waved to the audience, walked over and sat next to Jimmy Fallon.

"Welcome, Javier."

"Thank you, it's very nice to be here."

Javier then immediately turned to Bill, startling both Bill and Jimmy.

“I was watching the show back stage, and heard you talk about being a Boy Scout.”

“Yes.”

“I was one too!”

Javier fished a small Swiss Army Knife from his pocket and held it up, and the audience exploded in applause. Bill held up his small lockback, and after a short hesitation Jimmy held up the one Bill had given him, and with a dazed look on his face addressed the camera.

“What is happening?”

Bill responded to Javier.

“That’s amazing! Where did you go to summer camp?”

“Camp Tri-Mount, in upstate New York. Near East Jewett.”

“Me too!

Bill turned to Jimmy.

“Hey, Jimmy, I think that’s up near where you grew up. Saugerties, right?

Jimmy looked a bit confused.

“Yeah … that’s where …”

Javier cut him off to ask Bill a question.

“What camp site was your favorite?”

“Oh, I liked the lean-tos up in Seneca.”

“Me too!”

“How many times did you go?”

Jimmy looked on nonplussed as Javier responded, continuing the conversation with Bill as if no one else was in the room.

“Every summer from when I was 11 until I was 18. I did Order of the Arrow there when I was 15, and was a counselor up there for the next two summers. Made Eagle Scout just before I turned 18.”

"I only made it as far as Life Scout, but I did Order of the Arrow too. Spent as much time as I could canoeing on the lake and down at the rifle range."

"Me too! Those were my favorites! And the Trading Post too!"

"Me too!"

Jimmy broke in at this point.

"Boy, you guys are totally hard core. Really into it. Do you do a good turn daily?"

Javier and Bill both nodded and replied.

"Try to."

"Yes."

Javier turned to Jimmy.

"I can tell you that Scouting was an experience that prepared me for life like no other. You learn not only woodsmanship and things like that, but also about the importance of character, integrity, community, self-sacrifice and preparation. People have been asking Bill how he could do what he did -- risk his life to save those two people this weekend. I don't mean to speak for him, but I have to believe his Scouting experience played a huge part in that."

Bill nodded, and the audience broke into cheers and applause. Jimmy addressed them.

"Well, this has certainly taken an interesting turn. We started with a talk show and ended up at a Boy Scout Jamboree. We have to go to commercial, but then we'll be back for more."

The Roots dropped into "This Land Is Your Land." Jimmy held up his knife again, Bill and Javier did the same, and the show transitioned to a commercial."

***

After the show, Jimmy thanked Javier and Bill and left the set. Javier said his goodbyes to Bill and Howard and departed, and Mort came over to talk to them.

"Nice work, Bill. That was great."

“You think so? Seemed a little different from the way it normally goes when I watch it.”

“No, it was great. Jimmy likes it when it goes in a different direction sometimes – keeps it fresh. We’ve already loaded up some clips to our YouTube channel, and they’re getting a lot of views. Good stuff.”

After they left the set, Mort walked them to the exit to see them off.

“Well thanks again, Bill. You saved the day for me.”

“No problem, Mort, glad it worked out.”

“Check with Maggie and see what weekend will work for us to get together. I’d love for the two of you to join Kitty and me here in the city for dinner.”

“Oh, Maggie would love that. I’ll check with her when I get home and email you tomorrow.”

“Great. Howard, great meeting you too.”

Howard was looking out the door. Between the exit and the town car waiting for them was a TV crew – camera man, sound man, and a producer holding a microphone? The mic had a flag on it that said “PM Tonight.”

“It’s been a pleasure, Mort. Hey, what’s the deal with the TV crew there?”

“Ugh. Tabloid TV vultures. They like to stake out this exit sometimes and ambush our guests as they leave. Best thing to do is just walk right by them. You want me to get some security to help out?”

“No, I think we got it – no sense in making more of a ruckus than necessary.”

“Okay, they’re probably looking for Javier instead of you anyway. Well, listen, gotta run guys. Have to go talk to Jimmy about tomorrow’s show. Safe trip home. Bill, I’ll look for your email.”

They said their goodbyes and exited the building, walking quickly toward the car, trying to avoid the "PM Tonight" crew. Howard walked a couple steps ahead, and just as he got to the car door, the producer stepped directly in front of Bill and thrust the mic into his face.

"Mr. Ward. If I could have a moment, can you tell us what you think about the Boy Scouts' recent decision to allow gay men to be scout leaders?"

"What?"

"The Boy Scouts – deciding to let gays be leaders? How do you feel about that?"

"Why are you asking me?"

"Well, you just taped 'The Tonight Show,' and you were on with Javier Fernandez from 'The Gay Bachelor.' And you both talked about being Boy Scouts. So, what do you think of the Boy Scout ruling?"

"I guess I haven't really given it any thought."

"How is that possible? I mean, with your scouting background, and 'The Gay Bachelor,' and all. A lot of people on both sides are pretty upset. Do you support the decision or oppose it?"

The question annoyed Bill and rather than escaping into the car, he decided to respond.

"Look, first of all, I don't know why it matters what I think about it – I'm no one important. Second of all, I'm tired of every conflict or disagreement in our society being instantly turned into mortal combat. Why can't we just accept the fact that we can't always agree on everything all the time, and concentrate on being decent to one another? Try to get along. Mind our own business. Leave people alone and let them live their own lives the way they want."

"But ..."

“Whether you call it tolerance, or respect, or just manners, the only thing I know about any of that is that you have to give it to get it. Treat people the way you want to be treated. If you want to change someone’s mind about something, start with the things you can agree on. Isn’t that the only way to lay the foundation for reaching any kind of understanding?

“Look at how Martin Luther King convinced Congress to protect the civil rights of minorities, or the way Bono persuaded Senator Jesse Helms to support AIDS relief in Africa. They didn’t do it by arguing about their differences. They treated the people they were talking to with respect and courtesy, appealed to their human decency and found common ground.

“Anyway, those are the values Scouting taught me. That’s how I try to live my life every day. And that’s really all I have to say about it.”

“Well, that doesn’t really …”

Howard stepped between the producer and Bill, rose to his full height and looked at the producer.

“I’m sorry. I’m afraid we have to go.”

Bill used the interruption to slip into the car, and Howard followed. As the door closed and the car departed, the producer’s cell phone rang. It was his boss calling.

“Hi, Frank. Yeah, I just talked to that guy who’s on Fallon tonight. No, not the ‘Gay Bachelor’ guy, the other one. The hero guy. No, nothing, I got nothing from him – the man is boring. Yeah, we checked his background – he’s a nobody from nowhere. When he goes out on Saturday night, he paints the town beige. No, nothing we can use. But I checked up on that girl he saved from that car wreck – I think we got something there.”

***

Bill and Howard settled into the seat as the car made its way up the West Side Highway. They were quiet for a long time. Bill sat with his eyes closed, resting. Finally, he broke the silence.

"Okay, I'm glad that's over with. At least I hope it's over with."

"Probably. Me too. I hope so too."

"That last thing with those tabloid TV guys was something."

"Yeah, really? Martin Luther King and civil rights? Bono and Jess Helms? Man, you were rolling. Where did that come from?"

"Try not to sound so surprised."

"No, no, I'm not surprised -- I'm impressed."

"Well, nobody ever changed anyone's mind by calling them evil or stupid. Maybe I'm just tired, but it made me angry. Does everything have to be a big battle, with guys like that egging both sides on? Anyway, I hope they don't put me on their show."

"I wouldn't worry about it – I don't think you said anything they can use. Not the kind of thing they look for. With any luck, all the publicity will die down now and everyone will be back to normal tomorrow."

"I hope so."

"And it wasn't all bad. At least you got to see your best friend."

"Mort?"

"Yeah."

"Yeah, Mort and I go back a ways, and it was good to see him. But he's not my best friend."

"No?"

"No. You are."

"Huh."

Howard sat for a moment before speaking again.

"It's been a long time since I've been anyone's best friend."

"Yeah?"

"Uh huh."

They both sat in silence for a minute, and then Howard spoke.

"You know, to be honest I don't even like you that much."

Bill closed his eyes again, put his head back, and smiled.

"I know."

Chapter 7

Bryce walked back to his room at about quarter to midnight. He had just dropped Eve off at her dorm across the quad, after running into her at the library and offering to walk her home. The previous weekend, they had met up at a campus party Saturday night, talked and danced a little, and she left with her friends around 1 a.m.

They kissed a bit in the lobby of her dorm, and he was hoping she'd invite him upstairs. But she said her roommate was in her room, and she had an early class the next day anyway. So she left him with one more kiss and went back to her room alone.

Both Saturday evening and tonight the subject of his father had come up repeatedly. And not just with her – it seemed like everyone he knew was asking about his father and what happened Saturday morning. He found the attention a little puzzling, and a bit annoying.

He thought his father was an okay guy. But boring. His job, the books he read, the things he talked about, the car he drove, the off-brand discount clothes he wore – boring, boring, boring. It made him wonder if that's all there was after college – settle down, get married, have a couple kids, go to work, and become duller and duller until you die.

That wasn't for him. His major was marketing and media, and he was in the final stages of lining up a summer internship with MTV. With any luck, that would lead to another internship after his junior year and a full-time job offer upon graduation. Then it was off to New York and a career in the entertainment industry, making a lot of money and doing what he wanted. And never getting married – that was NOT in the plan.

His roommate Donnie was in the room when he got back, watching TV on his tablet. He and Donnie had been buddies since third-grade – school, Cub Scouts, high school athletics, double-dates for the prom – they had done it all together.

When they both picked Northern Connecticut for college, they immediately decided to room together. Despite everyone's warnings that it wasn't a good idea, it worked out well – they were a good match. Bryce was the party guy. Donnie was the stable one, engineering major. Bryce kept Donnie from becoming too stuffy and stale, and Donnie kept Bryce from going too wild.

It was unusual for Donnie to be watching TV, with his heavy course load. He looked up and greeted Bryce.

"Hey."

"Hey, what's up."

"Well, your Dad's on Fallon."

"What?!"

"Yeah, he just came on. It's pretty cool."

Bryce paused before responding as a wave embarrassment swept over him

"Roll it back so I can see the whole thing."

Donnie rewound the clip and they watched the interview with Jimmy Fallon, and then the conversation with Javier Fernandez through the end of the show. Bryce stood there transfixed to the laptop until the show was over and at then sat down on the bed.

"Turn it off."

"What's the matter?"

"Are you kidding me? I can't believe it. This is SO humiliating! The Boy Scout stuff, the knife – seriously what IS the deal with the knife thing? He talked about books, Donnie. And not just any books – a history of naval warfare by Winston Churchill? Who reads that? And it only got worse when the 'Gay Bachelor' guy came out."

"Come on, he wasn't so bad."

"Seriously? He's going to be a laughingstock – I'M going to be laughingstock."

Bryce sighed and closed his eyes, trying to contain his anger and mortification. He felt a fist slam into his shoulder, hard.

"Ow! What did you do that for?"

"Because you're an idiot, Bryce. I can't believe what a total dickhead you're being about your father."

"What do you mean?"

"You just have no idea what a good guy your Dad is, do you? Let me ask you something – when you graduate, how much will you have to pay back in student loans?"

"None – my parents are paying …"

"Exactly! Your boring Dad saved enough money so you don't have to pay for college. He could have bought cool cars, nice clothes, big vacations or a fancier house, or anything he wanted. But he saved that money for you."

"Well …"

"Shut up, Bryce. My father was a deadbeat and a drunk – he left my Mom and me when I was six and never came back. All those years since, your Dad has looked out for us – helped us when we needed it. Never made a big deal out of it."

"I …"

"You remember last summer when my car broke down right before we were supposed to come back to school?"

"Yes."

"Your Dad got his mechanic to open up on a Sunday and fix it. He even drove me to the parts distributor himself to get the parts so that it would be ready on time and I could get back to school. And he insisted on paying the bill."

"I didn't know …"

"Because he didn't tell you. And he asked me not to say anything either. And now – what he did on Saturday. Saving that lady and her kid. And you're EMBARRASSED about it? "

"I didn't ..."

"You're a spoiled, stuck-up, self-centered tool who doesn't know how good he has it."

"I'm … sorry."

"Don't apologize to me. I'm the not the one you've been slagging. I'd kill to have a father like yours. And if this is the way you're gonna be, I can't hang out with you anymore."

Donnie walked across the room, opened the door and turned around.

"Grow up, Bryce."

Donnie left the room, slamming the door behind him. Bryce sat on the edge the bed, stunned.

His phone beeped as he received a text message. It was from Eve.

"Just saw your Dad on Fallon – that's so hot!"

***

Tuesday

Bill was at his desk in his office at OpenSwitch by 8:30 a.m. Tuesday – just like every other work day. He'd gotten home around 9:30 the evening before. Maggie had made him a sandwich. He ate half, sat quietly in the kitchen for a little while, then went upstairs, took a shower and went to bed.

Maggie had set the DVR to record the Tonight Show. She watched it the following morning, after Bill left for work. She saved it for Bill, but he never watched it.

He spent the first couple hours at work getting caught up from the email that had built up the day before. Four or five people stopped by to say hello and talk about the weekend's events and his media appearances. He made small talk but didn't feed the conversation. Most of them got the message, congratulated him and left him alone fairly quickly.

At 10:30, he had his weekly meeting with his project team in a nearby conference room. As team leader, he was responsible for directing the work completed by the team. But he wasn't their actual manager – he couldn't make hiring and firing decisions, determine performance appraisals or manage personnel issues. That went to his boss, the group manager, Betsey Wetsel.

The focus of the meeting that day was an upcoming two-day spring planning session. All the teams in every department were tasked with developing a set of strategic objectives, with tactical plans for achieving them over the next six months. These plans were all folded into master plans for each group, department, function, division and up to corporate, and cross-indexed by discipline – finance, legal, engineering, sales and delivery, production, HR, etc.

The discussion took most of the hour and Bill looked at his watch and began wrapping up.

"Okay, so the meeting will be in the Somerville conference center on Tuesday and Wednesday. They're going to be long days, so I think we should have food brought in for lunches and snacks. Charlene and Jenny, would you mind making the arrangements?

Charlene Bogart and Jenny Stuart, the only female members of the 10-person team, looked at each other. Charlene responded to Bill.

"Are you asking us to do it because we're women?"

"No. I'm asking you to do it because you didn't like what I ordered last time. Pizza and subs from Little Quinceanera's. But if you prefer, I coul …

"No! No, no. We'll take care of it. Do you, uh, want us to get anything in particular?"

Bill was slightly taken aback by the forcefulness of Charlene's objection. Everyone else around the table chuckled.

"No, I trust your judgment. Just try to stay within the budget. Make it as nice as you can and order from wherever you want – within reason. No La Boulangerie du Bastogne, okay?"

"Okay."

"All right. Is there anything else we need to cover today? No? Okay, same time, same place next week, and the spring planning session in two weeks. Thanks, everyone."

The team members all filed out and headed back to their offices and cubicles. Bill sat for a moment, gathering up his papers. He looked up and noticed Jenny had remained.

"Something I can help you with, Jenny?"

"Yeah, I'm having a scheduling issue with our weekly Bravo Project checkpoint meeting on Thursdays. Those are my switchover days with my ex-husband and I have to leave at 3:30 to pick up my son from his afterschool program."

Jenny and her husband had divorced a year earlier and shared custody of their six-year-old son, Spencer. Her ex had Spencer Monday through Wednesday, and she had him Thursday through Saturday. They swapped off Sundays.

Bill responded.

"Well, the meeting runs 4 to 4:30, so that's probably not enough time for you to get all that done and get on the call. What if we shifted the meeting to 5, and you took the call from home?"

"That would be great, but ..."

"What?"

"Well, I don't want to inconvenience everyone else. I wish there was another way."

"Jenny, it's no big deal. We move things around to help each other out all the time. Charlene volunteers at her daughter's school two mornings a week – that's why we have our team meetings on Tuesdays instead of Mondays now. Dave, coaches Little League every spring, and leaves most days during the season by 4."

"Are you sure?"

"Seriously, it's not a problem. You have to be able to live your life too. We'll make it work."

"Thank you for understanding, Bill."

He returned to the paperwork on the table. She turned to leave and hesitated.

"What you did this weekend. That was amazing."

Bill didn't look up as he responded.

"Just trying to help someone out. Not a big deal."

Jenny walked out the door and headed toward her cubicle, thinking, "Why does HE have to be married already?"

Bill returned to his office, sat down and checked his email. A window popped up on his screen from the company's RightNow instant messaging system. It was Katey Perry, administrative assistant for Herve Pardon.

"Hi Bill. Herve would like for you to come by and see him."

Bill typed back.

"Sure. What time?"

"Thirty minutes from now."

"Okay, I can do that. Is there a topic?"

"He didn't say."

"K. I'll be there."

"TY."

Bill and Herve had joined the company at about the same time almost 25 years before. Part of the company's culture was to group new hires in "classes," like in high school and college. The goal was to encourage collaboration, identity, loyalty and esprit de corps. They were each also assigned mentors at that time – more experienced employees who provided professional advice and helped guide their careers.

The pair had actually been partnered as part of OpenSwitch's two-week new employee orientation program, sharing a room at the company's Employee Learning and Development Center in upstate New York. The two were very different, but bonded quickly. Bill was the steady, stable one, soon to marry his college sweetheart, while Herve was a playboy, always on the prowl for women.

Not even female colleagues were out of bounds for Herve, and although this led to some uncomfortable situations over the years, Herve somehow managed to not make any mistakes that were fatal to his career.

After employees of a class had been with the company for five years, they were each assigned a protégé of their own from an incoming class, and were supposed to help them get acclimated to the company. In many cases, these relationships lasted for decades, with rising executives providing ongoing career advice for their protégés, and even finding promotion opportunities for them. In many cases, the career progress of a protégé rested largely on his mentor's own fortunes.

That had been the case for both Bill and Herve. They had proven themselves as smart and capable, and advanced quickly to new and challenging assignments on both the merits of their accomplishments and the influence of their mentors.

Herve moved through the ranks in the Marketing, Sales, Technology Services and Supply Chain organizations, rising to one of the top spots in the company as Chief Value Officer. The CVO oversaw all activities related to marketing, communications, sales, digital media, sponsorships and strategic alliances.

Bill did tours in Business Development, Finance, Technology Services, and Research before moving into a key role as a director in a group that managed the company's mergers, acquisitions and divestitures. The group was tasked with identifying key technologies and companies to acquire to help drive new revenue opportunities and capture market share. It also was responsible for determining what products and divisions were no longer core to the business and should be sold off.

Bill's focus and discipline helped drive a string of successes for the company, until one particular divestiture became a problem. Negotiations had reached a critical phase for the sale of the OpenSwitch's wireline connector business to a competitor.

One of the Finance guys working on the deal confessed to Bill that the top executive leading the negotiations for OpenSwitch had been putting pressure on him to goose the projected revenue and profit numbers for the products in that business. The goal was to make it look like a better deal for the buyer and raise the sale price.

Bill understood this was a huge breach of ethics that could potentially ruin the deal or lead to a lawsuit. He immediately reported the issue to the top Legal and Finance officers in the company – he knew them both from previous deals, and they trusted what he told them.

They quickly investigated, took the executive out of his role, and ensured that the financial irregularities were fixed. There was no major damage – the problem had been caught before the numbers had been presented to the buyer, and the deal proceeded normally to a positive conclusion.

The executive was quietly demoted and sidelined into another role, but the damage to his career had been done. He had been on a fast track before this, and now would never rise above the level of director. The problem for Bill was that this executive's mentor was the CEO of the company, Stan Zbikowski. Stan was not happy about what happened and made it known to his direct reports.

That put a chill on Bill's career opportunities as well. Within a few months, he was demoted without explanation and moved to his current role in the Business Compliance and Process Controls group -- a virtual dead end. After that, his mentor stopped taking his calls, and many colleagues avoided him. Except Herve. Despite his other character flaws, Herve remained loyal to his friend and colleague, although there wasn't much he could do to help Bill.

The unusual thing was Bill still found a way to excel even when stuck in a corner. His co-workers and managers soon discovered that he had a real talent for refining business processes. Somehow, he could peer through all the documentation, the org charts, the PowerPoint decks and the spreadsheets, and create order out of the random chaos contained in them.

He was able to cull out the important data and improve any procedure, process or policy to make the organization work more effectively, economically and coherently. There was such clear logic to his work that some in the company considered him a genius when it came to business processes.

It was as if when he looked at a Gantt chart it was like he was seeing it in three dimensions. Of course, because of the mark on his record, it did him little good career wise. While he was considered a capable contributor with a gift for operational efficiency, it was understood by everyone – including him -- that he was unlikely to advance to any position of greater responsibility.

That had been five years ago, and Bill had been tempted to leave the company. But the job market was soft, and it was tough for men his age to find new opportunities – they were viewed as too old and too expensive. In addition, he was close to vesting for his retirement and equity in the company.

That was a lot of money to leave on the table, especially with two kids headed for college in the not-too-distant future. So, basically he was stuck. He did what he could to make the best of it, but he knew that for the near-term at least his career at OpenSwitch would remain at a standstill.

This year being their 25th year with the company for Bill and Herve marked a special milestone within the corporate culture for them. All members of that class would attend a special Silver Jubilee event near the end of the year, hosted by the company leadership and marked with honors, citations and gifts. In the past, it was something Bill looked forward to, but now he rarely gave it much thought.

Chapter 8

Bill finished up a few work items before heading up to see Herve up on the third floor. Herve's office was in a special wing where all the c-suite executives and senior vice presidents sat. At about 10 minutes beforehand, Bill headed out, walking along the corridor and across the open-bay cubicle area where most of the employees worked.

He stopped at the cube of Duane Burns, who he found staring into space. Duane was in his mid-30s, and had been with OpenSwitch for about 10 years. He had been on Bill's team for a couple years, and now worked in the Financial Reconciliation Department.

"Hi Duane. You okay?"

"Yeah. Yeah. I think so."

"What's going on?"

"Well … I think I just accidently had phone sex with Candace Garrett-McGinty."

Candace was the executive assistant for one of the product division general managers. Being an "EA" was a stepping-stone position that allowed a rising employee to see how senior executives operate on a daily basis. It's also a test – employees who passed usually ended up in their first junior executive roles, an important step on the corporate ladder.

"Uh, okay. How did that happen?"

"Well, I'm not sure really. She sent me some charts she was working on for her general manager for the spring planning, wanted me to check the financials. The file was zipped and I told her I couldn't get it unzipped. She told me how to do that, and then after I got the file unzipped, I couldn't get it up. So said she could help me get it up. It was just weird."

"Oy. Did she know what was going on?"

"Geez, I hope not.

"Well, I wouldn't worry about it then."

"Where you going?"

“Up to the exec wing on 3.”

“Good luck with that. Kind of like entering the bridge of the Death Star. Only less cheerful. Who you going to see?”

“Herv.”

“What for?”

“Dunno – his admin just asked me to stop by.”

“Oh hey, when you see Katey Perry, ask her if she kissed a girl and she liked it.”

“Yeah, you know, she doesn’t think that’s funny.”

“Everyone else does.”

“Well, I’d give it a rest – she finds out you’ve been telling that one, she could make things miserable for you. Never piss off the admins – particularly the ones who support the senior execs. They hold the keys to the kingdom.”

“Okay, Bill.”

“I have to go.”

Bill walked to the elevator bank, pressed the button and waited for the elevator. After about a minute it appeared, the doors hesitated and then opened. A woman he knew by sight but not by name was waiting as well, and he allowed her to enter before getting in. He entered, pressed the button for “3” and then waited. After about 30 seconds, the doors closed, the elevator hesitated, bounced once jarringly, and then began lumbering upward. Both he and the woman winced. He spoke to her.

“They need to do something about these things.”

“I know. I’m always afraid I’ll get stuck in one.

The elevator stopped at the second floor, the woman departed, the doors closed and the machine repeated its hesitation and lurch routine before continuing to the third floor. Bill exited the elevator and turned left toward the executive suites. When he arrived at Herve’s office, he found a young woman sitting in the secretarial bay in front of it. She was blonde, in her mid-20s and stunningly pretty.

"Oh, um, hello. I'm Bill Ward. I'm here to see Herv. Is Katey not around today?"

"No, Mr. Ward, she's working from home today. I'm Tawney, Mr. Pardon's EA. Do you have an appointment?"

"Call me Bill. Yes, Katey said he asked to see me."

"One moment, please. Let me see if he's ready for you."

Tawney got up, and walked to the closed door to Herve's office, and opened it slightly.

"Excuse me, Mr. Pardon, are you ready for Bill Ward."

Bill heard Herve respond from inside the office.

"Yes, just a moment. I'm just finishing up with Sondra."

After about 30 seconds, Sondra, a lovely young black woman exited Herve's office, smiled at Bill and spoke.

"You can go in, Mr. Ward. He's ready now."

"It's Bill. Thank you."

Bill walked into the office and found Herve sitting behind a large, dark wooden desk, starring at the ceiling. On the desk in front of him was a large Ziploc bag with something brown and clumpy in it. Herve spoke.

"Elephant poop."

"Excuse me?"

"Elephant poop. Someone actually brought a bag of elephant poop to a J-School readout today. Plopped it on the table right in front of me. Here it is."

J-School was a program the marketing department was running to try to get each of the product and brand teams to sharpen the focus of their messages and strategies. The objective was to help decide where to put the emphasis, and marketing dollars, for the remainder of the year.

The program included an intensive one-week, off-site meeting for each team, where they would brainstorm and review all their options. This was followed by a month of ongoing meetings and planning sessions, culminating in presentations of their finding and recommendations to Herve and other senior-level marketing executives.

Bill picked up the conversation.

"Uh, and WHY did he bring elephant poop to a J-School readout?"

"What his exact point is, I'm really not quite sure. Most of what he said after he dumped the bag on the table in front of us kind of went right by me. Something about real value versus perceived value, and the illegal trade in ivory tusks or something. Apparently, he was trying to be edgy, or clever or something. My understanding is that his teammates did everything they could to stop him, but he simply wouldn't be dissuaded."

"That's pretty bizarre."

"It's puzzling – what could possibly make him think that was a good idea? Well, I'll be talking to his manager about it shortly. I'm sure that young man will enjoy his new assignment – in Greenland."

"You're kidding, right?"

"About Greenland? Yes. But I plan to instruct his manager to tell him he has no future here and should probably start looking for opportunities outside the company. I'm told he drove five hours round trip to get this stuff."

"That's unfortunate. This is a guy whose brain was smart enough to figure out where to get the elephant poop for his presentation, but not smart enough to tell him not to do it."

Herve smiled.

"That's what I've always liked about you Bill. You see the nuances no one else does – even in elephant poop. I'm sorry, where are my manners? Please, have a seat."

Bill sat down in one of the guest chairs in front of the desk.

“Thanks, Herv.”

“Her-VAY.”

“Pardon?”

“Par-DOAN.”

“What?”

“Her-vay Par-doan. I’ve gone back to the traditional pronunciation of my name. Seems more authentic.”

Herve’s mother was American and his father was Haitian. He had his mother’s smooth good looks and his father’s dark eyes and straight black hair. He was a handsome man, tall and fit, and women found him exotic and exciting. Part of his success, both professionally and personally, came from meticulous attention to his image – everything from careful grooming, to the cut of his clothes, to his speech and mannerisms.

“Can I get you anything, Bill? A cappuccino, perhaps?”

“Oh, I’m fine – you don’t have to go to any trouble.”

“Really, it’s no trouble at all.”

Herve picked up the phone and called out to the secretarial bay.

“Tawney, would you please ask Angelica to prepare a couple cappuccinos for Mr. Ward and myself? Thank you.”

He replaced the handset and turned back to Bill.

“Well, never mind the elephant poop? How are you?”

“I’m good. You?”

“Great. Just back from vacation with Danielle and the girls. Spent a week on the Isle of Lucy in the Caribbean. Beautiful beaches. Great blues-jazz festival. You’d love it.”

“Sounds great. I’m sure I would.”

There was a long pause, and after about 10 seconds Bill broke it.

“So … is something on your mind?”

“No. No, I just wanted to see how you are. That was quite an adventure you had this weekend.”

“Oh, I’m fine. It really wasn’t that big of a deal.”

“Well, I saw the media coverage, and your appearances on ‘The Today Show’ and ‘The Tonight Show’ yesterday. It certainly seems like a big deal. The floor has been buzzing about it all day.”

“Well, I’m really just trying to get back to normal. My neighbor Howard says this will probably be the end of it.”

“Your neighbor Howard – who is he?”

“Public relations guy. He’s an executive at BKP Communications.”

“Oh. Well, good – glad you were getting some professional advice. You know, you can always call on me for that kind of thing too.”

“Thank you, Herv, uh, Herv-AY. I did think of it, but he lives across the street and was right in the thick of it as soon as the TV trucks rolled in.”

“Ah, I see. Makes sense. And you were injured.”

Herve pointed at the bandage on Bill’s hand.

“Oh it’s nothing – just a few stitches.”

A young Asian-American woman – as beautiful as the first two -- quietly entered the office and placed a tray with two cups of cappuccino on the desk.

“Here you are, Mr. Pardon, Mr. Ward. Is there anything else I can do for you?”

Herve smiled, reaching for one of the cups.”

“Thank you, that will be all for now, Angelica.”

Bill responded politely.

“Yes, thank you.

Angelica departed and Bill spoke.

“Good grief, Herv – Her-VAY. It’s like Charlie’s Angels up here.”

"Bill, I can assure you Tawney, Sondra and Angelica are all very qualified young professionals. Tawney has been rising fast in our Marketing Events and Special Programs Department, Sondra is a financial whiz who is an up-and-coming star over in Accounting, and Angelica is working on her master's degree in supply chain economics."

"I'm sure they're all quite capable, Herve. I didn't mean to imply otherwise. You've always had an eye for … talent."

Herve laughed, and continued.

"How's the family? Maggie? The kids?"

"They're all great. Now that the kids are older, Maggie's started to dabble in work again – jewelry sales via network marketing. Bonsai Bear is the name of the company. She seems to be enjoying it and doing well at it. Bryce is in his second year at North Connecticut – he's majoring in marketing and media. And Olive is a junior in high school, so we're in the thick of the college hunt for her too."

"That's wonderful."

"How about your family?"

"Danielle is president of the Southerton Service Club, heading up their annual charity ball committee. Hetherington is in eighth grade at Chart Academy, playing soccer. And my baby girl, Beatrice is in second grade at Ridgebury Day School."

"That's great."

"So how are you doing, Bill? How's working for Betsey?"

"It's fine."

It wasn't fine, but Bill wasn't going to get into that with Herve. Betsey also was a member of their OpenSwitch class, and there was friction between her and Herve. Bill wasn't sure why, but was under the impression they had tangled a few times over the years. There was also a rumor that one of them had made a romantic advance toward the other a few years earlier at an off-site function and had been rejected. Herve would have told Bill about it if he asked, but Bill didn't really want to know.

Herve and Bill could both sense that that the discussion was running out of steam. Protocol dictated that Herve conclude it.

"Well, listen, I don't want to take up any more of your time, Bill. And I have another meeting momentarily. But I did want to make sure you're okay, after the events of last weekend."

"Thanks, Herve. I appreciate it."

"Let's talk again soon."

Herve rose from his chair and extended his hand. Bill rose as well and shook it, then smiled and departed.

***

Bill was back in his office just before noon. He ate the lunch he'd brought from home at his desk, as he normally did, continuing to work on his computer. Just as he was finishing eating, he heard someone in his doorway.

"You went to see Herve."

He looked up to see his manager.

"Oh, yes. A little while ago."

"Was it something you felt you needed to go over my head about?"

"It was nothing like that, Betsey. He asked me to come up to see him. He wanted to see how I was doing after what happened this weekend."

"Oh. That. Right. How … are you?"

"I'm okay."

"And you and Herve, you didn't talk business?"

"He asked me how things were going, I said fine, and that was the end of it."

"Okay. Fine."

"Something wrong, Betsey?"

"No, I would just appreciate it if you would inform me of these things instead of my having to find out elsewhere, that's all. I know you and he are … close … but nevertheless."

"I'm sorry, it didn't occur to me to let you know. As I said, it really wasn't about business."

"Well, in the future ..."

With that, she turned and left.

Bill turned back to his work, preparing for his meetings at 3:30 and 5.

***

"That Metal Show" host and radio personality Eddie Trunk was sitting in his office at about 3 p.m. when the phone rang. It was Jim Florentine, one of his co-hosts for the television show.

"Hey, Jim. What's up?"

"Hey, Eddie. What time do we need to be at the Garden tonight for the Slash show?"

"Well, the show is at 8, but I have to get there early. I'm recording a segment with Myles Kennedy for my radio program beforehand and he asked that I get there by 6:30 so we can get it done before his vocal warmups. We're going to talk about the tour and his upcoming record with Alter Bridge."

"Okay, you taking car service in as usual?"

"Yeah. We can pick you up at 5 if you can be ready by then."

"Yeah, that's great."

"Okay, see you then."

"Wait, Eddie, one more thing."

"What?"

"Well, you know how VH1 wants us to tape those six extra episodes for this summer between regular seasons?"

"Yeah."

"Well, I've been talking to the producers and we're having a hard time getting the guest slots filled out, because so many bands will be touring then."

"Yeah?"

“Anyway, I was thinking maybe we could get that guy Bill Ward on the show.”

“Bill Ward? From Black Sabbath? Are you kidding me? I would KILL to get Bill Ward on the show!”

“No, Eddie, not THAT Bill Ward.”

“What do you mean not THAT Bill Ward? Is there another one?”

“Yeah, did you hear about that thing that happened up in Connecticut over the weekend? Bad accident on the interstate? Some guy saved a lady and her baby from a burning car?”

“Yeah, I heard something about that. So what?”

“Well, turns out that guy’s name is Bill Ward too.

“So?”

“So anyway, they had him on ‘The Tonight Show’ on Monday. Turns out his a big fan of our show. The guy’s, like, a major rocker – Zeppelin, Aerosmith, Deep Purple. He was talking to Fallon all about TMS and how great it is and everything.”

“No kidding!”

“Yeah, it was pretty cool, and a lot of people saw it. Our social feeds on Twitter and Facebook are full of talk about it.”

“And you think he’d be good on our show.”

“He was great on Fallon the other night – you should watch it.”

“Okay, well, I will. And I guess we should look into having him on the show.”

“Alright, I’ll talk to our producers and have our bookers see if they can get connected with him.”

“Thanks, Jim.”

“See you at 5, Eddie.”

Chapter 9

Wednesday

Bill was in his office around 10:30 a.m., working on PowerPoint charts for a meeting later in the day, when the phone on his desk rang with an electronic warbling sound.

The phone was a large, angular, square device, about eight inches on each side. The whole thing was made of a pale tan-grey-beige plastic – a color called "putty" by the industrial designers who developed it. The face of the receiver was angled toward the user, so that it sat about three inches high on the top and about two inches on the bottom. On the left side, two indents held the large handset, attached to the receiver by a 10-inch curly cord.

On the right was a set of buttons for various functions of the phone – hold, conference, flash (for putting one call on hold while connecting another to conference), primary and secondary lines -- and several more functions that were no longer in use. Below the buttons was a speaker for hands-free calling. At the top was a small translucent window that displayed the number of an incoming call, and above that was the name and model of the device – MOLR VX7000.

The whole handset and the systems that supported it dated back to the 1980s, when it was designed by the first chief technology officer for OpenSwitch, Fred Molr. Fred was an engineering genius and the right-hand man of the company's CEO at the time, William Garvin III. The MOLR products were the first series of business telephones to capitalize on the features of the new, fully electronic PBX telephone systems then coming online, and they sold quickly because of their utility and durability.

The fact that they were still in use 30 years later was testament to how resilient they were – from the internal components to the mechanical package that contained them, they were built to last. And because of their simple, open electronic architecture they even worked well with the newer IP-based phone systems that came into use in the mid-2000s. In essence, they were virtually indestructible and obsolescence proof.

It was only their aesthetics that marked them as outdated and unfashionable. A few years earlier, they'd all been replaced up on the third floor with newer, sleeker telephones with wireless handsets and other modern features. Unfortunately, the new phones didn't seem to last more than six months without either an electronic or mechanical failure.

Some of them seemed to simply disintegrate from use, although that may have been more a factor of how hard frustrated executives slammed them down – or threw them across the room – than a flaw in design or manufacture.

The MOLR VX7000 was an artifact of an earlier time at OpenSwitch Technologies, like many other things at the company. The antecedents of the company dated back to the late 1800s, from firms that manufactured things like wire and components for telegraph systems and, later, early telephone equipment.

In the early 1900s, William Garvin, Sr., combined several of these companies to form the Garvin Telephone and Telegraph Manufacturing Company. Soon the company was making not only transmission wire, components and subsystems but entire telephone and teletype systems they supplied to regional service providers.

Shortly thereafter, the company entered the radio equipment business as the medium gained popularity for news, entertainment, and two-way communication by the police and military. By the mid-1920s, whole cities and regions across America and beyond were supported by Garvin telephone, telegraph and radio systems, and many homes featured Garvin telephone handsets and radio consoles.

Like many of his industrialist contemporaries like Thomas Edison, Henry Ford, Thomas Watson, Sr., of IBM and Fred Johnson of Endicott Johnson shoes, Bill Garvin, Sr., adopted a benevolent, patriarchal view of his responsibilities to his business and his workers. He implemented forward-looking human resources policies that emphasized fair wages and competitive benefits, including healthcare and retirement.

He set a high bar for employment, with applicants required to go through a lengthy series of tests and interviews, regardless of their experience or education, to ensure they were Garvin material. But once hired, they were virtually guaranteed unlimited opportunity based on their ability and employment for life as long as they did their jobs ably and conscientiously. In addition, Garvin provided ongoing education for employees – both in-house training programs as well as tuition-free higher education for those who qualified.

That generosity extended to the families of the employees as well, along with the communities where they resided. Garvin subsidized the building of schools and medical facilities, and sponsored parades, family days and other community events. The wives of employees enjoyed discounts on appliances and other durable home goods through cooperative arrangements with local retailers.

Garvin families could get special rates on loans to buy homes and automobiles through the company's credit union, and many local banks would match those rates in order to compete for the business. And the children of employees could apply for college scholarships, depending on their academic performance in high school.

This largesse was not driven solely by generosity, but by a philosophy that said it would create more loyal, productive, innovative employees. The thinking was that a worker who didn't have to worry about paying his mortgage or for car repairs could devote that energy to his work.

An employee with the opportunity to learn and grow could apply that knowledge to developing new products and techniques for making them. And the higher cost for benefits would be offset by higher productivity, lower employment turnover, and greater innovation driving both revenue and profit.

Garvin would even provide safety shoes and protective glasses to employees for personal use at home. The assumption was that it would result in fewer injuries from personal chores like mowing the lawn or maintaining a vehicle, eliminating days lost from work for those injuries.

Garvin Manufacturing's guiding principle was to do everything first rate – from designing and manufacturing its products, to maintaining its buildings, to treating its employees well. The logic was that first-rate companies with first-rate employees produce first-rate products, and that would keep them competitive and profitable.

Garvin Manufacturing's administrative buildings, sales offices, and manufacturing facilities sparkled, its employees stood sharp in their crisp business suits or spotless workman's clothes. They said you could spot a "Garvin man" just by the way he walked.

This philosophy was put to the test after the stock market crash of 1929 and the economic depression that followed, but Garvin Manufacturing persevered. While some operations were scaled back and new employment curtailed, everyone kept their jobs. Bill Sr. knew the depression would eventually end and demand for new products will resume, and he wanted to be ready.

Declining health forced Bill Sr. to retire in the late 1930s, and his son Bill Jr. succeeded him. By then Garvin Manufacturing was a publically traded company, with operations in countries throughout the Americas, Europe and parts of Asia.

Bill Jr. had grown up at his father's side, joining the company as a salesman after college and working his way through almost every operation in the business. When the board of directors met to decide on who should take over the company, Bill Jr. was the natural and obvious choice.

World War II was the jumpstart Garvin Manufacturing needed after the depression, as the company became a major supplier of telephone, telegraph and radio equipment to the U.S. government and military. Because the company had maintained and staffed its operations through the lean years of the 1930s, it was ready to produce what was needed quickly to supply burgeoning federal government operations and outfit the troops headed overseas to fight the war.

With the growing government orders, Garvin was able to invest in new manufacturing operations throughout the U.S. When the war was, over the company was prepared to ride the wave of the continuing economic boom that followed.

Bill Jr. invested heavily in newer electronic technologies for telephone switching as demand for communications services swelled to meet the requirements of growing business and personal use. The company continued to expand and prosper through the 1940s and 1950s, swelling to more than 150,000 employees in 40 countries.

In 1960, without any warning, Bill Jr. dropped dead of a heart attack at his desk. As the news spread, men and women stood in the hallways at sales office and manufacturing plants around the world and openly wept.

Once again, the board of directors moved quickly to appoint a successor and once again chose a Garvin, William III. After college he had served two-years as an enlisted man in the U.S. Army, and then completed an MBA at Stanford before joining the family business. Bill III possessed the same talents, intellect and character as his father and grandfather, and got to work quickly in identifying new challenges and opportunities for the company.

To help him with the task, he picked Army buddy Fred Molr – a graduate of MIT with degrees in electrical and mechanical engineering. Fred saw the coming wave of electronic data processing, as computers evolved from exotic, custom-designed devices for scientific research to general purpose systems used by businesses. As companies ranging from airlines to banks deployed these new systems to run their businesses, they needed data networks that could provide the speed, reliability and bandwidth required to transport their business-critical data.

Fred would go on to found and lead Garvin's Advanced Science Division, dedicated to deep research in everything from software development to material science to physics. The division was to become the key driver of innovation for the company over the next 25 years, as the company continued to grow and expand to become the global leader in technology for telecommunications and data communications.

It was during the transition in the early 60s that Bill III and Fred decided to rename the company, establishing a more current and relevant brand – OpenSwitch Networks.

***

Bill answered the phone on his desk.

"Good morning, this is Bill Ward."

"Mr. Ward?"

"Yes."

"Mr. Ward, my name is Walt Schraber. I'm the president of Schraber Knives."

"How can I help you, Mr. Schraber?"

"Please, call me Walt. I'm sorry to intrude, but we saw the news reports about you this weekend, and I noticed in one of them you seemed to be holding one of the knives we manufacture."

"Yes, I believe it is."

"It looked to me like it was one of our Tech-Force import models. three-and-a-half-inch, drop-point, half-serrated blade? Skeleton handle? Liner lock?"

"Yes, I think so."

"Well, Mr. Ward, we're getting quite a few inquiries on our Web site about our knife and how it performed for you in the situation you were in. I must say, by the way, that was a really incredible thing you did, saving that lady and her baby."

"Thanks, uh, Walt. But is there something I can help you with?"

“Well, we’d like to talk to you about your experience with our product, and also discuss the possibility of signing an endorsement deal with you.”

“Gee, I don’t know, Walt. I’m kind of hoping to put the whole thing behind me at this point. I really don’t want any more publicity.”

“I can understand how you feel, Mr. Ward. The last thing I want to do is invade your privacy. However, I just want you to hear me out. I think we can do this in a way that isn’t too intrusive.”

“Okay.”

“We’re an American company. We design all of our products in the U.S. and still make many of them here. When a news event like this happens, it can provide a real opportunity for us to raise our profile in the face of some pretty stiff competitors – some of whom have much bigger marketing budgets than we do. So we’d like to at least explore the possibility with you. Of course we’ll be glad to compensate you for your time and use of your name.”

“Well ...”

“Look, I’m not asking you to say ‘yes’ right this minute. I’d like to invite you to visit our factory here in Nerlinville, New York this Saturday. We’re in the foothills of the Catskills, not too far from where you are, I don’t think. Are you married?

“Yes.”

“Well, please bring your wife along. You can come in Friday evening and, we’ll put you up in one of the resort hotels here. She can enjoy herself there while we meet on Saturday, and we’ll all enjoy a nice dinner Saturday evening before you head home on Sunday. Please, won’t you at least consider it?”

Walt Schraber was persistent without being pushy and he seemed sincere. Bill wasn’t really interested in doing any kind of endorsement, but felt like he should at least hear him out. And Maggie might enjoy getting out of town after all the craziness and attention the previous weekend.

"Okay, Walt, let me talk to my wife and see if we're free this weekend and I'll call you back. Would it be okay if we brought our daughter along?"

"By all means."

"Okay, great, let me talk to them and I'll call you tomorrow."

"Thank you, Mr. Ward."

"Please, call me Bill."

***

At home that evening, Bill talked to Maggie and Olive during dinner about the phone call from Walt Schraber and his invitation for the upcoming weekend. They were both excited about a trip to a resort in the Catskills, so Bill said he would make the arrangements.

After dinner, Howard called Bill to tell him there had been something on tabloid TV show "PM Tonight" about Shannon Gales. According to the story, she had worked at a strip club while in college.

Bill sighed as he responded.

"How bad is it."

"Pretty bad. They had video of women swinging around poles and stuff. The place is called Jiggles, down near Scranton, Pennsylvania. They interviewed some sleazeball manager who didn't even know Shannon. Wasn't there when she was there, but that didn't matter. And they had some dirtbag ex-boyfriend of hers on. Apparently he's the one who tipped them off."

"They talk about me?"

"Thankfully, no. You gonna watch it?"

"No, I don't think so. But I am going to call Shannon. Okay if I give her your number, if she has any questions about how to handle this?"

"Absolutely. Tell her I'll be glad to handle any press calls on this. I don't think there will be much – this is the kind of thing that tends to blow up and die down fast."

“Okay, thanks Howard. I appreciate you letting me know about it.”

“No problem, Bill. Talk to you later.”

After he hung up the phone, Bill told Maggie what had happened. She was visibly pained by what Bill said, and agreed that it would be nice if he called Shannon to offer his support.

Bill took the phone into the living room and dialed Shannon Gale’s phone number. Her husband answered the phone and quickly passed it to Shannon.

“Hello?”

“Hi, Shannon. It’s Bill Ward. How are you?”

“Um, not great. I suppose you saw the thing on TV about me.”

“I didn’t see it, but I heard about it. That’s why I called.”

“Oh Bill, I’m so embarrassed. I want you to know it’s not like they described it on TV.”

“Shannon, you don’t owe me any explanations, and that’s not why I called. I just wanted to tell you I’m sorry it happened and to make sure you’re alright.”

“No, but I want to tell you. I only worked there for a very short time when I was in college. I needed the money and a friend of mine was working there – she said the pay was really good. And we weren’t dancers – we were just waitresses. As soon as I started working there, I hated it. The men there were awful to all the girls. And the managers were even worse. I worked there for two or three nights, and then I quit and I never went back.”

“Is there anything I can do?”

“I don’t think so. My stupid ex-boyfriend – he’s the one who told them about it. My husband wants to kill him.”

“Well, I can understand how he feels, but that’s probably not the best idea in the world.”

“I know.”

"Look, Shannon, I know this is embarrassing right now. But the truth is everyone has things in their past they're not particularly proud of – choices and mistakes they've made. As those go, this is not especially horrible. The people who know you and your character won't give too much thought to this. And everyone else, well, there's not much you can do about that, and it doesn't really matter anyway. I know it doesn't seem like it now, but in a week or two this will probably all blow over."

"Tell that to my mother. She's ready to kill me."

"I doubt that. She's probably just shocked and embarrassed too. I'm sure she'll get over it. In the meantime, if there's anything I can do, please let me know."

"Thank you, Bill. You're very sweet."

"Also, I have a neighbor – guy named Howard Jones. He's a public relations executive."

"Right. The man who was with you at NBC on Monday."

"Yes. He really knows his way around this stuff. He's been a big help to me over the past few days. He said you're welcome to call him if you have any questions about how to handle this or if you need any help."

"He seemed very nice. Maybe I will call him."

"I think that's a good idea – he can probably set your mind at ease. Well, listen, I better let you go. I'm sure you need to get Lucy down for the night and get some rest yourself. How is she?"

"Bill, she's just fine. Thank you for asking."

Bill gave Howard's telephone number to Shannon, and they said goodbye and hung up.

Chapter 10

Saturday

Bill and Walt Schraber sat in Walt's second-floor office at the Schraber Knives factory. At the front of the office was a large window looking out onto the manufacturing floor of the factory. The rear wall behind Walt's desk was exposed brick.

Walt sat in a leather rolling office chair behind a large wooden desk, with Bill across from him in one of the matching leather guest chairs. On the walls were displays of various Schraber products, past and present. On the desk in a small display case facing Bill was a 10,000-year-old obsidian knife.

After breakfast with Maggie and Olive at the hotel – a very nice resort called Oaks Lodge – Bill had traveled several miles to the Nerlinville plant, arriving at 9:30 a.m. Maggie and Olive remained at the lodge, with an agenda for the day including horseback riding and a visit to the hotel's spa.

Walt had greeted Bill at the front desk of the Schraber facility, and after a few minutes chatting they toured the manufacturing plant. It was a Saturday, so there weren't many people on the shop floor -- just a few technicians performing maintenance on some of the equipment.

There also were a couple production operators working on some special orders, so Bill was able to observe the manufacturing process and how the craftsmen worked as they machined, cleaned, assembled and sharpened knives in preparation for final inspection, packaging, shipment and sale. Some of the process used computer-controlled machines for the general cutting and shaping, but all final work was done by hand.

The shop floor was meticulously laid out for efficiency, with materials, operating stations, tooling and other facilities all carefully arranged. The factory, which was clean and well maintained, was clearly an older facility, but the equipment was all up to date and well serviced.

After the tour, they settled into Walt's office for conversation.

“Well, that’s the factory, Bill. What did you think?”

“Very impressive. How long have you been in business?”

“My grandfather, Walt Senior – I’m Walt the Third – started it back 1919 when he came home after World War I. He served in the Navy on a battleship as a machinist mate, and when he got out he decided to use the skills he learned during the service to set up a small machine shop. Initially he just repaired farm tools and woodsmen’s axes and saws, and eventually began making his own products.

“Over time, hunters and other outdoorsman started bringing him knives for sharpening and repair, and he eventually started making those as well. People really liked them and demand grew, and eventually in the mid-1920s he was able to expand the shop, add more machinists, moving almost exclusively into making knives, primarily fixed-blade knives for hunting but also pocketknives, penknives, and specialty knives for the building trades.

“We nearly lost the business during the Depression, but Grandad was able to hang on with the help of my father. Dad joined the company when he turned 18. In the late 30s, we caught a break when the U.S. government gave us a big contract to make knives for the military – bayonets, switchblades, Marine fighting knives. The contract got huge when World War II started, and we were able to open this facility in 1943. We’ve been here ever since.”

“Do you do all your manufacturing here?”

“No, this is our U.S. base of operations. We have design, development, marketing, sales, finance and operations all headquartered here, along with the manufacturing facility downstairs. Everything we make is developed here. But we have three major product lines. We have our general consumer line -- mostly hunting knives, and knives for craftsmen and professionals – carpenters, electricians, and so forth.

“Those are manufactured in Asia, but under strict supervision from us – we have a management team at the overseas manufacturing facilities at all times, ensuring the quality of the materials and proper production, as well as to ensure the workers are being treated properly. My son, Walt IV, is over there on a two-year assignment right now.

“Then we have a P&M line for law enforcement, firefighters, EMTs and the military – everything from assisted-open tacticals to fighting knives to specialty multi-tools. We make most of those right here, under contract to federal, state and local government agencies. If their departments or service branches don’t provide them, first responders and service members can purchase them privately from us for wholesale plus 10 percent. We also offer several models from that line – like the one you have – in an import line that’s made in Asia.

“Then there’s our top-of-the-line collector’s line. Mostly commemorative models, special editions, special orders by military, police and sportsmen’s groups. These are presentation models made from the very best materials. We make all of those here.”

“Wow.”

“We’re a small company, Bill, and we don’t have aspirations beyond serving our customers and making the best products we can. We employ 250 people here in Nerlinville, and a couple hundred more around the U.S. and Canada supporting our sales and marketing efforts, and several thousand in Asia.

“It’s a tough market, with a lot of much bigger players who can beat us on price and volume. But we’ve built a global development and manufacturing operation that lets us do business the way we want to, the way we feel is best for customers, our employees and our communities. We don’t really have any other ambitions, and since we’re a private company we can operate the way we want without pressure from investors.

"Where we have an advantage is in the quality of our products and in service. We offer a lifetime guarantee on every product we make and sell – if it ever breaks or if you're unhappy for any reason, send it back and we'll repair or replace it for free. That builds a lot of loyalty with our customers."

"Walt, that's really all great. But I'm not sure where I figure into all of this."

"Like I said, Bill, we're in competition with a lot of much larger companies, so we need to look at every opportunity we can to gain an advantage. What you did last weekend has attracted a lot of attention for our products, and we'd like to offer you an endorsement and consulting opportunity."

"What would that involve?"

"Well, I would have my marketing team pull together a range of activities – from appearances in our booth at the larger sportsmen shows and professional events, to advertising, perhaps even some select speaking engagements. Really, it would be whatever you're comfortable with."

"I see."

"We'd also like to ask for your input on some of our current products, as well as new ones under development. For example, if there are any improvements we could make to the knife of ours you have now, we'd like to know about it."

"Well, I would have to think about it, Walt. I'm really not interested in any more publicity. I've kind of had my fill of it, to be honest."

"I understand. The reason I invited you up here this weekend was so you'd have an opportunity to see who we are and what we're all about. We don't want you to do anything that makes you uncomfortable, and I think you can tell from what you've seen today we take a pretty dignified approach to what we do."

"Yes."

"I will tell you, we're interested in having you involved in whatever way and at whatever level you want to be. I can promise you it won't take more of your time than you want to commit, and we can do most of it on weekends. If all you want to do is a few ads, or a couple personal appearances at exhibitions, or whatever, that's fine. And I want you to know, we'll be glad to compensate you fairly for your time and use of your name. Depending on what you decide, it could run well into five figures per year."

"It's a lot to think about."

"I know it is. And don't feel like you have to make a decision right now. Let me have the team pull together a proposal as kind of a menu, and you can review it and let us know what you think. Then we can draw up a contract for the activities you're interested in. "

"That seems reasonable."

"Okay, well then why don't you head back to the lodge and spend some time with your family. I'll swing by with my wife, Evelyn, and our daughter, Jeanine, at 6 and we'll all have dinner together. Jeanine is our CMO."

***

Sunday

The Wards started the drive home Sunday morning after breakfast. The first hour was spent on narrow, winding two-lane roads through Sullivan and Orange Counties before they reached the highway.

Maggie looked over her shoulder at Olive, who was dozing in the back seat, to make sure she wasn't listening before she spoke to Bill.

"So, what did you think?"

"About what?"

"About everything – Walt, the company, what they want you to do."

"Oh, I don't know. What did you think?"

“Well they were very nice – Walt, Evelyn, Jeanine. Olive and I had a wonderful time at the resort yesterday and dinner was lovely. It was very kind of them to do all that for us.”

“Uh huh.”

“So. Are you going to consider their offer.”

“Yes, consider it. Definitely.”

“But you’re not sure if you’ll do it?”

“Well, I have to see the details. They’re supposed be getting some different options together. But I’m not real comfortable with the whole ‘endorsement’ thing. Public appearances, advertising, all that. It’s just more attention, and I’ve had enough of that.”

“So are you saying you probably won’t do it?”

“Actually, as much as I don’t want to, I don’t know how I can turn it down.”

“Why?”

“Well, the money they’re talking about is pretty substantial. And with one kid in college and another headed there soon, it’s hard to say ‘no.’”

“Well, we’ve saved for college for them.”

“True. But I’m not sure it’s enough. Also with my job situation, I’m not sure how much longer I’m going to last at OpenSwitch.”

“What do you mean?”

“Well, you know how tough it’s been for me the past few years. Not much in the way of career prospects there.”

“You could have left and found something else.”

“I know, and I considered it. But a lot of my equity in the company is either unvested or under water, and I have a lot of my retirement tied to my Silver Anniversary date. So quitting now would mean leaving a lot on the table.”

Over the years, prior to his demotion, Bill had regularly received awards of stock options and restricted stock. But those awards came with limits on when he could cash out the options or take possession of the stock. By the time some of it had matured, the options were actually worth less than the value when awarded because the stock price had dropped so much. That meant they were essentially worthless until the stock price rose. With the restricted stock, he had to wait as much as four years for it to vest and he could take possession.

In addition, over the years, OpenSwitch had been gradually dialing back on the benefits it provided to employees, including discontinuing its pension program and shifting to a 401K structure. Some older employees like Bill were grandfathered in for certain added contributions to their retirement funds, but only if they reached the 25-year mark with the company.

"So you've been hanging on all these years for that? I know you haven't been happy there for a long time."

"I didn't really think I had a choice. I couldn't jeopardize the financial security of our family. And now, well, my career prospects aren't very good at OpenSwitch or anywhere else."

"You couldn't find another job?"

"Eventually maybe, but I'm not what most people are looking for. Too old. Too male. Too expensive."

"And you think your job is at risk now?"

"Well, the company hasn't grown revenue in more than three and half years, and now the profitability is starting to get soft. They've been cutting costs wherever they can, and that includes laying off people like me. That's what we are to them – cost."

"Can they really do that? It sounds like discrimination."

"They work pretty hard at disguising it, but it's exactly what it looks like."

""I didn't realize it was that bad there."

"Well, I don't talk about it much because I don't want you to worry about it. But under the circumstances, I think I have to consider Walt's offer when I get the details."

"I don't want you to worry either. My jewelry business is starting to pick up and I can work more at that."

A few months earlier, Maggie had joined a network marketing company called Bonsai Bear that sold jewelry through personal contacts and parties, like Tupperware. The company's products were becoming very popular and selling well. She had become a "Bonsai Bear Creative Artist," as their sellers were called, mostly to have something to do, earn some money, and dip her toe back in the work world. With her graphic design background and her personality, she found quickly that she was pretty good at selling jewelry and that she enjoyed it.

"That's sweet of you, Maggie. I know you enjoy your jewelry business and if you want do more of it because you like it, that's fine. But I don't want you to think you *have* to do it."

"I know. I just want you to know I can contribute too, and you don't have to carry the whole load yourself."

"I appreciate that. But look, let's just take it one step at a time. We'll see what Walt has to offer and go from there. As for what happens at OpenSwitch, I'm just taking it a day at a time."

"Okay."

Olive was not asleep in the back seat. She heard the entire conversation.

Chapter 11

Monday

Maggie stood in front of the bathroom mirror in her underwear, putting on her makeup. She had a meeting with a prospective client for a Bonsai Bear party later that morning, so after she got Olive off to school she came back upstairs to get dressed.

She stood back from the vanity, looking at her appearance in the mirror and frowning. Like many women her age she had a few lines around her eyes, but not many. Like most women her age, she'd put on a few pounds around her chest, belly, hips and thighs, but not as much as most.

She was still a very attractive woman, who could easily pass for 10 years younger and still caught men's attention without trying. Bill still told her she was beautiful – or he had, until recently, as she had increasingly brushed off his compliments. He had been completely sincere about it. That was one thing about Bill – the man had absolutely no guile whatsoever. He never said anything he didn't really mean.

But it was more than her appearance that made her frown, although she was less than happy about the age lines and extra pounds. What made her unhappy was the stage of life she found herself in, her changing relationship with her children, and the state of her marriage to Bill.

She and Bill had met in college. She was a sophomore and he was a junior. She had first noticed him while walking back from class with a couple of her friends. It was a warm spring day, and he and about a dozen other guys were playing touch football on the quad between their dorms.

She remembered seeing him there, stripped to the waist, dripping with sweat, consumed with the joy of physical play in the warm sun. She and her friends stood watching for a while before he noticed them and smiled directly at her. There was such sweetness in that smile.

A few nights later, she saw him at a dorm party where he was playing drums with his band. Sitting behind that drum kit, again with no shirt and soaked in perspiration, he was about the sexiest thing she'd ever seen. Again, he noticed her and smiled, and on a break between sets he sought her out to talk. He looked her right in the eye when he spoke with her, and asked about her. Only when she asked about him did he share anything about himself, and then only modestly.

Early the next week, he asked her out for the following weekend, and soon they were seeing each other regularly. It quickly became obvious how different he was from the other boys she had dated on campus. Most of them were jocks and other BMOCs, who were quick to rush her into bed and just as quick to lose interest. They were exciting at first, but her experiences with them left her feeling hollow.

Bill was completely the opposite, always sweet, tender and a gentleman. He never rushed her in any way, and his affection for her was warm and genuine. Only once did she see even a hint of anything other than gentleness in him and it wasn't toward her. They were at a party on campus when an old boyfriend of hers made a crude remark.

Bill quietly rose from his seat, put down his beer, got within three inches of the guy's face and politely asked him to apologize immediately. The other buy was four or five inches taller and 20 pounds heavier than Bill. But something in Bill's eyes told everyone who witnessed the confrontation that he was ready to take the other guy apart if he didn't do as asked. The ex-boyfriend mumbled an apology and quickly left the party.

The incident left Maggie breathless. Bill had literally defended her honor, and was willing to back it up with physical violence if necessary. No one had ever done anything like that for her before.

They dated through the remainder of the term, he visited her regularly over the summer, and in the fall the relationship intensified. By the end of the term they were talking about a future together, and during the holiday break he traveled to her home, spoke privately with her father, and proposed on Christmas Eve – down on one knee, by the fireplace, ring in hand, in front of her entire family.

He graduated in the spring, took a job with OpenSwitch, and visited her at school through the following year. Their wedding was two weeks after her graduation that May. They settled quickly into newlywed life, and she had worked full time for the first several years.

She loved her job as a graphic designer at an advertising agency, and the double income from their jobs allowed them to save quickly for a house. But she quit when the babies came along -- she wanted to be home with her children. It was her choice, and Bill would have supported her no matter what she had decided.

She loved her mommy time with Bryce and Olive, every moment. The opportunity to be there from the time they were babies through school was precious and perfect, and she wouldn't have traded it for anything. But as they grew older, they had needed her less and less. Bryce was now out of the house and away at college, and Olive would be gone before long.

As the children exercised their independence, she found she had less to contribute to their lives. And as she had devoted herself to the children and Bill had poured himself into work, a gap had grown in her marriage. As a couple, they had become distant and dull. And she had found herself feeling empty, lonely and a little bored.

With nowhere else to express her frustration and growing anxiety, she had taken it out on Bill, constantly criticizing and complaining. It got to the point where he couldn't open his mouth to say something without her contradicting him and finding fault. What was worse, her attitude toward Bill had started infecting the children as well, especially Bryce. In response, Bill had grown ever more quiet.

Deep down, she knew the biggest source of her dissatisfaction was within herself, and she had taken both negative and positive steps to address it. At the previous spring's Memorial Day block party, one of the neighborhood men had propositioned her. She'd had a little too much to drink and he'd caught her alone for a moment. She initially found the prospect and the attention exciting, and had briefly considered taking him up on his offer, as she had grown disinterested in both Bill and their marriage.

But she had just as quickly dismissed the idea. The guy who hit on her was legendary in town for running around on his wife, and Maggie didn't really want to become his latest conquest. And if the affair became known, which was almost certain, it would have devastated her children and destroyed Bill. For all his patience, that would be the one thing he couldn't abide and it might have ended their marriage.

At about the same time, she had signed up with Bonsai Bear and was thriving on it. With her design sensibility and her social skills, she was a natural seller for the jewelry. Within six months she had quickly built out her network, booking parties and growing her commissions.

While she found some fulfillment in selling jewelry, she still had to reckon with the state of her marriage and her role in how it got the way it was. She knew that she was the one who widened the gulf between her and Bill. If she was bored and disappointed with their marriage, most of that was on her.

If Bill was a little dull, it was selflessly toiling away at a job he hated year after year to provide for his family that had largely made him that way. Despite that one flaw, if you could call it that, he had very few others. He was a kind and loving father, and a gentle and faithful husband, and a decent man of quiet character and principle.

If she had forgotten any of that, she was quickly reminded of it by the events of a week ago. What Bill had done that morning out on that highway shouldn't have been a surprise to anyone who really knew him, least of all her. It was perfectly consistent with his nature and disposition.

Something else she realized was just how close she had come to losing him that morning. If it had taken him just a little longer to get that woman and her child out of that car, or if the fire had moved a little bit faster, he could have been gone without any warning.

Maggie sighed, leaned forward and finished putting on her makeup. Somehow, over the years as their lives had changed, she had lost sight of what was important and of the sweet man she had married. As she dressed and prepared to leave for her meeting, she decided it was time for things to change in her marriage and her life, and that change had to come from her.

***

Late April, Thursday

Derbeville First Selectwoman Tricia Guarino looked at the agenda for the town council meeting to see what the next item was for discussion. The meeting was held in the cramped council chambers on the second floor of the town hall, which included the desks of the five council members facing a small audience seating area. Other than the council members, the only other people in attendance were the town attorney, the town clerk, and a couple of local residents who were regulars at these meetings.

Tricia rapped her gavel to get the attention of the other four council members who had been chatting quietly with each other.

"Our next order of business is a resolution naming local citizen Bill Ward as grand marshal for our annual Memorial Day parade and ceremonies, along with a citation honoring for his act of courage earlier this month. You all have the full text of the resolution and citation in your packets and I've entered a copy for the record with our town clerk. Therefore I'm making a motion that we waive the reading and move to discussion. Second?"

Selectman Matt Corvo seconded the motion, all members voted in favor and Tricia continued.

"Thoughts? Comments?"

Tricia expected no opposition to the resolution and was surprised when Selectwoman Paige Cantwell spoke up.

"I have some concerns."

"Oh … okay. What are they, Paige?"

"Well, I'm just not sure why we're choosing this man for recognition. For openers, the incident in question didn't even happen within the town limits."

The other council members looked at each other puzzled before Tricia responded.

"Are you serious?"

"Yes, of course I'm serious."

Selectman Stan Stern commented.

"Last year's honoree was Marine Lance Corporal Marty Thomas, who we recognized for saving two members of his squad when they were attacked by insurgents in Afghanistan. So I don't know why the location where the incident occurred is relevant."

Paige responded.

"Well, in addition, I don't know what distinguishes this man other than that one incident. I've never heard of him before this. Who is he anyway?"

Tricia responded.

"Well, by all accounts he's a solid citizen, serving in the community for years by volunteering for youth activities and other civic duties. He's active in his church and well thought of by his neighbors. In addition, I think the events of several weeks ago speak for themselves – he saved a woman and her daughter from a burning car just before it exploded."

"Yes, but the facts notwithstanding, do we really want to be reinforcing this type of patriarchal cultural stereotype where women are vulnerable and need to be rescued by some man swooping in like a knight in shining armor. Personally, I find it very inappropriate and distasteful."

"Are you kidding? I don't really see how gender stereotypes enter into this at all."

“Well, I just think there are other individuals who are better role models and more deserving of honoring than so-called ‘war heroes’ and macho men like Mr. Ward. For example, local resident Lydia Cartwright has just completed a tone poem on the five key principles of holistic veganism that’s been published by Berkeley College press and will be performed this summer at the Woodstock Institute. I think that’s much more worthy of our recognition and promotion.”

“For Memorial Day?”

“Yes, I think it’s about time we put to rest such outdated notions as commemorating death and destruction, and replace them with something more life affirming and wholesome.”

The other council members looked at each in in disbelief. Tricia sighed and then spoke.

“Okay, if there are no other comments on this resolution I make a motion to call for a vote of the council.”

The other three council members said “seconded” practically in unison. The resolution passed by a vote of four to one.

***

To: First Selectwoman Tricia Guarino and members of the Derbeville Town Council

Thank you for your letter of April 29 inviting me to serve as grand marshal for this year’s Derbeville Memorial Day parade and ceremonies, and your gracious offer of a personal citation regarding the incident of last month. As a long-time citizen of Derbeville, I am deeply honored and gratified by this offer.

However, I think it’s important to keep the focus of Memorial Day where it properly belongs – on the men and women who serve in our nation’s armed forces, and particularly those who have made the ultimate sacrifice in defense of our freedom and security.

As a private citizen, any actions of my own pale in comparison to contributions our brave service members make daily, and especially those who have given their lives to protect us all.

Therefore I feel I must respectfully decline your offer and suggest you select a more worthy person for this important honor.

Regards,

Bill Ward

Chapter 12

Early May, Saturday

Richard's Barber Shop in Derbeville might have been the coolest barber shop in the world. This was a real barber shop, not a salon. A striped pole stood out front, and the walls inside were decorated with posters, autographed photos and paraphernalia from the Jets, Giants, Mets, Yankees, Islanders and other sports teams, as well as popular entertainment figures ranging from Barney Fife of "The Andy Griffith Show" to heavy metal band Metallica.

A television mounted in the corner near the ceiling would alternately be tuned to the latest sporting event, an old movie, or a Seinfeld re-run. Beneath the TV stood a large bird cage with four parakeets contentedly fluttering about. Nearby was a small refrigerator, with a coffee maker on top.

Richard Camerari was the owner and head barber of the shop and his son, Richie, manned the second chair. Richard was imposing in appearance – big and tall, and his size and Yonkers accent would have made him seem even more formidable if it weren't for his gentle manner. Richie was a shorter and slightly thicker version of his father, with full sleeves of tattoos on both arms but the same calm disposition as his father.

The mirror in front of Richard's chair was decorated with ticket stubs and other memorabilia from concerts and sporting events he attended. Richie's was covered with stickers from heavy metal and hardcore bands he was into – Tool, Disturbed, Godsmack, and Hatebreed.

Saturdays were their busiest day, but by afternoon the crowd had thinned out. Bill Ward was in the first chair getting his monthly haircut from Richard. In the second chair was Marty Thomas, getting a buzz cut and chatting with Richie. Marty was home on leave from the Marines, and he and Richie were talking about Afghanistan.

Marty had done two combat deployments there, and Richie had served there as well for a year with the Army Rangers. One tour was enough for Richie, and he left the Army afterward, returned to U.S., attended barber school and joined his father at the shop.

Marty was the same age as Bill's son Bryce, and Bill had coached the boys in youth soccer when they were in elementary school. He and Marty had arrived at the barber shop at about the same time, and had greeted each other warmly.

Tony Bastaldo entered the shop, grunting a hello, just as Richard and Richie were finishing up with Bill and Marty. Tony was an older local resident, a large man with a reputation as a loudmouth and a bully. He eyed Bill and Marty as they rose from the chairs and listened to them talk, but didn't say anything.

"So how much longer will you be home, Marty?"

"I have about another week here. Then I'm heading down to Washington to visit a couple buddies of mine who are recovering at Walter Reed. After that, I go back to San Diego to get ready for my next deployment."

"Where are you headed?"

"Can't say too much, but it's back in the sandbox."

"Well, I know you have a lot to do and want to spend as much time with your folks as you can, but if you have a chance to stop by the house I know Maggie and Olive would love to see you. And if there's anything we can do for you while you're away, please let me know."

"Are you kidding, Mr. Ward? The packages your wife has been sending me are epic – candy, magazines, beef jerky, homemade cookies. The other guys are so jealous when I get one, but she always puts in plenty to share."

"Well she loves to do it."

Richard was at the register, ringing up Bill's haircut.

"That's 19."

Bill reached into his wallet and pulled out two twenties and four singles, and handed them to Richard.

"That's all set, Richard. And I've got Marty's too, okay?"

Marty started to protest.

"Mr. Ward, you don't have to do that."

"No. It's the least I can do. It's nothing, really."

"Well thank you."

"Just enjoy your time off and take care of yourself when you head back out."

Bill said his goodbyes to Richard and Richie. Marty and Richie bumped fists and hugged, and Richie told him "Be safe, bro." As Marty and Bill left the shop, Tony settled into the first chair with a heavy grunt and let Richard pull the cape over him. After the door had closed and Richard started trimming his hair, Tony opened his mouth.

"Geez, can you believe that guy?"

"Who?"

"That guy. Who just left. What's his name? Ward?"

"What about him?"

"Goin' around acting like he's some kinda big shot or something."

"What are you talking about?"

"That thing he did last month at that car accident. Big whoop. And now he thinks he's some kind of hero or something."

"I never heard him say anything about it."

"He don't gotta say nothing. Look at the way he acts. Buying that kid's haircut for him and all. Going on TV. With that gay guy."

"So what?"

"And the town council, blowing smoke up his ass. Asking him to be the leader of the Memorial Day parade. Gonna give him a medal or something too. And he says no. Too good for it, I guess."

"Aw, you don't know anything about it, Tony."

"I know a big phony when I see one. What a jerk."

Richard stopped cutting Tony's hair and stepped back.

"Listen, let me tell you something about that guy. A couple years back, I broke my leg. They set me up with a walking cast so I could work, but I couldn't do much else. Richie was away in the Army, so he wasn't around to help."

"So?"

"That guy, Bill Ward, found out and guess what? He comes to my house every Saturday all summer long and cuts my lawn for me. Didn't say anything about it, didn't want anything for it – just came and did it."

"Yeah, so what?"

"So, I didn't see you doing anything like that. And what he did out on that highway last month. I don't know too many guys who have the balls to do something like that, risking his life to save that lady and her baby. Certainly not you!"

Tony grunted, and Richard continued.

"That guy is my friend and he's a good guy. You? You don't mean nothin' to me. We could use a lot more like him and a lot less of you. Your haircut is finished. Now get out of my shop and don't come back."

"You can't talk to me that way! I've been coming to this barber shop for 20 years."

"And that's 20 years too long. I'm sick of your attitude and I'm sick of your mouth. Now, get the hell out!"

"I'm not paying for this haircut!"

"It's on the house. Small price to pay if I never have to see you again."

Tony stood up from the chair and said nothing for a moment, looking from Richard to Richie, as if he was trying to decide what to do next. Richie spoke up first.

"You better go."

"What, you gonna do somethin'?"

"I don't think I'll need to. But if you don't leave now, I might have to pull my Dad off you."

Tony threw the cape on the floor and stomped to the door.

"Wait'll I tell everyone how you treat customers around here!"

Richard stooped to pick up the cape, and muttered in response to the closing door.

"If anything, it'll be good for business, knowing they won't run into you here."

***

Late May, Friday Evening

Bryce used an old cloth diaper to wipe dried polish off of his car. He'd been working out in the driveway at the Ward's home for hours, just routine maintenance and cleaning. His father had made it clear when he handed down the used Toyota Camry to Bryce in his senior year of high school that he would be responsible for the car – cleaning it, caring for it, doing whatever mechanical maintenance he could perform himself and scheduling any other work with their mechanic.

That morning, Bryce had drained the oil from the car, replaced the oil filter and refilled the crankcase with new oil. His father had done the family's other two cars earlier, so the drain pan, tools, and supplies were already out. Do all three at the same time and you only have to clean up once, his father always said.

He also had replaced the engine and cabin air filters, vacuumed the interior, and then cleaned the dashboard and other vinyl surfaces with Armor All. After a break for supper, he washed the car and dried it with a chamois, and now was applying a coat of polish. On Monday, he was scheduled take it over to Hank's Tire Shack to get the tires rotated.

Working on the car had taken up a good part of his day. In the past, he had kind of resented his father for making him do it, but now he kind of liked it. He found the activity therapeutic, and was pleased at what he could accomplish with a little effort. And unlike, most of buddies, he'd learned how to care for an automobile through the experience.

His summer was shaping up a little differently than he had planned. The MTV internship had fallen through, so he wouldn't be living in New York. But his father's friend, Mort, had lined up a part-time co-op job for him, working in the marketing and promotions department for "The Tonight Show" at NBC. It was only a couple days a week, and unpaid, but the experience would be great. And Mort said if he did a good job he would try to set something up for the next summer, full time with pay.

He'd gone in for the first time the previous week and gotten acquainted with his manager and colleagues. He even met Jimmy Fallon briefly, and when Jimmy found out who he was, he'd made a point of telling Bryce what a good guy his father was.

The internship office at his college had arranged a fellowship that would pay his travel expenses in and out of New York City for the co-op position. And since he was only doing it three days a week, he was able to pick up a part-time job as a lifeguard at the neighborhood pool to make a little cash.

So, he'd be spending the summer living at home. Which, as it turned out, wasn't really a bad thing. His parents and sister seemed to really enjoy having him around, and he was a little surprised at how much he was enjoying it too.

***

TJ pulled into the driveway at the Ward's house, stopped the car, and got out. As he walked up the driveway, he greeted Bryce.

"Hey, Bryce."

Bryce didn't even look up as he responded.

"Hi, TJ. Olive's in the house."

"K. I'm playin' at the Palace Ballroom tonight – big party, if you want to come by."

"Thanks."

TJ shrugged, went up the front steps and knocked on the door, and Maggie answered, greeting him with a big smile.

"Hi, TJ, come on in. Olive's upstairs getting ready. I'll let her know you're here."

"Thanks."

"What are you and Olive doing tonight?"

"I got a gig at the Palace Ballroom – it's a club downtown. An all-ages show, so Olive can go. They got three acts performing tonight, including me, and the headliner is national touring artist Hevi Lode. He's from Oakland."

"Oh, well that sounds very nice. Let me get Olive."

"Okay, thanks – we gotta get goin'."

Bill heard the conversation from the living room. He had a clear view of the front hall way and the stairway to the second floor. In a few minutes, Olive came downstairs and he got up to say goodbye to her and TJ.

Olive was wearing a pair of shorts, sandals, and a midriff top, not the kind of thing she normally wore, but it was what the girls who went to these parties wore, and she wanted to look nice for TJ. He had been acting kind of strange for the past few weeks – different from when she first started going with him.

She'd met him at a party a few months earlier, a party she wasn't supposed to be at, if her parents had known about it. He was cute, and showed a lot of interest in her, which attracted her to him right away. Her best friend, Jade, had been there and had the exact opposite reaction, and giving her a hard time about it on the way home.

"You better watch out for that boy – he's bad news."

"He seemed really nice to me."

"Yeah, well, they always do when they want somethin', and you know what he wants."

"He wasn't like that."

"No yet. But you watch out. White boy, thinkin' he's a rapper."

"Eminem is white."

"That boy is not Eminem!"

Bill took a look at Olive's outfit and said one word.

"Nope."

"But, Daddy!"

"Honey, I'm sorry, but you're not going out dressed like that."

Maggie tried to intervene.

"Bill, don't you think … "

"Honey. Please. Olive, you need to go change."

TJ was about to explode and couldn't contain his anger.

"But we'll be late and I'll lose my spot!"

Bill eyed him calmly and responded.

"Well son, you can either wait for Olive or go on ahead without her. It's your choice."

Olive had a look of panic in her eyes. She ran up the stairs, shouting behind her.

"I'll be right down. Five minutes!"

Bill went back in the living room while TJ stewed and paced in the hallway. Maggie went upstairs to help Olive change.

Five minutes later, Olive flew back down the stairs wearing jeans and a cute blouse, with the same sandals.

"I'm ready!"

TJ stormed out the door.

"Let's go!"

Olive ran after him, and Maggie called after the pair.

"Have fun! Home by midnight!"

TJ walked quickly down the driveway, with Olive running behind him. Bryce was crouched down, working the dried polish off the car's rear quarter panel when TJ passed him.

"Your old man's real piece of work, you know that?"

Bryce looked at him sideways and responded.

"What did you just say?"

TJ stopped, started to say something, and thought the better of it.

"Nothin'."

"Yeah, that's what I thought. Get out of here, TJ."

TJ turned to leave and shoved Olive toward the car.

"Let's go."

Olive stumbled and fell to one knee, and TJ grabbed her arm and yanked it hard.

"Come ON!"

Olive yelped in pain and pulled her arm close to her chest. TJ heard Bryce speak close behind him.

"Hey, TJ."

TJ whirled to face Bryce and started to yell "What!?,"when a fist slammed into his chest just below the breastbone, knocking the wind out of him. He doubled over gasping for breath, and Bryce brought his knee up hard into the bridge of TJ's nose, cracking the cartilage with an audible snap.

TJ fell back on the grass, still gasping and with blood streaming out of both nostrils. Bryce was instantly on top of him, pounding his face and chest with punches. TJ was yelling and trying to catch his breath, and Olive was screaming. Bryce stopped and his head snapped around as he heard his father's voice behind him.

"Bryce! That's enough."

His father was standing on the front porch, with his mother behind in the doorway. The wild look in Bryce's eyes faded and he climbed off of TJ. Bill walked down the steps and over to the garage, grabbed one of the clean diapers from the rag basket, and walked over to where TJ and Bryce were.

Bill spoke to Olive.

"Olive, go in the house."

Olive ran to the house, where Maggie was waiting to put an arm around her. They disappeared inside.

Bill knelt down next to TJ and gently helped him sit up. He used the diaper to blot the blood from TJ's nose and tilted the boy's head back to stop the bleeding. After a few minutes, when TJ had gotten his breath back and the bleeding had subsided, Bill whispered something to him.

TJ nodded, slowly got up from the ground, walked to his car and got in. He slammed the car in reverse, sped out of the driveway, shifted to drive and floored the gas pedal, disappearing around the corner down the block.

Bill walked over to Bryce.

"Are you okay?"

"Yeah. Dad, he ..."

"I saw what he did."

"Okay."

"Where did you learn to fight like that."

"Gym class last semester, for my Phys Ed requirement. Krav Maga – Israeli martial arts. I got an 'A'."

"I would imagine so."

"What, ah, what did you say to TJ before he left?"

"I told him the next time he laid a hand on Olive like that, I wouldn't stop you. And then I suggested he leave and not come back."

***

Two blocks from the Ward's house, TJ was pulled over by the police for running a stop sign. There was an open can of beer in the cup holder on the center console of his car, and the officers quickly discovered that his registration and insurance were expired.

A subsequent search of the trunk revealed a large Ziploc bag full of marijuana, cocaine and oxycodone pills.

TJ wouldn't be going to California for a while.

***

Bill walked upstairs and stopped outside of Olive's room. The door was open, but he knocked before entering anyway. Maggie was sitting next to Olive on the bed. Olive had been crying.

"You okay, sweetie?"

"Yes. Is Bryce okay?

"He's fine."

"I thought he was going to kill TJ."

"I don't think he would have done that. But it's probably just as well that I stopped it when I did."

"Yeah."

"I'm sorry about what happened. Has TJ ever done anything like that to you before?"

Olive hesitated before answering.

"Well, not really. But lately, he hasn't been as nice to me. Sometimes he's a little rough. But not like tonight. Not like that."

"Okay. I want to make something clear to you. No matter the circumstances, it is not okay for a boy to treat you like that. Never. That's not the way a man – a real man -- behaves. Do you understand?"

"Yes."

"Maggie?"

Maggie nodded. Bill turned back to Olive.

"Olive, until you turn 18, your mother and I are going to have an opinion about who you are allowed to date. From now on, TJ is not welcome here and you are not allowed to see him. Once you're an adult, who you see is no longer our prerogative. But I want to be clear, what happened tonight – what he did – that's never acceptable. And your Mom and I will always have an opinion about that."

"Yes, Daddy."

"Okay then."

Chapter 13

Memorial Day

The holiday festivities were in full swing in the Ward's neighborhood, Acorn Park. Memorial Day marked the start of the summer season in their end of town, with a full day of activities and events for all the local families.

The day started with the annual Derbeville Memorial Day Parade, with all the usual participants taking part in the trek down Main Street – middle school and high school marching bands, Little League teams, troops of Brownies, Girl Scouts, Cub Scouts and Boy Scouts, veterans groups, Revolutionary War and Civil War re-enactors, the Corvette Club, the Shriner Mini-Bike Patrol, an array of military vehicles from the local museum, and local elected officials as well as those seeking office, bag pipers and veterans groups. Bringing up the rear of the procession was a fleet of fire trucks and other emergency vehicles, horns blaring and sirens wailing.

After the parade, the residents of Acorn Park returned to the neighborhood for an afternoon of eating, socializing and fun. One of the larger cul de sacs, Paradise Court, was blocked off and a big tent erected at the end of the street, covering a small stage with an open area in front of it, and tables and chairs in the rear.

On the stage throughout the afternoon, there was entertainment for the children, including clowns, a magician, local dance school performances, and a martial arts demonstration by students at Master Chi's Tae Kwon Do Academy. Outside the tent, there were games and races with prizes.

Later in the day, a dozen neighborhood men manned their grills, serving up hot dogs, hamburgers, Italian sausage, and barbecue chicken. Several of the guys had set up a barbecue pit and roasted a whole pig. The women arranged tables full of salads, side dishes and desserts. There were coolers full of soda, lemonade and ice tea, while for the adults there was beer on tap and wine to pour.

As the afternoon faded into evening, the younger children were sent home for baths and bedtime, attended by babysitting middle-schoolers. The teenagers departed for the neighborhood pool, where they would have their own evening of entertainment with a DJ and dancing. The adults remained at the tent, where the wine and beer continued to flow. At 8:30 p.m., a band called The Dead Lunchladies, consisting of amateur musicians from the neighborhood, took the stage.

Many of the women liked to dance the more they drank, and more than a few of the men would join them. As the evening wore on and the alcohol took effect, the party got more and more raucous. The Dead Lunchladies were actually not bad. Band leader and guitarist Stu Guffin was a pretty accomplished player who had toured with some minor-league pro bands when he was younger before he gave up the road for the steady life of a tax accountant. And he had gathered around him a group of fairly competent players.

They majored in playing songs from various eras and idioms that people like to dance to, from "Honky Tonk Woman" by the Rolling Stones to Maroon 5's "Harder To Breathe." If a song had a good beat, and it would make the women shake it, they would play it. By pre-arrangement, at various points they would invite other members of the neighborhood with musical ability to come up and sing a song or play a solo. As the evening wore on, the band tended to sound better and better to the whooping, ever-more-tipsy audience.

***

The Wards had skipped the parade, but came down the street for the barbecue and entertainment, hanging close with the Joneses and socializing with other families they were friendly with. At dusk, Olive and Jade exited for the party at the pool, with Bryce and Jade's older sister, Jasmine, going along to serve as hosts and chaperones.

Maggie and Judy huddled at the far end of the tent where the music wasn't quite so loud, talking and laughing. Bill and several other neighborhood men were chatting over beers.

"I dunno man, I can't figure it out. No matter what I do, my yard is a mess."

"I know, right? Mine looks like a missile test range. Bill – your lawn looks like an ad for a fertilizer company. What's your secret?"

"Yeah, right? It's embarrassing. You're making us look bad, dude."

Bill thought for a second and then responded.

"It's really not that complicated. Just a shot of pre-emergent in the spring – you have to time that just right for it to be really effective. I usually go the first or second week of April, depending on how warm and wet it's been. Then spot treat for dandelions and other broadleaf weeds periodically throughout the spring and summer, a shot of winterizer in the fall and that's it."

"Spot treat?"

"Yeah, Weed B Gon or one of the other selective topicals will do it. Hit every dandelion as soon as you see it. Otherwise one becomes two, two become 10, and 10 become a hundred. It's basically an arms race."

"Can I use Roundup?"

"No! Roundup kills EVERYTHING. You want something that only kills the weeds but doesn't harm the grass."

"Well that explains it. Bob used so much Roundup last year his yard was like scorched earth. We started calling him Agent Orange."

"Shut up, Frank! Anything else, Bill?"

"Well, you know, little things. Vary your mowing pattern so you don't get ruts. Mulch your leaves in the fall – that's like free fertilizer. And every three years or so, I aerate and overseed the lawn in the fall. That helps break up the dirt and bring in a fresh crop of grass."

"Aerate and overseed?"

“Oh yeah, you HAVE to aerate and overseed. It really helps maintain a nice, tight healthy lawn, with thick grass that helps choke out the weeds. But other than that, just the bare minimum of fertilizer spring and fall. It’s really not complicated.”

“What about watering?”

The band had just finished its first set, closing out with Power Station’s cover of “Bang A Gong,” which really got the crowd wound up and yelling for more. Stu promised they’d be back in a few minutes to play more, exited the stage and walked to the back of the canopy where Bill and some of the other men were standing.

“Hey, Bill. Sorry to interrupt guys.”

“Hi Stu.”

“Say, someone told me you play drums.”

“Well, I used to. Years ago.”

“Would you be interested in coming up and playing a song with us?”

“Wow – I don’t know. It’s been a long time since I sat behind a kit.”

“Aw, that’s okay. It’ll be great. Please? We’d love it.”

“Uh, okay, I guess maybe. If it’s okay with your drummer.”

“Great, we’re back up in about five minutes. Why don’t you come over and I’ll ask Dan to get you set up?”

“Okay.”

Bill followed Stu to the front of the tent, where Dan – the band’s drummer – and the rest of the group’s members were joking and laughing with some of the neighbors. Stu walked up to Dan, and Dan looked at him and Bill, slightly puzzled. Stu spoke.

“Hey Dan, I asked Bill to sit in on drums for a song. You don’t mind, do you?”

Dan DID mind, but he was caught off guard and didn't want to be a jerk. Bill realized that Stu hadn't arranged things in advance with Dan and felt awkward about the situation, but didn't know how to back out. Dan responded to Stu.

"Um, okay."

"Great! Why don't you show Bill your kit and get him ready to go?"

From across the canopy, Maggie saw Bill climb the stage and looked at him quizzically. He looked back with an "I'll tell you later" shrug, and started to survey the drum kit.

It was a *very nice* drum set -- a top-of-the-line DW Collector's Series five-piece kit with gorgeous mahogany and maple shells, chrome hardware, two bass-drum-mounted toms and two floor toms. Accompanying the kit was a DW six-and-a-half-by-14-inch snare and Bosphorus hi-hat, splash, crash and ride cymbals, all mounted on heavy-duty stands. Bill inhaled deeply as he took it in.

"This is a gorgeous kit, Dan."

"Thanks. I just reskinned the bass drum and tuned all the toms and the snare."

"I appreciate you letting me take it for a spin. I'm really sorry about this."

Dan had recovered from his surprise and realized Bill was just as caught off guard by Stu's suggestion. He responded to Bill's sincerity with good humor.

"Well, just try not to make me look bad, and bring it back with a full tank of gas."

Bill laughed as he sat down on the motorcycle-style airlift drum throne, adjusted the height, tapped the kick drum pedal sharply a couple times and rapped a quick run around the drums and cymbals to hear their individual timbres.

The other members of the band remounted the stage and went through the routine of tuning and warming up. Stu looked over his shoulder and spoke to Bill.

"You ready to go?"

"Ready as I'll ever be. What's the tune?"

“How about ‘Keep Your Hands To Yourself’ by the Georgia Satellites?”

“Seriously?”

“I know. But the girls like it. You know it?”

“Yeah, I think I can find my way through it.”

Stu turn back around to the front of the stage, walked to the mic and addressed the gathering crowd.

“Alright! We’re back! You ready to party?”

The crowd hooted and cheered in response.

“Okay, we have another guest joining us on stage here. On drums, Mr. Bill Ward!”

The crowd shouted its approval, to Bill’s surprise. Stu gave a four count, started the opening riff of the song and began singing the first verse. When he got to the sixth line, Bill and the band hit the downbeat on cue, and launched into the instrumental bridge leading to the second verse.

To his own surprise, Bill’s drumming was tight. His time was good, his fills worked, and he and the bass player were able to lock up nicely to drive a cool groove for the dancers.

“Boy, this feels good,” Bill thought.

Five minutes later, the band ended the song to cheers and yells from the crowd. Some of the women had moved down front and were really getting carried away. Stu and the other band members looked back at Bill and gave him a thumbs up, and he smiled back.

He was a split second away from rising off the drum stool when without warning Stu launched into the intro riff of “Give It Away” by the Red Hot Chili Peppers. Stu looked back at Bill with a wink, and Bill shrugged and got ready.

On the third turn through the riff, Bill snapped off a series of snare hits and the band launched in to the song to shouts from the audience. Whether it was the beat or the alcohol, or the collective effect of both, the crowd danced harder and yelled louder than they had all night. As the band wound down the song, the crowd yelped and roared. Stu looked over and shouted to Bill.

"One more? How about 'Rockstar' by Nickelback?"

Bill instantly stood up and responded.

"No. Thanks. It was great. But this is Dan's gig. He should play it."

He stepped away from the drum set and handed the sticks back to Dan.

"Thanks for letting me sit in. That's a fantastic kit. I appreciate you sharing it with me."

Dan blinked at Bill's graciousness and his compliments about the drums.

"You're welcome, Bill."

As Bill exited the stage, Dan thought, "Man, that guy is good!"

***

Bill walked to the back of the tent where Maggie, Judy and Howard were standing while the band banged its way through Buckcherry's "Crazy Bitch." Maggie was the first one to greet him, somewhat breathlessly, when he arrived.

"Bill, that was … that was …"

Judy jumped in at that point.

"Bill, that was amazing! I had no idea you could play drums so well."

Howard then commented with some consternation.

"Yeah, uh, what the hell was that? Where do you get off, all these years, not letting me know you were cool?"

Bill responded.

"Aw, come on guys. It wasn't that great. I haven't picked up a pair of sticks in over 10 years."

Howard replied.

"Nevertheless, that was pretty impressive. Everyone here seemed to like it."

"Credit goes to the alcohol. At this point, they'd like a chimpanzee banging on a bongo."

The two couples chatted for a few more minutes, and then Howard announced that he and Judy were calling it a night – he had an early meeting the next day. Judy asked Maggie to walk down to their house with them for a quick look at the new curtains in the living room. Judy wasn't sure if she should keep them and wanted a second opinion. Bill offered to come along, but Maggie told him he didn't have to and that she'd be right back.

Bill walked over to one of the kegs, grabbed a cup and drew a beer for himself. Then he settled down in a chair at one of the empty tables near the back of the tent. For late May, it was a warm, muggy night, and he was still perspiring from his exertion on the drum kit. He was glad he and Bryce had put in the air conditioners earlier in the day at home, as it would make sleeping more comfortable for everyone that evening.

One of the neighborhood women, Marguerite Des Barres, approached his table. Marguerite was a tall, attractive woman in her late 40s, but looking much younger. She wore a sleeveless top that was cut low and open at bottom showing her slim waist. Her long, slit skirt was tight across her waist and hips, accentuating her figure.

"Hi Bill. Mind if I join you."

Bill looked slightly startled, but responded politely.

"Please, have a seat."

He rose to hold her chair for her.

"Oh. Such a gentleman."

Bill didn't know Marguerite particularly well – they didn't really travel in the same social circle. But he was aware that she and her now ex-husband both had reputations for infidelity – occasionally with other people in neighborhood. They'd split up about a year before, with him moving out and her remaining in the house.

Bill didn't really pay much attention to the rumors about the Des Barres. It didn't concern or interest him, and he wasn't the kind of guy who traded in gossip. But he had become aware of Marguerite's presence while he was playing with the band.

For most of the evening, she had been dancing near the front of the stage, spinning the hardest and yelling the loudest. While he was playing, he glanced up a few times to notice her looking directly at him.

"That was really great, you playing with the band. I had no idea you were such a good drummer."

"Oh. Thank you. It's been awhile since I've played. I'm surprised I didn't tank."

"No, you were wonderful."

There was a long pause before either of them spoke. Bill wasn't much for small talk, so he felt no obligation to fill silence as sipped his beer.

"You're really a very interesting man, Bill Ward. I haven't really known you before this, but you seem to be full of surprises."

"Oh. Uh, thanks."

Bill felt Marguerite's bare foot rubbing against his ankle. He moved his foot. Then he felt her hand on his knee, under the table, and then on his thigh. He looked at her with puzzlement and mild annoyance.

"Marguerite. What are you doing?"

"Oh, I just want you to know, you know … if you want."

Bill got up from the table and put down his beer. As gently as he could, he responded.

"All the same, Marguerite, you're right – you don't really know me. That's not who I am. Have a nice evening."

Marguerite was confused by his response and watched him walk away. Men simply didn't reject her that way.

Maggie had returned from the Jones' house and Bill saw her walking across the tent toward him. She saw Marguerite sitting at the table he'd just left, looking puzzled. Bill walked to meet Maggie.

"Time to go."

"Oh. Okay. Let me just grab my dessert tray and we can go home."

The party was still in full roar when they left.

Chapter 14

Bryce and his pal Donnie Walbridge stood by the refreshment table at the neighborhood pool, watching the younger kids have fun. By mutual agreement, the adults and teenagers separated at dusk on Memorial Day for their own separate parties. The adults didn't want the kids seeing them dancing and carrying on, and no teenager in the world wanted to see his parents doing that.

The adults always deputized a couple of the college kids in the neighborhood to supervise the teen party, and this year Bryce had drawn the duty, along with Jasmine Jones from across the street. Donnie had tagged along, but had to head out shortly for home.

For the most part, the kids were behaving well and having a good time – swimming, dancing to the DJ, enjoying the refreshments. Some of the older teens clustered in huddles, self-segregated by gender, occasionally venturing across the invisible demarcations between the groups to ask someone to dance or just talk.

Five of the older boys had come over to Bryce and Donnie. They were bored and wanted the older guys to buy some beer for them, but Bryce declined and Donnie backed him up. One of the more aggressive boys, Jeff Smith, confronted Bryce and pushed back.

"Aw come on! What's the big deal?"

"I said 'no,' Jeff. Not a good idea. Too many younger kids around."

"Well, we'll just get it on our own then."

"That's up to you. But if you leave the party, don't come back."

"Why, what are you gonna do about it?"

Bryce gave him a cold look and replied evenly.

"I'm not going to tell you twice, Jeff."

Jeff got a look of mild desperation in his eyes. He knew he had pushed too far, but didn't know how to back down without embarrassing himself. The other boys grew uncomfortable with the exchange. Bryce hadn't threatened Jeff, but he didn't really have to. They all knew about the fight between Bryce and Olive's ex-boyfriend a few weeks before, and that it wasn't a good idea to cross Bryce. One of more serious boys in the group, who had always looked up to Bryce and Donnie, finally spoke up.

"Hey, if Bryce says 'no,' then it's 'no.' That's it. Come on, Jeff."

The five departed for a dark corner of the pool area. Donnie spoke to Bryce.

"Well, that went well."

"Yeah. Funny. A year ago, I would have just bought it for them. I hope nobody saw any of that."

"Well, someone did."

"Who?"

"Jasmine."

Jasmine was standing near a table on the other side of the pool where her sister Jade, Olive and their friends were talking and laughing. She was a beautiful girl, tall and athletic. She'd lettered in volleyball and track in high school, competing well enough to qualify for a partial scholarship at Yarborough College, where she had begun attending the previous fall.

Bryce had been attracted to her throughout high school, and even made a few small attempts to get her attention, but she hadn't returned his interest. She thought he was conceited and arrogant at the time, which was largely true. She was serious and mature for her age even in high school, a good judge of character, and had no time for any boy who was so full of himself.

Bryce looked across the pool at Jasmine and saw her looking in his direction, but he quickly glanced away when their eyes met. He had seen her only briefly since they had both left for college the previous fall. If she had been pretty before, she was even more so now, and he would have loved to ask her out, but he knew from prior experience that he didn't have a shot.

His relationship with Eve at college had ended after they had only gone out a few times. Although she was very cute, he found her to be shallow – it turned out the main reason she was interested in him was because of his father's new-found fame. In the past that really wouldn't have mattered to him – in fact, he probably would have used it to his advantage. But when she had finally invited him up to her room just before the end of the semester, she was surprised when he declined. So was he.

Donnie's voice stirred Bryce back to the present.

"She's been looking over here all night."

"Yeah?"

"Yeah. You gonna do something about that?"

"I don't know."

"You should probably do something about that."

"Maybe."

"Well, I gotta go. Early day at work for me tomorrow. I'll see you later."

"Okay. Say 'hi' to your mom for me."

Donnie walked around the pool to say good night to Jasmine. Bryce watched as she smiled at Donnie and gave him a hug before he left. After a few minutes, Jasmine made her way over to where Bryce was. She had noticed a pronounced difference in Bryce this summer. His cockiness had been replaced with a down-to-earth, polite confidence. She liked it. He'd always been handsome, but his new attitude made him very attractive to her. She walked up and greeted him.

"Hi."

"Hi."

"Thanks for helping out with the party tonight. Some of these kids can be a handful."

"It's no problem. Glad to do it."

"I appreciate the way you handled those boys a few minutes ago."

"You heard that?"

"Yes."

"Well, I just didn't think it was a good idea for them to be drinking here. I wouldn't want anything to happen."

"Well, thanks. I'm not sure I could have been as persuasive as you were."

"Don't sell yourself short. The Jasmine Jones I know can be pretty determined."

She smiled, and there was a short, awkward pause. He made an attempt at small talk.

"So, how was school?"

"Good. Really good. I can't believe I'm already done with my first year."

"Yeah, it goes fast. I can't believe I only have two years left myself. Classes went well?"

"Yes, very well. I've decided to double major in biology and chemistry."

"Whoa. Heavy load. What are you thinking about for a career?"

"Well, maybe med school. Or maybe I'll get a Ph.D. and teach college. I still need to figure it out."

"Well, you have time. How's your summer going?"

"Fine. I'm working at Pottery Pier. I worked there last summer and they took me back. How about you? I heard you got an internship."

"Yeah, just part time, a couple days a week. At NBC in New York. And I'm lifeguarding here at the pool. Nothing too exciting."

"I heard you pulled a toddler out of the deep end the other day after he fell in when his mother wasn't looking. "

"It was no big deal. He was a just little scared."

Jasmine smiled at him.

"Well, my, my, Bryce Ward. It sounds like modesty and lifesaving are kind of the family business over at your house these days."

"Really. It was nothing."

"And I know about what you did when that boy got rough with your sister last weekend."

"Aw, man. You didn't see that, did you?"

"No, but Jade told me about it."

"Yeah, I'm a little embarrassed by it. I don't usually do stuff like that. I haven't even been in a fight since the ninth grade. But he had it coming. Nobody touches my sister like that."

"Well, I thought it was … gallant."

"Uh, thank you. I just wouldn't want you to think I go around getting in fights all the time. I don't."

"I don't think that."

Bryce looked down, a little embarrassed by the attention. When he looked up, Jasmine was still looking at him smiling. He blushed. She broke the silence.

"Well, I suppose I should make the rounds, make sure nobody is getting into trouble."

"Oh. Sure. Hey, uh, would … would you like to maybe do something Friday night? Maybe go to a movie or get something to eat. Or something."

"Oh. Um, no."

He looked down again, embarrassed, thinking he had misread her.

"Oh. Okay."

"I have to work Friday night."

"Oh."

"But I'm free Saturday."

"Oh! Good. Okay. Good! I'll call you tomorrow. Good."

"Great."

"Good."

Jasmine turned to walk away. Bryce paused for a minute and then called out.

"Wait. I'll come with you."

***

Bill was sitting in bed, reading a book by the soft glow of a lamp on the night table. It had been a long day and he was tired, but still too restless to go to sleep. Maggie was in the bathroom getting ready for bed. Olive was home from the party and in her bedroom down the hall way. The last he saw Bryce, his son was standing on the Jones' front porch talking with Jasmine.

The door to the bathroom opened and Maggie stood there silhouetted against the light behind her. She was wearing a short, pink, opaque chemise that fell just to the top of her thighs, and in the light filtering through it he could see each curve of her body. Maggie had always had a nice figure, but in the past six weeks or so she had lost about 15 pounds through diet and exercise. And she looked good -- really good. Bill sat stunned for a moment before speaking.

"Wow."

"You like it."

"Uh. Yes."

There was a short pause and then Maggie spoke.

"Something wrong?"

"No. No. Nothing's wrong. It's just …"

"What?"

"What is this, Maggie?"

"What do you mean?"

"Why are you doing this?"

Maggie started to get upset.

"Doing WHAT? What's the matter? You don't like it? You don't like … me?"

"No, of course not. That's not – "

"I guess you'd rather be with Marguerite!"

"What?"

"I saw her with you tonight, at the party. That skank."

"Maggie. You know better than that."

Maggie paused.

"I know. Then … what? What's the matter?"

"I don't know. It's just ever since the accident everybody … everybody … treats me different. Like I'm not the same guy I was before. Like they're … surprised or something. That's what really hurts my feelings – they're surprised. I had kind of gotten used to being written off, having nobody care what I think. "

"Nobody didn't care …"

Bill cut her off.

"And NOW – now some people are nicer to me, like they never knew me before. Some people aren't as nice to me, like they're jealous or something. People I don't even know have an opinion about me. And everybody acts different toward me. Even you … for the past month or so, you've been doing it too. Being ignored is one thing. But I can't even deal with all this weird attention I'm getting now. And now … this, from you.'"

"This what?"

"This! You haven't acted this way with me in … years."

Maggie startled slightly, and then sighed.

"I'm sorry. It's not what you think. I think I've just realized that I've been taking you for granted. I haven't been happy. About a lot of things, for a long time. And I took it out on you. And when I thought about the fact that I could have lost you that day … that I came very close to that … I decided I wanted to change things. Make things better between us. I just want … I just want us …"

Maggie was crying, and Bill spoke to her softly.

"It's okay. I understand. I'm not complaining. I just want to make sure it's really me you want to be with, and not this stupid … 'hero' people keep talking about."

"It's not. It's just you. And me. And if anything, what happened last month made me remember what kind of man you really are, the man you've always been, and how important you are to me. I had lost sight of that. And I'm sorry. I'm sorry for taking you for granted."

Maggie pulled herself together, and Bill spoke.

"You okay?"

"Yeah. I'm fine. I'll go change."

"I didn't say I didn't like it."

"What do you want me to do?"

"Come to bed."

***

Maggie lay in Bill's arms in the warm, drowsy afterglow of their lovemaking. The intimacy had been heated and cleansing after their argument.

"Maggie?"

"Yes."

"Two things."

"Yes?"

"You should wear that thing you had on tonight more often."

"Okay. And?"

"The hero sex thing? I'm kind of okay with it."

Maggie giggled and snuggled closer.

***

Tuesday Evening

After helping clean up dinner, Bill headed for the basement. Maggie looked over as he opened the door and spoke.

"Where are you going?"

"Downstairs. Got something I want to do."

"Oh. Okay."

About a half hour later, she heard noise coming from the basement. First there was a "thump," followed by a "thump, thump, thump," and then a "bap" and a "crash." The noise continued and soon settled into a steady rhythm. "Thump, bap. Thump, bump, bap. Thump, bump, bap, thump. Thump, bump, bap. Thump, bap. Thump, bump bap. Bap, thump, bump, bap, bap, thump, bap, bap, bap, bap, crash ..."

The sound grew louder and the patterns faster as they continued. Maggie walked across the kitchen. Buddy was lying across the doorway to the stairs and she had to ask him to move to open the door. He looked up and rose painfully, then crept off to the family room to settle back down near the couch. She snuck down the stairs and peered around the corner.

Bill was sitting behind his drum kit, set up over by the oil tank. It was the first time he'd set it up in more than a decade. For years, it had been stored neatly in its cases on the top of the shelves over in the back corner of the basement.

It was a set of Premier drums in black, with 14-inch and 16-inch toms mounted on a 24-inch bass drum, an 18-inch floor tom, all with three-ply birch shells and basswood braces. The kit was finished off with a five-and-a-half-by-14-inch brass snare drum and Zildjian K cymbals all the way around. It was a true player's drum set, known for its sweet, rich tone, and Bill had always loved it.

Bill was sitting on the drum throne, headphones on, eyes closed and head methodically nodding as he played along with whatever song he was listening to. After about a minute, he looked up, saw Maggie watching him, stopped and pulled off the headphones. He greeted her a bit sheepishly, as if he'd been caught doing something he wasn't supposed to be doing.

"Hi."

"Hi. What's this?"

"I don't know. I just felt like getting them out and playing them. Felt good to play the other night. Do you mind?"

"No. Not at all. You sound good."

"Thanks. Not exactly ready for 'Tom Sawyer,' but it's coming back to me."

"I'm sorry. 'Tom Sawyer'? By Mark Twain?"

"No. Not that. It's, uh, a song. By Rush. It's very technical and … well, never mind."

"Well, I'm glad you're playing your drums again. Don't let me interrupt you."

"Thanks. I won't keep it up for too long."

"It's okay. Play as much as you want."

Bill pulled the headphones back on and settled back into playing. Maggie watched him for a few minutes, smiling, and then went back upstairs.

Chapter 15

Mid-June, Tuesday Night

"That Metal Show" returned from its first commercial break of the night, and as the heavy chords of the interstitial music by guitarist Bumblefoot faded, the camera focused on host Eddie Trunk, flanked on the right by co-hosts Don Jamieson and Jim Florentine. Eddie smiled and addressed the camera and the studio audience.

"Welcome back to the first episode of our special summer edition of 'That Metal Show.' Once again, we want to thank our guest musician for the evening, guitar virtuoso Steve Vai, for joining us."

The camera cut to Steve Vai sitting with a guitar across his lap and an amplifier half-stack behind him. Steve was seated on a metal platform attached to the right-hand side of the bleacher seats holding the audience. He nodded and smiled back to Eddie, and the crowd yelled and applauded with approval. Eddie started speaking again.

"I wanted to mention that Steve told us on the break that he'll be touring the U.S. and Canada this fall in support of his latest record, 'Wave Form.' So watch for upcoming dates to see Steve in a city near you.

"Now, we have a great show prepared for tonight. Joining in just a little while is co-founder and guitarist for legendary band Rush, Alex Lifeson ..."

The audience, packed into the bleachers, erupted in sustained shouts of approval and applause, and Eddie signaled them to quiet down.

"... Wait ... wait ... but before ... before we bring out Alex, we have another very special guest this evening, Bill Ward."

The audience broke out in applause again, but Eddie quickly cut them off.

"Now ... now ... I have to explain, and I mentioned this earlier, our guest tonight is not THE Bill Ward, legendary drummer for Black Sabbath. It's ANOTHER Bill Ward. Jim, maybe you'd like to explain."

“Sure, Eddie. A lot of people might remember this guy. A few months back, he rescues this lady and her kid from a really bad car wreck. Freakin’ nearly got killed doin’ it too – the car exploded just after he got them out. Hardcore, right? But anyway, it’s in all the news, and a couple days later, Jimmy Fallon has him on ‘The Tonight Show,’ and while he’s there he starts talking all about our show. Turns out he’s a heavy rocker and never misses ‘That Metal Show.’ So we thought we’d invite him to come on.”

Eddie picked it back up.

“So, I hope everyone will please welcome our first guest of the evening, and of this special summer season of ‘That Metal Show.’”

The theme music for the show blared loudly as Bill Ward entered the studio from behind the audience, walking through a space between the two sets of bleachers. The audience members rose to their feet as if on cue, yelling, stomping and applauding. Those closest to the aisle reached over the railing to shake Bill’s hand as he made his way toward the hosts.

Bill settled into a chair at Eddie’s left, and it was instantly apparent how different he appeared from everyone else in the room. Eddie and his co-hosts were dressed in black t-shirts featuring logos for hard rock and heavy metal bands ranging from Megadeth to Five Finger Death Punch, jeans and sneakers or boots. The audience, men and women alike, were dressed like the hosts, with many adding black leather jackets or vests to their outfits.

Bill was wearing a navy blue blazer, a light green polo shirt, pressed khakis with a brown leather web belt, and loafers. Despite his incongruous appearance, Bill actually looked and felt quite comfortable. He was relieved when all the publicity had died down after the accident, but when Eddie Trunk had called him personally to ask him to be on TMS, he just couldn’t say no.

Eddie turned and addressed him.

“Welcome to the show, Bill. Thanks for being here.”

"Oh, thank you for having me. I can't believe it. This is incredible."

"It's a little different than watching it on TV, I guess."

"Absolutely – larger than life. Being here with you guys, in person, is just great. And the audience is terrific. And Steve Vai – holy cow!"

"Are you a fan?"

"Oh yeah. I think I first heard him on Frank Zappa's 'Tinseltown Rebellion' record. Then the Alcatrazz stuff was great, and then there were the iconic records with David Lee Roth – what a great band, with Billy Sheehan and Gregg Bissonette."

The camera cut to Steve Vai, who responded.

"Thank you. Thank you very much. That's very kind of you."

Bill continued.

"No really, amazing stuff. And then there's your solo work – mind blowing. 'Passion and Warfare' and 'Alien Love Secrets' are in regular rotation in my car. Don't even get me started. And the G3 tours with Joe Satriani. And what a really sweet story about the two of you."

Steve smiled and spoke again.

"Stop, I'm blushing. But really, thank you."

"Who's going to be on tour with you? I assume Dave Weiner, and Phil Bynoe or Bryan Beller on bass."

"Yeah, can't tour without Dave. And Phil's in the lineup this time."

"And what about Jeremy Colson. On drums, that guy. Animal.

"Yeah, he's an animal."

"No, I mean he's like Animal, from the Sesame Street band. And I mean that in a good way. I love that guy – what a drummer!"

Steve laughed, and the audience laughed and applauded. Eddie tried to regain control of the conversation.

“So maybe you can tell us how the whole Fallon thing came about.”

“It was a fluke, really. I was at NBC to be on ‘The Today Show’ with … with the lady I helped out at the accident, and I ran into my college roommate, who is the producer for ‘The Tonight Show.’ Turns out they had a guest cancel for that evening and he asked me to do it.”

“And how did the topic of ‘That Metal Show’ come up?”

“Jimmy was asking me what I like to do, what I’m interested in and so forth, and one of the things I mentioned was your show. It’s my favorite. I never miss it.”

“Well, lemme tell you, that gave us a big boost. Lots of talk on Facebook and Twitter.”

Jim Florentine jumped in.

“Yeah, I was reading that the show you did with him was the most watched one of the season so far.”

“Well, I would guess his other guest, Javier Fernandez, probably had more to do with that than me.”

Eddie responded.

“Nevertheless, a lot of people saw it, and heard about us. We appreciate you flying the heavy metal flag on network television.”

“My pleasure, really. I really enjoy your show. I love getting to hear from artists I love, and learning about new bands. And one thing I can say about you guys and heavy rock fans in general – you’re so authentic and passionate about the music. I think that’s one of the things I like about it.”

“Well thank you. And I think it speaks volumes about the genre that a guy like you can be just as passionate about it. I mean, you don’t look like us – I think this is the first time anyone’s ever worn Dockers on our show.”

The audience laughed. Eddie continued.

"But it's pretty clear you're the real deal – a lot of heart. And, based on what you did – saving that lady and her baby – some pretty big balls."

The audience shouted and applauded. Bill responded.

"Thank you, Eddie. I'm not sure that one has anything to do with the other, really, but I will say most of the fans of heavier music I know – despite the clothes, the tattoos and the attitude -- are the most generous people you'd ever want to meet. They'd give you their last dollar if you needed it."

"Tell us a little about your musical roots – what you started out listening to, and what you listen to now."

"Well, I was very fortunate to have an older cousin – Bobby -- who turned me on to some really cool stuff when I was 10 or 11. Rolling Stones, Led Zeppelin, Cream, Santana, Deep Purple, Uriah Heep, Jethro Tull, Black Sabbath. He was a huge influence on me – got me started playing drums and gave me my first drum kit."

"Wait -- you play drums, like Bill Ward of Black Sabbath?"

"Well, I play drums. But not like Bill Ward. I wish."

The hosts and audience laughed. Bill continued.

"But when I was younger, playing drums was a big part of my life. I played all through high school and college, and some after."

"What was the name of your first band?"

"Last Child."

"Cool name!"

"Yeah. Aerosmith was obviously a big influence for that one. We did a few by them, some Zeppelin, some newer bands at the time, like Ratt and Motley Crue."

"Do you play now?"

"Well, I hung it up for a while. Family, career, kids – you know, not really any time for it. But I just started playing again."

"Do you play with a band."

"Oh, quite a few. I was just playing with Steve the other night."

The camera cut to Steve Vai, and he responded.

"Wait. Was I there?"

"Not in person. But it's amazing what you can do with an iPhone and a great music library these days."

Everyone in the studio laughed. Bill continued.

"Hey. I have a surprise for you guys. If I could ask your hostess, Jennifer, to bring it out?"

"Oh … okay. Uh, Jennifer can you come on out?"

The game show theme music they used for hostess Jennifer Gottlieb's entrances played, and she walked in via the same route Bill had followed. She was wearing a Metallica t-shirt cut down into a halter, over tight leather pants and knee-high boots with spike heels. The audience shouted their approval as she made her way toward the front of the studio, carrying a metal tray covered with a piece of cloth. When she reached Bill and the hosts, she smiled, looked at Bill with a sparkle in her eye and spoke to him.

"Hi Bill."

"Hi, Jennifer."

"Hi, guys."

Eddie smiled slyly, raised an eyebrow and spoke.

"Boy, it looks like the two of you really made a connection."

The audience laughed. Bill responded.

"Oh, nothing like that. I'm married, and she's young enough to be my daughter. But she's very nice, and agreed to help me out."

Jennifer jumped in.

"Yeah, you know, it was nice to have a conversation with a guy who actually looks me in the eye when I'm talking to him for a change."

The audience laughed again, and Eddie rolled his eyes and spoke.

"Alright, alright. So what is this Bill?"

"Well, you guys all saw I had a gift for Jimmy Fallon on 'The Tonight Show,' and I couldn't come here without something for you. So here it is."

Jennifer lifted the cloth to reveal three knives in presentation boxes.

"I've been working with a company called Schraber Knives, and this is actually an improved version of the one I use on weekends. It has brass bolsters, a smoother opening and locking action, and a high-quality carbon steel blade that will really hold an edge well. On the butt of the frame is a hardened stud for breaking glass in an emergency."

Eddie blinked and responded.

"Well, this is great, really nice of you."

"Oh, and we have one for every member of the audience tonight. And you too, Steve!"

The audience broke out in applause and shouts, and Steve fired off a quick guitar riff with a whammy bar dip at the end to punctuate his approval. Eddie, Don and Jim each retrieved a knife from the tray, marveling at them and thanking Bill. Jennifer smiled at Bill and departed from the set.

Eddie signaled a commercial break and Steve Vai played a shredding guitar solo to segue to the advertisement. When the commercial break was over, the camera focused back on Eddie.

"Welcome back to 'That Metal Show.' I'd like to bring out our next guest, a real treat for us. He's the guitarist and cofounder of one of the most epic hard rock and progressive rock bands for more than 40 years. Please welcome Alex Lifeson.

The theme music played as Alex Lifeson emerged from backstage and made his way between the bleachers toward the hosts. The audience was on its feet, roaring and applauding. He took a seat between Eddie and Bill, nodding, smiling and greeting the hosts. Eddie signaled the audience to simmer down and addressed Alex.

"Alex, welcome to 'That Metal Show.' It's really a thrill to have you with us. Truly an icon."

"Oh, thanks for having me."

Alex immediately turned to Bill.

"Hey, that was really nice for you to bring gifts for everyone tonight."

Bill smiled, and then jumped.

"Oh. Hang on."

He reached into one of the inside pockets of his blazer and pulled out one of the Schraber knives in a gift box, and handed it to Alex.

"Here. Sorry. I almost forgot."

The audience and the hosts laughed. Alex smiled and spoke to Bill.

"Wow. Thank you. You know, knives are kind of a big deal up in Canada – part of our frontier heritage."

Bill responded.

"Oh, you're welcome. I've been a really big fan ever since I was a kid. You guys were a big influence on me, musically."

Eddie broke in, trying to regain control of the conversation.

"As a drummer, I'm sure Neil Peart made a big impression on you, Bill."

"No doubt, although a lot of what he does is far beyond me. I must have listened to 'Tom Sawyer' like a million times. I think there's one snare hit of his I can do."

"You mean one fill?"

"No, I mean one actual hit. Bam. That's it."

Everyone laughed. Eddie continued.

"Alex, it's difficult to think of another hard rock or heavy metal band that has such a rich legacy of music as Rush. Is there any particular record or period in the band's history that's your favorite?"

"That's really hard to say, Eddie. With our first two records, Rush and Fly By Night, we were just getting started, and we were young and it was exciting and it was all new – getting signed, touring the U.S. So that's really special."

"True."

"With 'Caress of Steel,' I think we were really starting to explore who we were musically and artistically, even though the record label was less than thrilled with it. And then there was '2112,' which was the record that really made us as a band."

Bill broke in here.

"You know, I have to tell you, Alex, for me there are certain records that when you hear them for the first time they make an instant, lasting life-long impression on you. They make you stop and say, 'Wow, this changes everything – this is totally different from everything that came before it. These guys have invented something totally new.'"

"I suppose that's true."

Bill continued.

"Whether it was the first Led Zeppelin record, or 'Van Halen I,' or Aerosmith's 'Toys In The Attic,' you just totally stop in your tracks. For me '2112,' maybe more than any other record, did that. My cousin played it for me and I must have listened to side one about 10 times. It was … otherworldly."

The audience shouted and applauded in approval, along with the hosts. Alex responded to Bill.

"Thank you, Bill, that's very kind of you."

"And then I turned the record over, and there's a whole second side of great songs!"

Eddie addressed Bill.

"So you're quite a Rush aficionado then, Bill?"

"Well, I have everything they ever recorded – I think I may have stuff they don't even know they did."

Everyone laughed. Eddie continued.

"Any particular favorites?"

"Oh, I love them all in many ways, some more than others certainly. I think with 'Hemispheres' you guys were in what I would call your 'earnest' period, where you wrote music that was a little beyond even you yourselves."

Alex laughed.

"That's right, we did."

"With 'Permanent Waves' and 'Moving Pictures,' you started making music that was a little more approachable for a mass audience, yet without dumbing it down at all. Then in the early 80s you moved into a more synth-based sound that some didn't like as much, including you, Alex."

Alex popped up.

"That's true."

"But if you listen to those records, still a lot of great stuff – 'Mystic Rhythms,' 'Distant Early Warning,' 'Subdivisions,' awesome songs. And continuing, you came out with records like 'Power Windows,' 'Presto,' 'Roll The Bones,' right up through 'Clockwork Angels.' Every one of them, through every period, is worth listening to."

"Thanks. I appreciate that."

"We all have our favorites and some we may not like as much as others. But in end there's just no such thing as a 'bad' Rush record. There just isn't."

The hosts and the audience shouted and applauded in approval. Alex visibly blushed, and when the audience quieted down, he responded.

"I … wow … thank you. Thank you very much. That means a lot to me, and I know it will to Geddy and Neil too."

Eddie jumped in.

"I don't know if anyone could have said it better. Thank you, Bill. Now, Alex – after finishing a rather lengthy world tour last year, there have been some rumors that Rush won't tour any more. There was something in at least one music magazine to that affect attributed to Neil. Can you comment or respond to that."

"Well, I think what Neil said was taken a little out of context, but ..."

Chapter 16

Mid-July, Early Sunday Morning

Howard woke from a deep sleep to see his daughter, Jade, standing over his bed.

"Dad! Mom! Get up! There's a fire over at the Ward's!"

Howard looked at the clock, which said it was 12:45 a.m. He got up and moved to the front bedroom windows that faced the Ward's house. He could see nothing but flames all along the front of the house.

Judy was starting to rise from the bed and he spoke to her before bolting from the room.

"Call 911!"

Howard ran downstairs and out the front door dressed only in his pajamas. He was focused on the fire as he reached the bottom of the front porch steps, but his head snapped around when he heard tires screech and looked just in time to see a car down the block speeding away and turning the corner.

He ran across the street to the Ward's driveway where he saw that the flames were restricted to the front lawn and had not reached the house yet. He ran up the front steps, pounded on the door, and then ran back down to the shrubs along the foundation, where he located a garden hose attached to a spigot. He turned the water on and exited the shrubs, uncoiling the hose behind him as he turned on the nozzle and directed a stream of water at the base of the flames closest to the house.

Behind him he heard the front door open and glanced over to see Bill Ward emerging, wearing only boxer shorts and a t-shirt.

"Howard! What …?!"

Bill froze for a moment as he saw the flames whipping eight feet in the air, and then quickly spun around, ran back in the house and returned with a fire extinguisher. He immediately began helping Howard extinguish the blaze. Within about a minute, Bryce had joined them after retrieving a second fire extinguisher from the garage, and they all heard sirens approaching the house.

Several fire trucks arrived and the firefighters quickly exited the vehicles and got the blaze under control. Howard, Bill and Bryce moved to the driveway to stay out of the way and allow the firefighters to do their work. They were joined by Maggie and Olive, and a few minutes later, Judy and her daughters walked across the street.

Jade huddled with Olive as Judy reached for Maggie and gave her a hug. Jasmine moved over to Bryce and silently took his hand. Other neighbors had gathered on their own front lawns and porches to see what was happening, but most kept their distance to stay out of the way.

The fire chief and a police officer walked over to talk to them. The chief spoke first.

"I'm Chief Brenda Brady. This is Officer Wade Tuttle. Who is the homeowner?"

Bill responded.

"My wife and I are."

"Well, fortunately the fire was contained to the lawn. Good thing you got to it when you did or it could have spread to the house."

"Do know how it started?"

"We don't know the details yet, but it's pretty clear it was intentionally set. You can still smell the gasoline. It appears to be an act of vandalism. I don't think they meant to burn your house down. You can see by the char pattern they were trying to spell something out."

The firefighters had set up large utility lamps to light the areas and in the burned grass four letters about 10 feet long were visible. They all looked and Howard spelled it out, out loud.

"F-U-U-K. Those idiots."

The fire chief responded.

"I think they meant to write …"

Howard cut her off impatiently.

"We KNOW what they meant to write, chief!

"I'm sorry. Who was the first one to see the fire?"

"My younger daughter did."

"And who are you?"

"I'm Howard Jones. This is my wife Judy and my daughters, Jasmine and Jade. We live across the street."

The chief turned to the younger girl.

"Jade, can you tell me what you saw."

"I had been reading in my room and just turned out the light about 15 minutes before. I wasn't quite asleep when I heard people running and laughing outside. I looked out the window and I saw the fire. And I went and got my Dad and Mom."

"What happened next?"

Howard responded.

"I told my wife to call 911 and I ran out of the house. When I got to my front yard, I heard a car down the street. I didn't get a good look at it, but they were taking off in a big hurry. Then I came over here, knocked on the front door, got the garden hose and tried to put out the fire. Bill and his son came out and helped me, and then you folks arrived."

"Okay, did anyone see or hear anything else?"

Everyone shook their heads. Officer Tuttle continued the questioning.

"Do you have any idea who would do something like this? Had any problems with anyone lately?"

Jade responded.

"I know who did it."

Everyone looked at her, and Officer Tuttle continued.

“Who.”

“It was those boys – friends of TJ’s. Robert Perkins, Juan Alvarez and Tryone Green.”

“Who is TJ?”

Bill responded.

“TJ Simmons. My daughter’s ex-boyfriend. He was arrested on drug charges a couple months ago and has been in jail ever since.”

“And you think those boys hold you responsible for that somehow?”

“I really couldn’t say.”

Officer Tuttle returned his attention to Jade.

“How do you know those boys did it?”

“They came into the restaurant Olive and I work at a week ago. Goodfellas Pizza in town. We were both working there and they were giving Olive looks and cracking jokes and laughing the whole time. I didn’t hear most of it, but when Olive was in the back I was cleaning off a table near them, I heard them say they were gonna get back at her for what happened. Then they saw me, stopped talking. But I know it was them.”

Olive started to cry and Maggie put her arms around her. Bryce looked stunned. Officer Tuttle’s radio crackled and he grabbed the handset attached to his shirt to give a quick response, then turned back to the Wards and Joneses.

“Excuse me, I have to take this.”

He moved about 10 feet away to talk with whoever was on the radio, and the fire chief continued to talk with the group. Bryce looked at his father.

“Dad. I’m so sorry. I didn’t …”

“It’s not your fault, Bryce.”

Officer Tuttle returned to the group.

"Well, they got 'em. Just a few blocks from here. Another patrol car responding to the emergency call saw a car whipping by doing about 50 in a 25 mile-an-hour zone. They turned around and caught them. All three boys were in the car, gas cans still in the trunk and they all reeked of gasoline. They're lucky they didn't incinerate themselves when they set the fire. They're taking them in now."

Bill spoke.

"Did they say anything?"

"Enough to incriminate themselves. Listen, I'll need to get a formal statement from you, Mr. Ward. You too, Mr. Jones, and your daughter as well. We can go to the station and do it now, or first thing in the morning if you prefer."

Howard and Bill looked at each other, and Howard spoke to Jade.

"What do you think, honey?"

"It's okay, Daddy. We can go now. I don't think I can sleep anyway."

Howard turned to Bill.

"What about you?"

"Yeah, let's get it done."

"Okay, we'll get dressed and head over – you want a lift?"

"Nah, I'll bring my own car. That way you and Jade can go first, and then you can get her home.

"Okay, we'll see you there."

***

It was about 3:30 a.m. by the time Bill finished his statement at the police station. Judy had accompanied Howard and Jade to the station so she could take Jade home after she was finished. Howard stayed behind with Bill.

When they had arrived at the station, they were taken in past the front desk to the office area, which contained several interview rooms. As they walked through the open landscape office area they could see the three boys in custody through a large window that looked into a conference room. The police had confiscated their clothes as evidence, and they were dressed in orange prison jumpsuits and handcuffed to the table. One of the boys was white, one was Hispanic, and the third was black.

As they walked by, Jade glared at them angrily. Each of them looked up briefly to see Bill and Joneses walking by, looking down quickly when they saw Jade staring at them. To Bill, they looked lonely, scared and small.

Howard, Jade and Bill all made statements to Officer Tuttle and Detective Wayne Jeffries, who took over the investigation from the patrolman. After Bill was through, Detective Jeffries walked him and Howard back out through the office area toward the front desk. The three boys were still in the conference room, looking even more forlorn and hopeless.

Bill stopped to look at them for a minute. He recognized two of them – the white one, Robert Perkins and the Hispanic boy, Juan Alvarez, had played on the same Peewee Soccer team with Olive when they were in first and second grade, and he had been the assistant coach. He turned to Detective Jeffries.

"What happens to them now?"

"Well, with their confessions, the evidence we gathered, and your statements, they're in a lot of trouble. At worst, they're looking at felony arson charges, which could mean serious prison time."

"Are there any other options?"

"Depending on what the prosecutor thinks and what you want to do, we could charge them as minors with malicious mischief and vandalism, which are misdemeanors. None of them have been any in any serious trouble before. They all kind of have rough home lives – one's mother is an alcoholic, the other two have no fathers around. I think they basically got mixed up with the wrong kid in that TJ Simmons and now they're paying for it. I see enough of these kids come through here that I can tell the hard cases from the ones who aren't. Kind of a shame, really."

"What can I do to help them?"

Howard broke in, incredulously.

"Bill, are you serious? Those punks almost burned your house down!"

"Howard. I know. But that didn't happen. And I don't want to see three young lives damaged because of a stupid prank. I feel bad enough about TJ. The difference is, he deserves it. I'm not sure these kids do. And I'm willing to give them the benefit of the doubt."

Howard was speechless, and Bill turned his attention back to the detective.

"So what do I have to do?"

"Well, if you want the charges reduced, you'll have to speak with the prosecutor and get him to agree. My guess is under the circumstances he'll probably go along. If they plead guilty to the misdemeanors, they'll probably get fines and community service, and be ordered to make restitution. Their records will be sealed if they're convicted as juveniles, so it won't hurt them down the road."

"Okay, please let the prosecutor know I'd like to speak with him before they're charged. How soon can we talk?"

"Probably later this morning. He's going to want to charge them as soon as possible so they can be arraigned on Monday. I'll call you with the details later."

"Great. Thank you, detective. One more thing – may I speak with them?"

"I don't know, Mr. Ward. That's highly irregular."

"Please. It's important. I just realized a few minutes ago that I know two of these boys."

"Okay, but just for a minute and if anything starts to happen that might jeopardize the case, I'm putting a stop to it."

"It won't be a problem. I promise."

Howard spoke up.

"If you're going in to talk with them, so am I."

Bill looked at the detective and spoke.

"Okay with you?"

The officer sighed and shrugged.

"I suppose if I let you, I have to let him too."

Bill turned to Howard.

"Just behave yourself, okay? Better let me do most of the talking."

Chapter 17

Detective Jeffries led Bill and Howard into the conference room. Robert Perkins looked up at the men. He didn't know Howard, but he suddenly recognized Bill and groaned audibly. Juan Alvarez whispered to him.

"What's the matter?"

"That guy is Coach Ward. From soccer. When we were little!"

Neither of them had remembered that when they targeted his property for revenge, and their eyes got wide at the realization as they saw him standing in front of them. Bill spoke to the boys.

"Hello, boys. Robert. Juan.

He looked at the third boy and addressed him.

"I'm sorry, son. I don't think I know you. What's your name?"

Tryone starred sullenly at the table, refusing to make eye contact with Bill. Howard broke in.

"Hey boy! You look this man in the eye and answer him when he asks you a question! Got it?"

Tryone's head snapped up and he looked at Howard in surprise and then looked over at Bill.

"I'm … Tryone Green."

Bill continued.

"Looks like you guys have gotten yourselves into some serious trouble. Have you spoken with your parents?"

They all hesitated and then Juan responded.

"Yeah, they let us call them. They're all pretty mad at us – said there was nothing they could do until morning though. Get us lawyers or something. Except Tryone. His mom wasn't home and didn't answer her cell phone."

Bill spoke to all three boys.

"Well, I hope you understand how serious this is – the impact this could have on the rest of your lives. They're talking about charging you with arson, a felony. You boys are all over 18, so they can charge you as adults, and you could end up in jail."

Robert spoke.

"Yeah, we know. They told us. Guess that pretty much messes up my plans."

"What are your plans?"

"I'm an apprentice at my uncle's plumbing business. That's what I studied in high school, at Babbitt Tech. I'm supposed to take my license exam in the fall and move up to service technician. But now … I don't know."

Detective Jeffries responded.

"Yeah, if you're convicted, the state can deny you a professional license. That would be a shame. What about the rest of you."

Juan spoke.

"I'm supposed to start at Saugatuck Community College in September. I'm going to major in accounting, get my associate's degree and try to transfer into Northern Connecticut State in two years to complete my bachelor's."

Detective Jeffries replied.

"Well, they may not let you attend if you're convicted of a violent crime, and arson falls in that category."

Bill looked at Tryone and spoke.

"What about you, son?"

Tryone was speechless, but Juan responded for him.

"He's signed up to join the Marines. Supposed to leave for boot camp at the end of August."

Howard jumped in.

"Yeah, well you can forget that even if you don't get jail time. If you're convicted of a felony, the Marines won't take you – ever. No branch of the service will."

The boys all sagged in their chairs and looked forlorn. Bill spoke to them.

"Look, I'd like to think this was just a high school prank that got out of hand, and I'd hate to see something like that ruin your prospects for the future. The way I'm feeling about it now, I'm going to talk to the prosecutor about reducing or even dropping the charges against you. I don't know if he'll go for it, but I'm willing to try."

Robert looked up and spoke.

"You'd do that for us?"

"Yes."

"Why?"

"It seems like the right thing to do under the circumstances. But before I do, I'd like an explanation. I want to know why you did it. Why you wrote ... that word on my front lawn."

Howard spoke.

"Yeah. F-U-U-K. Seriously?"

Juan spoke.

"Yeah, Tryone slipped with the gas can on that one. It was supposed to be F-U-C..."

Howard interrupted him.

"We KNOW what it was supposed to be, dumbass!"

Bill broke in.

"Howard. Please."

Howard stopped, and Bill continued.

"So? I'm waiting for an explanation."

Tryone spoke.

"Well, we were mad. About TJ and stuff."

"TJ Simmons? What about him?"

"He's our friend. And, well, your son beat him up. And then he got arrested. And now he's in jail and probably going to prison. So we wanted to get even."

“Well first of all, the reason Bryce punched him out was because TJ put his hands on my daughter Olive and hurt her. Physically. Bryce was defending his sister.”

Robert spoke.

“I … we didn’t know that.”

“Well, now you do. As for him getting arrested, that was his own doing – we had nothing to do with it. My understanding is the police pulled him over for running a stop sign and found a big bag of drugs in the trunk. So that’s on him, not us.”

Robert spoke again.

“Yeah … I guess … yeah …”

“So your blame and your loyalty are misplaced. I won’t tell you that TJ isn’t your friend, but if he is I’d suggest you could choose your friends a little better.”

Juan spoke.

“I don’t know what to say. It was a stupid thing and we shouldn’t have done it. And now, I don’t know what’s going to happen to us. I’m sorry, Mr. Ward.”

The other boys piped in.

“Yeah, me too.”

“Yeah, I’m sorry too. Really sorry.”

Bill took a breath, and then spoke.

“Well, no permanent damage done. Nobody got hurt. That’s the most important thing. I hope you boys have learned your lesson. You’re not kids anymore. The choices you make and the things you do have real consequences.”

The boys looked like they were on the verge of tears. Robert spoke.

“What happens now?

“Well, the detective here says you’ll probably be held until Monday when they arraign you in Police Court in front of a judge. Depending on how they charge you, you could be released then. I’m supposed to talk to prosecutor later this morning – no guarantees, but I’ll see what I can do.”

“Thank you.”

“Okay, you boys try to hold it together until Monday. Oh, and if you do get out, don’t make any plans for next weekend. Other than to be at my house by 7 a.m. sharp on Saturday. We have a lot of work to do.”

Detective Jeffries gestured toward the door, Howard and Bill started moving toward it. Howard glared at the boys as he went. The detective followed them out and closed the door behind him.

***

Saturday Morning

The three boys arrived at the Ward’s house at 7 a.m., just as Bill had been told them to do. Bill had convinced the prosecutor to reduce the charges to misdemeanors and charge them as minors. After some questioning of Bill, the prosecutor and the boys, the judge consented.

But Judge Darrah Schukoth also gave the young men a stern talk, telling they had better stay out of trouble.

“You young men are very fortunate that the Wards are being so gracious about this. I’m not sure I would be if someone set my property on fire. But because none of you have a previous record, I’ll allow it. This time. But at your sentencing, I will put you on probation for a year, and you BETTER keep straight. I don’t want to EVER see any of you in my court room again. If I do it will a sad, sorry day for you, let me tell you that.”

In addition to probation, Judge Schukoth told them she planned to give them 100 hours of community service and order them to make restitution to the Wards for the property damage. Bill explained to her that they would be helping to repair the damage they had done, and the judge said that would be sufficient of it was okay with him.

“Mr. Ward, you look very familiar to me. Have you appeared in this court before?”

“No, your honor.”

“Have we met somewhere else?”

“I don’t believe so.”

“Very well, then. Thank you for being so forgiving with these young men.”

She dismissed the court, and it was only later in her chambers that she realized she recognized Bill from news reports several months earlier.

***

Bill and Bryce came out of the garage and met the boys in the driveway. Although it was still early, the day was already getting warm and the air was heavy with humidity, making it feel even warmer. Bill greeted them.

“Good morning, Juan, Robert, Tryone. Thanks for being here on time. We should get started – try to get as much done as we can before it gets too hot. Have you all eaten this morning?”

They all shook their heads, bashful. Bill continued.

“Well, we’ll get going and take a break in a little while, get you all something to eat. Bryce will bring the wheelbarrows and tools around from the shed. We need to cut out the damaged sod and rake out the soil. It’s the wrong time of year to plant grass – too hot to get the seed going – so we’ll have to leave it until the end of the summer, then bring in some fresh top soil, spread it, seed it and fertilize. Let’s get started.”

Bill, Bryce and the boys got to work and it went reasonably quickly with the five of them going at it. Bill would instruct them on what to do, patiently correcting them and providing pointers, and demonstrating how to use the tools for the greatest efficiency and least effort.

It was hard work, and the three boys were soon sweating and breathing hard. They started to overcome their self-consciousness and talk more openly with Bill as they worked. He asked them about what they were doing that summer and about their plans for the fall, and they shared details, joked and laughed. After about an hour they took a break for water and then went right back to work.

Bryce was much cooler to the boys than his father was, still not having forgiven them for the fire. But Bill had asked him to be civil to them, so he restrained his anger as they worked side by side in the yard. It was tough and tedious going – working yard tools under the burnt sod to loosen and remove it, loading it into wheelbarrows, and rolling them to the woods behind the house and to dump the contents.

By 9 they had made a good dent but still had a lot to do. Bill called for a break and they all walked around to the back of the house, where Maggie had set the patio table with dishes, glasses, cups and silverware, pitchers of water and orange juice. The five sat down, and Maggie came out the back door from the kitchen smiling and carrying a platter of freshly made bacon, egg and cheese breakfast sandwiches. Bill introduced the boys to Maggie, and she greeted them sweetly.

"It's nice to meet you all. If you want to wash up before you eat, there's a bathroom just inside the back door. There's plenty of food for all of you, and more in the kitchen, so eat as much as you like and let me know if you need anything."

Bill, Bryce and the boys got up and entered the house. The boys took turns using the bathroom to wash their hands, while Bill and Bryce used the kitchen sink. They returned individually to the patio table and dug into the food, continuing their conversations about the work to be done and summer activities.

Bill left the table to get more orange juice from the kitchen for the boys, and the table grew quiet in his absence. The boys were a little intimidated by Bryce. After about a minute, Juan broke the silence by asking Bryce a question.

"Hey, uh, can I ask you something?"

"What?"

"Why, um … why are your parents being so nice to us?"

Bryce answered matter-of-factly.

"Because they're nice people."

"But after what we did to your house?"

"What you did didn't change who they are. They're taking it for what it was – a stupid thing a bunch of teenagers did. They're willing to let it go at that."

"Well … thanks."

"Don't thank me. I still think you're a bunch of idiots. But I guess you're trying to make it right, so I'll see how I feel about it at the end of the day."

They fell silent as Bill returned, and the small talk resumed when he again asked them about the things going on in their lives. After about a half hour they went back to work. They worked through the rest of the morning, taking breaks every hour or so for rest and water, and then got right back to it. At 1, they stopped for lunch, again served on the patio, with sandwiches, potato chips, water and ice tea.

Chapter 18

By about 2:30 Bill, Bryce and the three boys had most of the sod torn out, leaving a large brown scar in the front yard where the grass had been removed.

Bill stood on the sidewalk surveying the damaged landscape of his yard. He let out an audible sigh, and then heard Howard's voice behind him.

"Kind of looks like an artillery test range."

"It'll grow back – just takes a little work."

"More like a lot of work. What is it you always tell me? It takes three years to establish a new lawn."

"Yeah, well. I've got the time, and I've got help. And I'm not going anywhere."

"But I have to look at it every day – think of me."

Bill knew Howard was joking and smiled at the effort to cheer him up.

"The only alternative is to put in fresh sod, and that's way too costly. I wish I could speed things up, but there's nothing I can do."

"Oh, I wouldn't say that."

At that moment, a truck from Nick's Lawn and Garden Center came down the street and stopped in front of the Wards' house, just a few feet from Bill and Howard. The back was loaded with rolls of fresh sod. Almost as if on cue, about a half-dozen men from the neighborhood came down the block carrying yard tools and pushing wheelbarrows. Bill looked at Howard.

"What's this?"

"Oh, I was talking with some of the guys in the neighborhood, and we agreed we couldn't stand to look at this eyesore all summer. So we decided to give you a little hand."

"Howard, this is expensive. I can't accept this."

"Don't know as you have much of a choice, Bill. It's done. So you might as well be gracious and accept it. About 30 families chipped in to cover the tab, so there's really nothing to worry about."

"This is too much."

"Look, Bill, you're a good guy. You're always looking out for everyone else around here, so just take a little kindness in return for a change."

"But …"

"I told you, it's done. Look, you don't want to offend anyone, do you? If you refuse this, you're going to look like a real jerk."

Bill sighed.

"Okay. I guess you're right. I wouldn't want to hurt anyone's feelings."

"Well, then let's get to work – I don't want to be out here all day."

The neighborhood men, the three boys, and Bill and Bryce began unloading the truck, preparing the soil and rolling out the sod. Maggie and Olive watched from the porch, and Judy, Jade and Jasmine came across the street to join them. Bryce brightened when he saw Jasmine, and she stopped to talk with him. They chatted for a minute and she gave him a quick kiss before trotting off to the porch. Bryce winced as he saw Mr. Jones frown slightly at the display of affection.

The men and boys worked hard through the afternoon heat, prepping the yard and laying the sod. Nick from Nick's Lawn Center had accompanied the delivery and stayed to supervise the installation of the sod, offering Bill advice on watering and other care for the fresh grass.

Maggie and Judy provided a steady supply of water and iced tea to keep them from getting dehydrated. By about 6:30, the work was complete and the guys paused to survey the work and chat. Olive and Jade pulled up with a carful of pizzas from Goodfellas and everyone adjourned to the backyard to eat and relax. There were several coolers of bottled water, soda and beer waiting.

Everyone lounged on the patio, eating, drinking, talking and laughing. Dan, the drummer from The Dead Lunchladies, was there and Bill invited him down to the basement to see his drum set. One of the boys, Robert, overheard their conversation and crept down the cellar stairs behind them. Dan sat behind the kit and played a few patterns, looking up after a couple minutes and speaking to Bill.

"Man, sweet vintage drum set, Bill. It sounds so good. What year?"

"Thanks. Not as nice as yours, but I like it. It's from the mid-70s – my cousin gave it to me."

"It's great. I love the tone of those shells. You might get a little more punch, though, if you switched out the heads on the toms to hydraulics. The ones from Evans are pretty sweet."

"Is that what's on your kit? I was thinking about getting a set of those. I liked the way your heads felt and sounded."

"Yeah. Let me know if you get some, and I'll help you install them. I can nerd out on drum stuff forever."

The men looked up and noticed Robert standing there quietly. Bill spoke to him.

"Hi Robert. Do you play drums?"

"Yeah, a little. I started a couple years ago. I'm not very good."

"Would you like to try mine out?"

"Um … sure. I guess. That would be great."

Dan stood up from the drum throne and handed the sticks to Robert. Robert sat down tentatively, tried to get comfortable, and started rapping out a couple different patterns. His performance wasn't bad, but a little self-conscious and tentative. He looked up at the two men after a minute, who shrugged and nodded. Bill spoke to Robert as he walked around to stand behind him.

"Pretty good. May I make a few suggestions?"

"Uh, sure."

"Okay, first, I think you need to raise the seat a little bit and pull the throne in a little closer to the kit – you seem to be reaching too much."

"Okay."

Robert made the adjustments and looked up. Bill continued.

"Now, when you swing your stick to hit the snare, I want to cut the distance of the stroke by about half the height. You'll still get plenty of power, but there's a lot of wasted motion in your swing and it's throwing off your time just a bit."

"Okay."

"Now, try it again."

Robert ran through some of the same patterns he had played before. But this time they were tighter, the time was better, and he played with more confidence overall. He looked up and smiled. Bill turned to Dan.

"What did you think?"

"Much better. I think he might be gripping the sticks a little too tight, so that's something else to work on. But much, much better."

"Yeah, I think so too."

Robert spoke to Bill.

"Do you think … could you maybe give me some lessons?"

“Well, I don’t know if I’m really qualified to teach you. But I’d be glad to show you a few things. Let’s look for an evening in the next week or so. In the meantime, think about some songs you’d like to learn and bring the recordings with you when we get together, and we can talk about those.”

“Wow, that would be great! Thank you!”

“A plumber and a drummer. That’s a great combination, Robert.”

Robert smiled and got up from the drum kit, and the three headed back upstairs. On the way up, Dan spoke to Bill.

“Hey, I wanted to ask you something. Stu’s got some gigs lined up for the Lunchladies, and I can’t make all the dates. Work has me traveling through the end of the year. Would you be interested in subbing for me?”

“Wow, Dan, that’s very generous of you. But I don’t want to horn in on your thing.”

“You’re not horning in – I’m asking you. Can’t think of anyone I’d rather have do it.”

“Well thank you. That’s very kind of you to offer.”

“I’ll send over the calendar with the gigs I can’t make, and you can decide if you can do them. I already talked to the other guys, and they’re fine with it.”

“Well, great. Thanks. It would be fun to play out again.”

***

By 8:30 most of the neighbors were shuffling off home, and the Wards started cleaning up the patio. Howard, Bill and one of their neighbors, Mark Price – a CPA from down the block -- had a side conversation and each agreed to take an interest in one of the three boys and help them along the way. Howard took Tryone, Mark took Juan, and Bill took Robert. They said they would reach out to the boys regularly and provide advice and support.

The Joneses stayed behind to help with clean up, and after the backyard was tidy, the trash stowed and dishes washed, they departed. Bill and Bryce circled around to the front yard to collect the wheelbarrow and a few remaining yard tools for storage in the shed. Bill stood with his hands on his hips while Bryce stowed the yard gear.

"Well, that's that."

"Yeah, quite a day. I have to grab a shower and change. I told Jasmine I'd take her to a late movie tonight."

"Where do you get the energy?"

"Well, I have youth on my side."

Bill laughed, and Bryce continued.

"Hey. You know, I don't think Mr. Jones likes me too much."

"You're dating his daughter. He'd be suspicious of any guy under those circumstances. Even one he likes otherwise."

"Yeah, I guess. But, well, I mean, it's not like I'm like …TJ … or anything."

"That's probably why he tolerates you as well as he does."

"I suppose."

"Look, as long as you're a gentleman with his daughter and you treat him and Mrs. Jones with respect, he'll come around. Just give it some time."

"Okay, Dad. Thanks."

"I can't believe we're even talking about this."

"Yeah, me neither."

"A year ago, you'd have run away if I brought up the subject of your social life."

"Well, you didn't bring it up – I did. And it's not a year ago."

***

Bill opened the bathroom door and walked painfully to the bed, slowly backed up to the edge on his side and slowly sat down. After everyone had left and he had finished in the yard, he had come upstairs, showered and changed, and then gone back downstairs. He tried to watch television for a while, but found he was too tired to do even that. He finally gave up at around 10 and headed upstairs to get ready for bed. As he had sat downstairs, his muscles had begun to stiffen up and walking up the stairs was slow and painful.

Maggie looked over at him as he groaned and he swung his legs up on the bed.

"Tired?"

"Oh, you have no idea."

His face, neck and arms were sunburned, but he hardly noticed that compared to the muscle aches and soreness.

"Thanks for everything you did today. The food, the water, all that."

"Are you kidding? I'd much rather do that than what you guys were doing outside. You looked like a prison chain gang out there."

"Well, it was a lot of work, but we had a plenty of help and got it done. The boys did a good job. And Howard and the guys from the neighborhood were great. I can't believe they did that."

"We have nice neighbors. We're very blessed in that way."

Bill winced as he slid under the covers, put his head back on the pillow and closed his eyes.

"Oh … uh … oh …"

Maggie watched him in his discomfort and spoke to him sympathetically.

"Sweetie, I know it's Saturday night and everything, but I think I better give you the night off."

"No … no … it's okay … I can …I can …"

Bill was asleep. Maggie leaned over, gently kissed him on the forehead and turned off the lamp on the nightstand.

Chapter 19

Early August, Thursday Morning

Duane Burns stood in the doorway of Bill's office, talking about an argument he had with his wife the previous evening.

"I'm telling you, I just don't know what she wants. No matter what I do, it's the wrong thing. I don't help out enough with the house and the kids. So I try to help out more – do the dishes, the laundry, drive the kids to their stuff. And THAT'S wrong."

Bill listened patiently, and responded.

"Have you talked to her about it?"

"That's just the thing. I try to talk to her about it. Or rather get her to talk to me about it, and I can't make sense of it. 'Do this.' 'Don't do that.' She says she wants us to talk more, but what she really wants is for her to talk and for me to listen."

"What's wrong with that?"

"Well, nothing as far it goes. But I asked her this – who listens to me?"

"And what did she say?"

"She just kind of blinked at me, like it had never occurred to her. Anyhow she wants to talk about problems, but she doesn't want me to make any suggestions about what to do about them. And no matter what she says, I'm supposed to know what she means, even if what she says isn't what she means. And feelings – we're supposed to talk about feelings – what is that?"

"Hmm."

"And then it finally hit me. And I told her, Franny-Jo, sweetheart, your solution to all our problems is for me to be … more like you. I'm a guy and guys don't do ANY of that stuff you're talking about. We don't talk about feelings – we try not to HAVE any. We don't read minds and we don't know what you meant – we just know what you said. And if you bring us a problem we're gonna FIX IT because that's what WE DO!"

"How did she take it?"

"Not well. But here's the thing – an hour later, when we're in bed, she comes at me guns hot, ready to go. It's like that all the time. She's at me about every little thing all day, but at night she's ready to go, two, three, four nights a week."

Bill rubbed his eyes before he responded.

"Why does everything always come back to that with you?"

"Not everything. Not all the time."

"Yeah, actually, everything, all the time, Duane."

Duane paused for a minute, thinking about it, then shook his head and shrugged his shoulders.

"Huh. I never really thought about it. Maybe she's just bored and needs something to do. Hey, maybe I could get her into that thing your wife does, with the jewelry. What is that – Teriyaki Turtle? Kamikaze Koala? Something like that?"

"Bonsai Bear."

"Yeah, right. Anyway, I gotta get up to '3' for a budget prep with Candace Garrett-McGinty. Something's not right with the numbers."

"What's the problem?"

"I don't know. We go through this every quarter leading up to our earnings reports. What they're asking for isn't what the numbers show. And making matters worse, the SEC is starting to give us a raised eyebrow about some of it. I want to see if we can flatten it out before the next cycle and not end up with a federal investigation on our hands."

“Well if anyone can sort it out, you can. You’re the best finance guy I know. Just go easy with Candace. Remember what happened last time we talked about this.”

“I know. That’s why we’re doing it in person. Gotta go or I’ll be late.”

Duane walked down the hall and around the corner to the elevator bank leading to the upper floors of the building. Full trash cans and recycling bins lined the hallways as he went, evidence of cutbacks in janitorial services and garbage pickups. Every third ceiling light along each hallway had been removed – allegedly to conserve energy – and one of every remaining two was either burned out or flickering. Employees joked that it looked like the set of a low-budget horror film.

He waited in the elevator lobby for a car to arrive, noticing a large gash in the wall between the elevator doors. It had been made by a mail cart months before and remained unattended. Just before an elevator arrived, he was joined by a very visibly pregnant young woman, an administrative assistant for one of the managers on his floor. He smiled and greeted her.

“Hi, Renee. How’s it going?”

“Okay, I guess, Duane.”

“You must be getting pretty close. When are you due?”

“Any minute now. My due date was Tuesday. I had contractions yesterday and I went to the hospital. But they stopped, so they sent me home.”

“Why didn’t you just stay home today?”

“I can’t. The way they have the maternity leave structured now, I can’t take any time until the baby comes. So here I am.”

“And your boss wouldn’t swing with you on it – give you an extra day or two?”

“Funny.”

“Yeah. Right. What was I thinking?”

The elevator car finally arrived and the doors slowly opened. Duane allowed Renee to enter first and then followed her in. He was closest to the buttons so he reached over to push the one for his floor, asking her where she was headed.

"3?"

"No, I'm only going to 2. Normally, I'd just take the stairs, but I can't anymore."

"No problem."

Duane punched the buttons and the two waited for the doors to close. The elevator jumped and hesitated before starting to rise. Renee winced.

"I HATE when it does that."

"Yeah, me too. But you know what they say about the elevators in this building – they're slow, but they're unreliable."

Renee laughed at the joke and responded.

"Well, I hope not today."

Suddenly, the elevator lurched, hesitated in its climb and then stopped with a hard bounce. Duane reached over and tapped the buttons a couple times, with no effect. After about 30 seconds had passed, he started to get nervous.

"Looks like we're stuck. Hopefully not for long."

Renee gave him a very concerned look before responding.

"That's not the worst of it."

"What?"

"I think my water just broke."

Duane felt the blood drain from his face, but tried to compose himself and reassure Renee.

"Okay. Okay. Don't panic!"

"I'm not panicking. YOU don't panic!"

Below the elevator buttons was a small door with a picture of a telephone receiver on it. He opened it to find a handset and receiver. On the inside of the door was a sticker that said "In case of emergency, dial 9999 for Security." He picked up the handset and listened, hearing a dial tone.

"I'm calling Security."

He dialed the number and after a few seconds dropped the phone and cursed. Renee looked at him.

"What?"

"Straight to voicemail."

Renee was beginning to get scared. Duane disconnected the call and started dialing another number. Renee spoke.

"Who are you calling?"

"Bill Ward."

***

By most outward appearances, everything was fine at OpenSwitch. The company continued to put out glowing annual reports and snappy announcements about new products, acquisitions and competitive wins. But within the company a rot had set in a few years ago, and had gradually become more and more obvious to those on the inside.

It started about five years earlier with the retirement of CEO Stan Zbikowski. Stan had been the first "outsider" to become CEO at the company, with Bill IIIs retirement more than a decade earlier. Stan had overseen a significant expansion of the company into new technology areas, through organic growth and acquisition, renaming the company OpenSwitch Technologies to reflect that broader mission.

This had opened up new opportunities for OpenSwitch, but also put new market and cultural strains on the company. The policies of the founding family began to fade with these new pressures, new ideas, and new attention from clients and investors on the company's performance.

When he retired, Stan left a company that seemed to be in reasonably good shape to his hand-picked successor, Cassandra Petticoat-Primrose. She was a fast-riser in the organization and one of the first female senior executive vice presidents in the company's history.

Sandy, as she was known, had risen through the ranks of sales and marketing by virtue of intelligence, talent and relentless drive. She was identified early through the mentor-protégé system of the company as a high-potential employee – a "heatseeker," as they were called – and was regularly rewarded with promotions and greater responsibility. But the project that really got her noticed was her management of the acquisition of a company called Synaptic Networks.

At the time, Synaptic had a very hot technology called Nightrain that was poised to take off fast with the growth of online commerce. It was a highly encrypted but very efficient method of processing online financial transactions, with applications in industries as diverse as banking and energy trading. But Synaptic was small, and needed the global reach of a company like OpenSwitch to establish its protocol as the foundation for a whole new set of online services.

With the deal, Sandy effectively made her bones at OpenSwitch and was quickly promoted to senior executive vice president in charge of assimilating Synaptic into OpenSwitch's operations. The position put her firmly on a track as successor to Zbikowski as CEO. Because of the pressure to perform in order to cement her destiny as leader of the company, however, she drove the new Synaptic Division hard, alienating the senior managers and top technical leaders who came over with the deal.

Within two years, many of them had left, taking their talent, customer relationships and technical expertise with them. Hardly anyone at the top of the business noticed, however, and Sandy's star continued to rise with senior management and the board of directors.

When Stan retired and Sandy was named as new CEO, no one was surprised. The naming of the first woman CEO at OpenSwitch was widely applauded by shareholders, employees, major media, Wall Street analysts and industry observers.

It wasn't long, however, before cracks started to appear in the veneer. Because of a series of bad calls, industry shifts, and technology trends that had occurred over a few years, OpenSwitch began losing market share and its revenues started to fall off. With each successive report of quarterly earnings, the numbers looked worse until Sandy had presided over 19 straight quarters of revenue declines.

The company tried to shore things up through large-scale stock buybacks to bolster the share price and by boosting dividends and profits through increasingly stringent cost-cutting efforts. Products, technologies and whole divisions were sold off, many of them profitable and thriving, but OpenSwitch needed the cash. Capital budgets for everything from retooling in manufacturing operations to facilities maintenance were cut to the bone, but with only limited positive effects on the financial results.

Throughout it all, layoffs became common, impacting mostly older employees with many years of service. These job cuts were dribbled out in small numbers to conceal them from the outside world, but employees could plainly see what was going on.

The laid off employees were supplanted by offshoring work to low-cost countries and hiring younger employees, often only on temporary contracts that offered low pay and no benefits – a process pejoratively referred to by veteran employees as "downsourcing." The recruitment of these younger workers was done under the guise of bringing in fresh skills, but while many of the new hires brought new abilities and vitality, they lacked the knowledge and perspective that comes with experience.

Frequently, an older more experienced worker would be asked to help educate newer employees, only to be terminated shortly after completing the task. And the new hires weren't fooled by what they witnessed and experienced at OpenSwitch, perceiving very quickly that the company had no real interest in investing in them for the long term. To the contrary, the objective was clearly to grind as much work out of them as possible, without offering any hope of increased reward or opportunity.

Most of the young recruits left after only a year or two – which, again, was part of the true agenda at the company. Senior management viewed employees not as talent, but simply as cost, and didn't want anyone sticking around long enough to move up the pay scale.

As a result, morale among employees began to crumble. Those who had opportunities elsewhere took them and left as quickly as possible. Those with more limited prospects hung on as best they could, literally watching the company fall apart around them. Broken office equipment and furniture weren't replaced, and laying claim to items departing employees left behind became a ritual.

The physical environment itself was depressing. The bathrooms stank, the walls and halls were marked and messy, the carpets were stained and worn, and the food in the cafeteria became so bad that most employees stopped buying it.

The only places where these conditions weren't present were the executive office areas and in the briefing centers were customers were entertained. Those facilities were kept in pristine condition, marking a stark contrast that was noticed and noted by regular employees.

Although the company had a good technical strategy and a sound technology roadmap, execution was poor. The employees had become so disenfranchised by the constant abuse that most simply turned in a minimum performance. There was no point in showing initiative or taking a risk, because they knew such efforts would not be rewarded.

In the senior executive suite, what was once drive had turned into aggression, aggression became predation, and predation gave way to panic. Sandy browbeat and abused her lieutenants for better results, and they in turn did the same to their subordinates. A few leaders refused to engage in such behavior, but they were a marginalized minority and had no way to stop it.

Nothing worked. It was only a matter of time before the cracks would start to show ever more visibly to the outside world, and when they did, no one would be safe. Not even Sandy. And she knew it.

***

Bill was in his office having a brief meeting with Charlene Bogart and Jenny Stuart from his team when the phone on his desk warbled an incoming call. He glanced at the small window display that showed who the caller was and frowned slightly in confusion. Charlene spoke.

"Who is it?"

"Says 'Elevator 1-A.'"

Bill answered the phone.

"Hello?"

"Hi, Bill? It's me, Duane."

"Duane? Why are you calling from the elevator."

"We're stuck."

"Who's stuck?"

"Me and Renee Aviles. And she's having a baby. Like, right now!"

"Did you call Security?"

"I tried. Nobody answered."

"Okay, hang on a second. I'm going to get you some help."

Bill looked up and addressed the women in his office.

"Jenny, would you please go down to the Security office and tell them we have two people stuck in elevator 1A and one of them is a pregnant woman who is labor. If no one is there, go to Facilities."

Jenny gasped.

"Oh geez, okay."

Bill turned his attention the Charlene.

"Charlene, I'd like you to go call 911 and tell them the same thing. Tell them we need an ambulance and someone who can help get them out of the elevator. Then go wait for them by the front entrance and bring them to the elevator lobby."

"Okay."

Both women ran out the door, and Bill again spoke into the phone.

"Duane, help is on the way, so hang on. How is Renee doing?"

"She's okay, I think. But listen, if the baby comes I don't know what to do."

Duane's voice was tense but under control. Bill knew the best thing he could do was stay on the line.

"Listen, you were in the delivery room when your kids were born, right?"

"Sure. Both times."

"Then you know what to do. Renee's going to do all the work. You just have to help her out as best you can, keep her calm, and catch the baby when it comes. You can handle that, right?"

"Well, it's not like I have much of a choice, right? Yeah, I can do it."

"Okay, just hang in there. I'll stay on the phone with you until help comes."

***

It took the firefighters roughly 15 minutes to get to the OpenSwitch headquarters building and they immediately got to work trying to evacuate Duane and Renee from the elevator. The OpenSwitch security manager and building superintendent had offered their assistance, but were waved away by the firefighters and stood meekly to one side.

The emergency workers sent Charlene back to Bill's office to tell him to hang up the call with Duane so they could call from a phone in the lobby and communicate directly with the trapped co-workers. After telling Duane what was happening and hanging up the phone, Bill left his office and headed for the elevator lobby, stopping at a vending machine along the way to buy a bottle of water. Once he arrived at the elevators, he waited quietly and stayed out of the way.

After working on the elevator for about 90 minutes, the firefighters were finally able to get it to return to the first floor and they began prying the doors open. A firefighter talking with Duane on the phone throughout the event had reported regularly on what was going on inside. Renee's labor had progressed and her baby had been born inside the elevator about an hour into the ordeal.

As the doors opened, EMTs rushed in and quickly put Renee and baby on a gurney, and removed them from the elevator. Renee was crying and repeatedly thanking Duane as she and the baby were wheeled out. The baby was quiet but seemed fine, looking up with big, dark eyes and swaddled securely in Duane's sport coat. Bill could see Duane sitting on the elevator floor next to a large bloody spot. He appeared to be in a daze, but called after Renee.

"Oh hey. No problem. It's … I'm glad it … glad … everyone's okay. You, um, can, um keep my jacket. I don't need …"

A second pair of EMTs turned their attention to Duane, telling him to remain seated while they checked him over. Bill walked to the elevator door, and Duane looked up blankly and greeted him.

"Oh. Hi, Bill. How are you?"

"I'm fine. How are you doing?"

"I'm, um, okay. I think. No, I'm fine."

"Good, good."

"She's uh … she said she's naming the baby after me."

"That's nice."

"Well, it's a girl, so … but, I'll, uh … she doesn't have to … that's not … I'll talk to her. Hey, can I have that bottle of water?"

Bill looked to one of the EMTs, who nodded.

"Sure. I brought it for you. Here."

"Thanks!"

Duane gulped the water, and Bill continued.

"Sounds like you did a pretty good job in here."

"Yeah. Yeah. You know, it was kind of like you said. She did all the work. I just had to help out, keep her calm, take care of the baby when she came out. I cut the cord and wrapped the baby up in my jacket."

"You cut the cord? With what?"

Duane reached in his pocket, pulled out a slim Swiss Army knife and held it up.

"It's the one you gave me for my birthday two years ago. Been carrying it ever since. I keep the blade real sharp like you told me to. Thought it might come in handy someday. I didn't think …"

"Nice work, Duane."

Bill turned his attention to the EMTs.

"How is he doing?"

One of them looked up and responded.

"He'll be fine. A bit dehydrated. That water will help. He's probably in shock a little bit. We're going to take him in to the emergency room, get him checked over a little better. You want to come along?"

"Yeah, but let me follow in my car. That way I can take him home after they let him go."

The EMTs helped Duane to his feet. They wanted to put him on a stretcher, but he insisted on walking out to the ambulance. The EMTs flanked him on either side as he walked, a bit wobbly but otherwise okay. He called over his shoulder to Bill.

"See you there."

"Okay."

Bill pulled out his cell phone and placed a call.

"Hi, Howard. It's Bill. Hey, listen, I may need your help with something."

"Oh, no. What have you done now."

"Not me this time. A friend of mine. Everyone's okay though. Listen, can you head over to the emergency room at Stanhope? I'll call you from the car to explain and meet you there."

Chapter 20

Late August, Wednesday Afternoon

Bill exited the elevator into the first floor lobby of the professional building and began walking toward the exit. He'd spent the last several hours giving a deposition to the lawyers for the family of Roberto Gonzales, the young man killed in the highway accident the previous April.

The lawyers were friendly, but businesslike, explaining that they were speaking with all the witnesses and participants in the accident, discussing in detail what they had each seen. The lawyers told him that his comments would be recorded and were a sworn statement, meaning he was expected to tell the truth as best he could recall it.

The resulting information would be used to determine the legal course of the matter. In the event of a lawsuit, it would be shared with the court and with the attorneys for the opposing party, in this case the trucking company and its insurance company.

The lawyers explained that if the Gonzales family filed suit, he might be called to testify as witness in court. They then introduced the court reporter who would record his deposition. She administered the same oath witnesses swear to in court to him, affirming his intention to tell the truth. The deposition then began, with her recording it via a small digital recorder.

The lawyers asked him to recount what had happened the morning of the accident, including what he was doing at the time, where he was going, with all times, locations and other key details he could remember, what he had seen and done at the accident scene, and what happened afterward.

Bill recalled the events as best he could, remembering most details fairly clearly. Occasionally, the lawyers would interject a question or ask for more detail, and near the end of the interview they circled back to a couple points he had been fuzzy on to see if the continuing conversation had jogged his memory.

When they deposition was completed, they thanked him for his cooperation and told him they would be in touch. He said goodbye to them and the court reporter, and left their offices. Recounting the details of the accident had been stressful and draining, and he was in a bit of a fog as he walked toward the exit of the building.

Ahead of him in the lobby he noticed a small group of people moving toward him, but didn't really pay much attention to them. When they were about 10 feet from him, he heard one of them shout.

"YOU!"

The shout startled him, and he looked up to see a small, older woman in the middle of the group pointing a finger at him, her eyes blazing. She shouted again.

"You! The hero! You saved the girl and that baby! You couldn't save my son? Why didn't you save my son?"

Bill stood frozen as the woman melted down, sobbing and shouting as two members of the party took her by the arms and half led, half carried her from the building. The others in the group followed them toward the door. There was a bench against the wall near Bill, and he sat down on it. The shock of the woman's outburst drained what little energy he'd had left, and he sat hunched forward with his elbows on his knees and his head in his hands.

A few moments later, he heard a gentle male voice above him.

"Mr. Ward?"

He looked up to see a man from the group with the woman, but said nothing. The man continued.

"Mr. Ward. I'm Benny Gonzales, Roberto's brother. I want to apologize for my mother."

Bill opened his mouth to speak, but was unable to say anything. He just sat there, looking stunned. Benny spoke again.

"I hope you can understand. My mother is crazy with grief. 'Berto was her baby. The pride of the family. The first one of us to go to college. He had a great job as a teacher, met a nice girl he was going to marry next year. When he was killed in the accident, my mother just collapsed and she's been inconsolable ever since."

Bill finally found his voice and responded.

"I'm … I'm so sorry. I wish … I wish I could have …"

"Mr. Ward, we've seen the accident report and everything. There was nothing you could have done. 'Berto was killed immediately. I'm grateful you were able to save the young woman and her baby."

Bill finally regained his composure, thought for a second and spoke again.

"My wife's older brother was killed by a drunk driver when he was in college. I don't think her parents ever recovered. I remember her father telling me once, 'You expect to bury your parents. You don't expect to bury your children.' All these years, they've grieved for their son. So I can appreciate what your family -- your mother -- is going through."

"Thank you for understanding."

"Not a day goes by that I don't think about that accident, and about your brother and your family. In my mind, I know there was nothing I could have done, but in my heart I wish I could have. I'm so very sorry for your loss."

Both men looked at each other with understanding, communing in their shared grief. Benny sat down on the bench next to Bill. They sat silently for a few moments. Benny quietly put a hand on Bill's shoulder, the men continued to sit in silence together in the quiet of the hallway for a while.

Chapter 21

Early September, Friday Afternoon

Bill was in his office talking with a co-worker named Gar Lewis, who was a senior manager in the Communications and Public Affairs Department. Gar was doing most of the talking, filling Bill in on a project they had both been asked to help out with, unexpectedly and at the last minute.

Bill had found out about the project earlier in the day, when his manager had urgently called him to her office. She had just learned out about the project as well, which was on the brink of failure and under a very tight deadline. She was in a near panic, and asked Bill to get involved immediately.

Bill had asked Gar to fill him in because he knew Gar would tell it to him straight, without glossing over any of the problems. They had worked together before, and trusted each other for their mutual competence, insight and integrity. Gar was taking him through it.

"So I'm in my office yesterday, minding my own business, trying to get some work done, when my computer screen lights up with about a half dozen Right Now instant message windows. Some of them were from people I didn't even know, and all of them were demanding I immediately drop what I was doing and join a teleconference about something called the 'Simplified Coverage Model.'"

"Had you been involved already?"

"Nope. First I heard about it. Apparently it was this big, super-secret project. So I responded, you know, 'Sure – I was just sitting here with nothing to do, hoping you'd all ask me to get involved in your thing.' And I get on the call and they lay it out for me."

"What did they tell you?"

“Well, you know our sales coverage model is really complex. We’re a big company, with a lot of different products and services. And we have a really big sales team, divided by geographies, brands, and industries, with all kinds of people involved – managing directors, account supervisors, brand specialists, technical support specialists, delivery specialists, industry specialists, pricers, you name it. So figuring out who should be involved on any given deal is really difficult to determine sometimes. And this is important because it determines who gets paid for what.”

“Right.”

“So, about six months ago, the VP of Sales Operations decides they’re going to completely redesign the whole thing. Take a fresh look at it, try to make it easier for everyone to navigate and understand, create some new online tools to make it simpler to register, qualify and progress deals, make sure the right people are involved at the right time, and that everyone gets paid the right way.”

“VP of Sales Operations – Anthony Bambino? From our OpenSwitch class?”

“Yeah, BamBam Bambino.”

“BamBam?”

“Yeah. Remember?”

Bill had forgotten the nickname, but he remembered Anthony from their early days at OpenSwitch. He, Gar, Herve, and Anthony all started at the company about the same time. He remembered Anthony as eager to the point of aggressiveness, very cocky and not quite as smart as he thought he was. Anthony would often charge into a situation and try to take command without fully understanding what was going on, sometimes with disastrous results.

Anthony quickly gained a reputation as a bully and a ball hog. He had a talent for contriving to be seen as having the "big idea," while coercing others to do the actual work while he paced on the sidelines making unhelpful suggestions and demanding status reports. Then, when the project was completed he would either take all the credit if it was a success or blame the team if it was a failure.

It was hard to understand how he had risen to a VP position, until you remembered he was one of the current CEO's protégés.

Bill continued.

"Is Anthony even qualified to develop a program like this?"

"Anthony isn't qualified to run a Jamba Juice. But that's beside the point."

"So what happened next?"

"Well, they've been working on this thing since last spring, they finally got it all ginned up and blessed by their management team, and they decided to test it a little with some of the senior sellers – the guys on our top accounts -- and see what they think. Well, it stiffs right out of the box. The sales execs say it's even more confusing than what they have now, and the tools don't work the right way. It's just a mess."

"Okay."

"So this wave of irony rolls over me. What they're telling me is, after six months of their hard work and good intentions, the new 'Simplified Coverage Model' is too complex. So I put my head down on my desk, and thought, 'I'm Dilbert. I am Dilbert, in the saddest, most unfunny way possible.'"

"Yeah."

"Well to make matters worse, not so cleverly hidden inside this thing was a scheme to raise quotas and lower commissions for everyone."

"They do that and the sales guys will quit."

"I think that was the general idea – thin the herd, get rid of some of the more highly compensated sellers, bring in some new guys at a lower cost. Of course, the people they tested this with are the top sellers in the company. Well, they saw through that in a heartbeat and said they'd quit on the spot if that wasn't fixed. You have any idea what that would do to our fourth-quarter sales this year?"

"Yeah, and it would probably blow out the first and second quarters next year too, and we'd never be able to make up the deficit. It would effectively tank our revenue for this year and next. So then what happened?"

"I let them talk for a little longer, until they finally got tired and asked me if I had any suggestions."

"What did you say."

"Well, I told them right off the bat they might consider making it less complicated, or else stop calling it the 'Simplified Coverage Model.' They didn't think that was funny at all."

"Yeah?"

"And I said get rid of the bogus scheme to rip off the sellers or their coverage model would be simplified like they couldn't have imagined."

"So what did they say?"

"They didn't think that was funny either. They said they really need help from Communications to fix it. And I told them, 'Look guys, there's no special magic communications BS that will make this better. You want to fix this, you need to fix the process.' And then I asked them if they had involved you guys in Business Compliance and Process Controls, and they got real quiet."

"They hadn't told us until today."

"Bill, they hadn't told anybody! BamBam is an egomaniac and idiot, and he specifically told his Sales Ops team to exclude all the major functions that SHOULD be involved in something like this – Finance, Legal, HR, Comms, and most of all you guys. I mean, this is what YOU do – you re-engineer business processes."

"Good grief. Why all the secrecy?"

"Sandy told him to get it done, so I guess he figured he had carte blanche to do whatever he wanted. I think he kind of fancies himself as sort of an Italian film genius, like Federico Fellini or something, with this unique vision for his masterpiece that only he can fully understand, and therefore he didn't want or need anyone else's input."

"Seriously?"

"In reality, he's more like Francis Ford Coppola disappearing into the Philippine jungle with his cast and crew to make 'Apocalypse Now,' and now 15 months later the studio is wondering if they're ever gonna get their movie."

"Oy."

"Oh, it gets better. This thing has to be all wrapped up and finished, ready to go and blessed by the end of next month or they won't be able to use it when the put the new sales plans in place in January. And if that happens, the CEO is going to blow a gasket – as if she needs another excuse for that."

"So what's the plan?"

"Well, there's a full-day review on Monday, with all the right players this time. After that, we should have at least some initial ideas on how to get this thing back on track. My part is relatively simple – it really all comes down to having something to talk about. But you've got a lot of work to do to fix this thing. You think you can at least have some ideas pulled together by Monday?"

"Well, I'll have to take some time to look at the project plan today and over the weekend, but I should have something to discuss by then. It won't be pretty, but I can at least see if I can figure out what the biggest problems are and start thinking what to do about them. You think they'll listen to us?"

"At this point, I don't think they have a choice. They've screwed this up so badly, they're about ready to walk off a cliff."

"Well, good, that should make it a lot easier. If I have a choice between having a month to do the impossible or six months, I'll take the month every time – makes it less painful in the long run. Tell them to send me everything they have on this thing and I'll get started."

***

Mid-September, Monday Morning

Betsey Wetsel was in her office with the door closed, looking at a file on her computer and speaking on the telephone. She was talking with Butch Snyder, manager of IT Security Services for OpenSwitch.

"I don't understand what I'm looking at, Butch. There's nothing in here."

"There's nothing in there because there's nothing to see. We did a thorough check, going back six months."

"Nothing? He looks at nothing on the Internet?"

"Well, there are visits a couple times a month to a website called 'Business Process News.' And there's something called the 'Daily Bible Verse' he checks regularly. But that's really it. No Facebook, no Twitter, no Instagram – it's like he's got no online profile at all."

"Could he be hiding … other things?"

"Look, I know what you're getting at, and the answer is 'no.' We do this all the time, and we know all the tricks. If he were going to websites that violate our business policies, we'd see it. No gambling sites. No hate speech or violent stuff. No pornography. Not even a peek at the Sports Illustrated Swimsuit Edition. He's clean – there's just nothing here."

Betsey grunted.

"Okay. Thanks, Butch."

"You sound disappointed."

She ignored the comment.

"I'll be in touch if I need anything else."

Betsey hung up the phone, closed the file, and sat thinking for a minute. There was a knock at the door, and Betsey stirred from her thoughts to answer.

"Come in."

Jenny Stuart poked her head in the door.

"You wanted to see me?"

"Yes, Jennifer. Come in. Close the door behind you and have a seat."

Jenny flinched at the formality of her full name. No one called her that. She sat down and Betsey spoke to her.

"I want to ask you about an incident with your project supervisor, Bill Ward, a few months ago."

"Incident?"

"Yes. I understand that he asked you and Charlene Bogart to make arrangements for food at a day-long team meeting. That seems a little inappropriate to me, and I'd like to know if that caused you any discomfort or embarrassment."

"No, not really."

"No? Being asked to perform a subservient task. Some people might call that a little sexist, don't you think?"

"No. He made the arrangements himself the time before. It was just our turn. We all share those kinds of duties on our team."

"So you didn't find that offensive at all?"

"No. He wasn't asking us to do anything he hadn't done himself. And knowing Bill and his character, he had no ulterior motive in asking us to do it. He asked Duane and Al to do it for the next meeting."

"I see. So there's nothing in Bill's … management style that you find demeaning or patriarchal?"

"To the contrary. I find him to be very sensitive to all of our team's members, as employees and as human beings. He understands the challenges of balancing our professional duties and personal responsibilities, and works very hard to be as accommodating as he can be."

"My, my, you seem to be quite the little fan of Bill, don't you?"

"If by that you mean I respect him as a supervisor and as a person, then yes."

Betsey paused for a moment and then looked directly at Jenny as she spoke.

"Is there something ... going on between the two of you?"

Jenny flushed as her discomfort and anxiety over the interrogation transformed into anger.

"Look, I don't know what it is you're looking for here, but I deeply resent that insinuation."

"That's not a denial."

Jenny got up from her chair and walked to the door.

"To answer your question directly, no, there is nothing going on between Bill and me. I don't know what you're up to, but I won't be any part of it. And I'm leaving."

After Jenny left, Betsey pulled up a spreadsheet on her computer containing a list of names. She scrolled down to Jenny's name and put an "x" next to it.

***

Late September, Saturday Morning

Bill sat uncomfortably on a plastic chair in the small examining room at the veterinarian's office, Buddy lying quietly at his feet, the dog's breathing a bit labored. Bill reached down occasionally to give Buddy a pat or a rub, and Buddy would raise his head slightly each time responding to the gentle touch of his master.

The symptoms Bill had noticed in Buddy in the spring had gotten progressively worse over the summer and into the fall. An earlier checkup had shone nothing unusual – just the normal signs of an aging dog. But Bill had noticed a dramatic increase in Buddy's lethargy and discomfort over the previous two weeks. Within the past seven days, it had gotten to the point where the dog would barely eat, which was completely untypical for Buddy.

After about 10 minutes the veterinarian, Ingrid Heikkinen, entered the room with a serious look on her face. She had been Buddy's vet since he was a puppy, and she knew Bill from all the regular office visits for checkups over the years. Bill rose to his feet and greeted her quietly. Buddy remained on the floor.

"Hello, doctor."

"Hi Bill."

"What can you tell me about Buddy?"

Dr. Heikkinen sighed and then responded.

"Well, I'm afraid it's not good news. The images show an enlarged heart. That's why he's had so much trouble breathing these last few weeks."

"Is there anything we can do for him?"

"Not really. We could do a few things to keep him going for a month or two longer, but there's really no curing this. Along with his other conditions, like the hip dysplasia, it's just old age catching up with him."

"Is he in pain?"

"He's in considerable discomfort – probably more than he's letting on."

"What can we do?"

"Well, I never like telling a pet owner this – it's the worst part of the job. But it may be time to let him go."

Bill took a deep breath. The news wasn't unexpected, but was painful nonetheless. After a moment, Dr. Heikkinen gently broke the silence.

"What do you think, Bill?"

Bill replied sadly.

"Look, if there was a pill we could give him that would make him better or at least a little more comfortable, it would be one thing. But if he's in pain and we can't fix this, I can't put him through any more of this. It would be selfish. Let's go ahead."

"Right now?"

"Yes. No point putting it off."

"Okay, can you help me lift him up onto the examining table?"

Bill nodded, and the both reached down gently to pick Buddy up. Buddy winced slightly as they lifted him and placed him on the table. Dr. Heikkinen turned away to prepare the syringe, and Bill placed his face close to Buddy's. Buddy looked into Bill's eyes and licked his chin, making Bill smile.

Dr. Heikkinen turned back to them and addressed Bill.

"Whenever you're ready."

"Will it hurt him?"

"No, it won't hurt him and it will be very quick."

Bill drew a deep breath, looked at Buddy, then looked at Dr. Heikkinen and responded.

"Okay."

"If you can just hold him while I give him the injection."

"Sure."

Buddy lay quietly as the vet administered the shot. Buddy stiffened for a second and then relaxed as he slipped away. Bill looked at Dr. Heikkinen.

"Thank you, doctor. May I have a moment with him?"

"Take all the time you need."

Dr. Heikkinen left the room. Bill looked at Buddy lying still on the examining table. He slipped his arms around Buddy' neck, pulled him close, and quietly wept.

***

Late September, Wednesday Evening

Bill carried a pot of coffee into the living room, Maggie right behind with a tray holding cake, plates, cups and utensils. Howard and Judy were sitting on the couch, waiting quietly and a bit nervously.

After the coffee and cake were served, Howard started the conversation.

“Hey, how are you doing? I know losing Buddy was tough for you. I know how much he meant to you.”

Bill drew a breath and then responded.

“Thanks for asking, Howard. I appreciate it. It was just his time. Now, you sounded pretty serious when you said you and Judy wanted to speak with us. What’s on your mind?”

“Look, we’re sorry to bother you on a week night and all, but we have something that’s been concerning us and wanted to discuss it with you.”

Maggie responded.

“It’s no bother, Howard. We’re always glad to see the two of you. What is it?”

“Well, it’s about Jasmine and Bryce. They were seeing each other regularly all summer, and even now that they both back at school it doesn’t seem to be cooling down.”

“Is there something wrong? A problem with Bryce?”

Judy spoke.

“No, we love Bryce.”

Maggie responded.

“And we adore Jasmine. So what’s your concern?”

Howard continued.

“Look, there’s nothing wrong. We just, well, from look of it, this thing has all the hallmarks of going the distance. And I … we just want to make sure we’re all prepared for that.”

Maggie responded.

"You think so? You mean marriage?"

"Yeah, I do. I can tell by the look in that boy's eye that he means business, and the same with Jasmine. Never seen her so serious about a young man before."

Bill spoke.

"Yeah, I see it too. It was the same with Maggie and me. I knew the minute I saw her she was the one."

Maggie seemed both surprised and flattered by that admission. Howard continued.

"I know what you mean. It was like that with Judy and me too."

Judy smiled and blushed. Bill spoke.

"Okay, so we think we know what this is. Knowing my son, it wouldn't surprise me if he walked across the street this Christmas to ask for your permission to propose, Howard."

Howard raised his eyebrows and responded.

"You think?"

"He hasn't said anything, but if I'm reading it right, yeah. But I'm still not sure I understand your concern. Has Bryce done something to make you uncomfortable?"

Howard replied.

"No, not at all. By all accounts, he's been an absolute gentleman, and as a father of two daughters I appreciate that. Frankly, he's maturing into a fine young man, and I'm glad my daughter is seeing someone like him."

"Then what's the issue?"

Howard stopped for a second, sighed, and then continued.

"Boy, you guys just don't see it, do you? I don't know why that surprises me – you two are the most colorblind people I've ever met when it comes to this sort of thing. Actually, I appreciate that. So let me spell it out for you. We're black. You're white. That complicates things."

Bill responded.

“Well, I don’t see why that matters. It’s certainly not an issue for us. And it’s the 21st century for heaven sake. It’s not like they’ll be the first interracial couple in America.”

“That’s true. But even now there’s a lot of ugly-ass stupidity and hatred in the world.”

Judy startled and interrupted Howard.

“Howard! Your language!”

“I’m sorry.” He turned to Maggie. “Please forgive me.”

Maggie smiled and replied.

“It’s okay, Howard. I understand.”

“Thanks, Maggie. But I’m not sure you do. Our perspective on this may be a little different than yours. Even in this community, our family has experienced bigotry and prejudice, simply because of the color of our skin. It’s usually not prevalent or flagrant, but it’s there, and we can’t ignore it. If Bryce and Jasmine get married, they’re going to experience it too, and so are you. And I want to make sure you know that going in.”

Bill spoke.

“Look, Howard, you’re right. Our experience has been different from yours, there’s no question about that. I don’t think we’ll ever know what it’s like to experience prejudice like you and Judy and your kids have. But we have had our own experiences with ‘ugly-ass stupidity and hatred,’ so to speak – undeservedly, and simply because of who we are. So I think on some level we can sort of relate, if not completely.”

Maggie scolded Bill.

“Bill! YOUR language!”

For whatever reason, the exchange broke the tension and they all laughed for a moment. Bill continued.

"I think the best thing for our kids is that they know the four of us are behind them 100 percent, no matter what. As long as they have that, nothing else really matters. One thing we've all learned over the past few years of being friends and neighbors with you is that we can always depend on each other."

Howard responded.

"Well, okay then. As long as we all know what we're getting ourselves into."

"Actually, I think you missed the biggest problem of all."

"What's that?"

"The prospect of having to look at me across the Thanksgiving table for the next 40 years."

Howard thought for a second and then spoke.

"You know, to be honest, I don't even like you that much."

"I know."

The women giggled.

Chapter 22

Early October, Tuesday Evening

Bill slid into the driver's seat of his car in the parking lot of Grace By Faith Community Church. He was dirty and tired, but he felt good. It was about quarter to 10, and he had spent the evening with some of the other men in the church helping Youth Pastor Gill Brynett build a halfpipe skateboard ramp in one corner of the church's gymnasium.

Gill had been using a weekly skateboard club as outreach to teenagers in the community, and it had garnered quite a following. Adding the halfpipe would make the ministry even more attractive to the kids, Gill said, and he had solicited money for materials from the Elder Board and recruited church members to help build it.

Bill liked Gill and appreciated his outreach to local youth. He also enjoyed putting his handyman skills to practical use in building the ramp. And the project had been a nice diversion from his job. He'd been working long days and weekends on the special project at the office, with little time for personal pursuits. But when Gill had asked for his help, he blocked the evening on his calendar and made sure he could be there to participate.

He started the car and reached for his phone to text Maggie that he was on his way home.

"Heading home – be there in 15 mins."

She texted back right away.

"Can you stop for milk and eggs?"

"Sure."

A couple miles from home he stopped at a small convenience store called the Dairy and Energy Mart, parked next to the building and went inside. A young black woman was standing behind counter at the cash register, reading a text book. He was a regular patron of the store, and he greeted her by name – Ivory – without having to look at the name badge on her shirt. She looked up, smiled and returned his greeting.

Bill made his way to the back of the store past several rows of groceries and merchandise that ran parallel to the front of the store. Directly ahead of him was a closed door leading to the back room, with a sign reading "Authorized Personnel Only." Before reaching the door, he turned right behind the last row of shelves.

Lining the back wall were coolers containing the store's refrigerated products. The eggs were on the bottom shelf behind the second door. He opened the door, pulled out a carton and turned to place it on the shelf behind him, allowing the cooler door to slip closed. He stooped to open the carton and inspect the eggs for cracks, which hid him from view at the front of the store.

A few seconds later, as he was about to straighten up, he heard the door swing open and someone walk in. Then he heard a man's voice shouting.

"Open the register! Give me the money! NOW!"

He heard Ivory let out a short yelp of fear, and then the sound of the cash register opening. In the corner above stockroom door was a curved security mirror that allowed the cashier to see what was happening in the back row of the store. From Bill's location, it also gave him a full view of the counter and the area in front of it.

In the mirror, Bill could see a tall, skinny man in faded jeans and a white tee shirt. The man had a scruffy beard and was wearing a dirty, tan baseball cap. He also was holding a gun. Bill knew who he was. Over the past month, there had been news reports about a series of armed robberies at small convenience stores around town. The robberies always happened between 10 p.m. and midnight, usually at small, independently owned stores like this one.

Each time, after cleaning out the register, the robber would march the cashiers into the backroom of the store and tie them up. The one detail that changed was that with each robbery, the thief had become progressively more violent – assaulting his bound victims with increasing ferocity. The previous week he had pistol-whipped a store owner, fracturing his skull and putting him in the hospital.

The man Bill saw in the mirror matched the description of the robber that had been shared in the news reports. Bill reached into his pocket and quietly pulled out his knife. It was his bigger, heavier weekend knife – he'd brought it along for the construction project at church. He slipped the blade open, being careful not to let it make its characteristic "snap" when it locked into place. He heard Ivory emptying the register and shoving the money into a bag, and then the man yelled again.

"Now! In the back!"

Bill marked their progress in the security mirror as they started moving toward the rear of the store. He noted that the man wasn't looking at the mirror, so he was sure the robber wasn't aware of his presence. At the end of the row was a display that extended about four inches beyond the width of the shelves. Bill pressed himself into the corner as far as he could, to provide as much concealment as possible, stooping to keep his head below the top of the rack.

As he heard them near the back of the store, Bill spun the knife in his hand so that the blade was facing up. He figured that would allow it to penetrate more quickly and deeply when he thrust it. He saw Ivory get to the door and start to open it. Then he saw the robber shove her forward.

As the robber moved past him, Bill swiftly and quietly stepped in behind him, and swung his arm in a low arc as if he was bowling, plunging the blade deeply into the man's right buttock. The robber had seen a flurry to his right and was just turning his head when his body exploded in pain and he dropped to the floor.

Bill followed up with a kick to the ribs, knocking the wind out of the robber, who collapsed on the ground. Bill then dropped on top of him, pinning the squirming, gasping man to the floor with a knee in his back.

The robber had dropped his pistol when he fell and it had skittered a few feet away, out of reach. Ivory glanced at it for a second, then reached down and picked it up. Bill looked up to see her pointing it at the robber. He spoke to her.

“Don’t shoot him.”

“I WILL shoot him if he gets up.”

“I won’t let him get up. And be careful. You might shoot me.”

Bill placed the point of his knife against the robber’s throat with just enough pressure to make it uncomfortable, and spoke calmly to the man twisting beneath him.

“Please stop struggling.”

With those words and the feel of the blade against his throat, the man went limp. He continued to groan and sob in pain. Bill looked up at Ivory and spoke to her.

“Go call the police. Tell them to hurry.”

Ivory went back to cash register, placed the gun on the counter, picked up the phone and dialed 911. She told the operator what happened and that Bill was restraining the robber until police arrived. Within a few minutes, they could hear sirens in the distance.

Over his shoulder, Bill watched Ivory pick up the handgun, remove the magazine and put it on the counter. She then racked the pistol’s slide back, locking the action open and ejecting the round from the chamber. She then placed the firearm and the single bullet back on the counter in front of her. Bill spoke to her.

“You seem to know what you’re doing there.”

“Uh huh. I was in the military -- MPs.”

“So you weren’t kidding when you said you’d shoot him.”

“Nope.”

Ivory looked out the window and then spoke again.

“Police are pulling in. When they come in, do exactly what they tell you.”

“Okay.”

Two police officers entered the store, guns drawn. They immediately walked over to Bill and the robber. One took Bill by the arm and guided him to his feet, while the other handcuffed he robber, who remained lying on the floor groaning. The first officer led Bill and Ivory outside and asked them to wait on a bench by the ice machine. More police arrived, along with an ambulance, and the additional officers and the EMTs entered the store.

Ten minutes later, a police detective pulled in and entered the store to speak with the officers who had been first to arrive. After they briefed him, he came back outside to speak with Bill and Ivory. He found them sitting on the bench where the patrolman had deposited them. Bill had a dazed looked on his face and had an arm around Ivory's shoulder. Ivory was wearing Bill's jacket and she had her head against his chest. He was speaking quietly to her and she was crying.

***

Detective Wayne Jeffries was standing in the squad room at the police station talking with Shift Sergeant Rich Halloran and the two patrolman who had been first to arrive at the robbery scene. Jeffries was the detective who arrived at the store shortly after the robbery and had recognized Bill Ward immediately from the incident in July.

The four police officers were discussing what procedures and forms needed to be completed, the condition and treatment of the robber, and various details of the incident. The thief was under police guard at Stanhope Memorial Hospital, where he had been admitted for his injuries -- three broken ribs and a serious puncture wound to the right buttock. Jeffries filled in the others on the background of Bill Ward and Ivory Jones.

"Yeah, he's the same guy from that accident out on the highway last spring and from that arson case in July. Nice guy, really. After the fire, he actually talked to the judge and the DA, went to bat for the kids who did it. Probably kept them out of jail. And now the thing with the robber tonight. Mr. Ward seems to be having a bit of a bad-luck streak."

Sergeant Halloran responded.

"Not bad luck for that young lady tonight. I'd say she had a pretty close call. How is she doing?"

"She's fine, considering. Pretty tough. Name is Ivory Jones. Former Air Force Military Police. Single mom – her husband was Air Force too, killed in Afghanistan two years ago. She's studying criminal justice down at Sacred Conception College, working at the convenience store nights. She interned over at the Milbury PD last summer. She'll be okay."

Another detective, Larry "Speed" Dirk burst through the door of the squad room and barged into the conversation. He had been running the investigation into the convenience store robberies for a month and had been off duty that evening, but rushed to the police station when he heard what had happened.

"Where is he? I want to talk to him!"

Jeffries and Halloran both looked at Dirk slightly annoyed. He had a reputation within the department for being overly ambitious and a bit of a cowboy. He wasn't a bad police officer – just kind of pushy and obnoxious. Sergeant Halloran responded.

"Where's who, Speed?"

"The suspect!"

"He's at Stanhope – admitted for treatment of his wounds."

"Not him. The other one – the one with the knife. I want to talk to him!"

Jeffries responded.

"He's waiting in the conference room. And he's not a suspect – he's a witness."

"Like hell. Assault with a deadly weapon, hindering an investigation. I want to get him in The Box and interrogate him."

"The Box? You mean the Interview Room? Save the TV cop lingo, this isn't 'Law and Order' ... Laurence."

Jefferies let the use of Dirk's full first name linger, knowing it would get under the other detective's skin. The response was angry and immediate.

"Don't call me that! You don't get to call me that. And I don't need you or this … civilian … getting in the way of my investigation."

Sergeant Halloran intervened.

"Seems to me like this guy did us all a favor, Speed. We've been trying to catch this robber for a month now, with very few leads and a suspect who's been getting more violent with each robbery. I'd say someone stopping this guy before he could hurt anyone else was a lucky break."

Dirk stopped to think for a second, and then responded.

"Well … maybe. But I still don't like it."

Police Chief Forgas entered the squad room and approached the officers and detectives.

"I just got off the phone with district attorney. He's very relieved that we caught the robber. Congratulations to all of you for your good work on this case. Speed, even though you weren't on duty at the time of the arrest, I want you to share in the credit with Detective Jefferies and the two patrolmen."

Dirk responded less than enthusiastically.

"Okay … Thank you."

"You've led this investigation from the start, and your work will help ensure we can put this guy in jail for a long time. There's more. The gentleman who was assaulted in the robbery last week died from his injuries earlier today. So among the charges the DA is filing the suspect is murder.

Dirk interrupted again.

"What about the other guy? The guy with the knife. Are we going to charge him?"

“The DA has no interest in pursuing charges against Mr. Ward, nor do I. Under the circumstances, I’d say it was a pretty gutsy move and it helped us stop a bad guy. Now, if you’d all work together to wrap this up tonight, I would appreciate it. Detective Jefferies, if you would please take formal statements from the witnesses and make sure they get home safely.”

Chief Forgas turned to leave, and speaking over his shoulder as he started to walk away.

“Speed, if I could see you in my office, please?”

***

Detective Jeffries took the witness statements as instructed, first from Ivory Jones and then from Bill Ward. He conducted in the interviews separately, and after Ivory was through he had a patrolman drive her home. He and Bill were wrapping up their discussion.

“I think that about covers it, Mr. Ward. Is there anything you’d like to add to your statement?”

“No … no, I don’t think so.”

He paused for a moment, and Detective Jeffries queried him.

“Are you okay, Mr. Ward.”

“Yeah, I think so. It’s just … a lot. I’ve never … hurt anyone like that before. There was a lot of blood. It was pretty scary.”

“Can you tell me why you stabbed him in the buttocks?”

“I wanted to stop him.”

“By why there?”

“I didn’t want to kill him.”

“How did you know to do it there?”

“I don’t know. I probably saw it in a movie or something. Am I … am I in any trouble?”

"No, Mr. Ward. We won't be pressing any charges against you. From all appearances, you did what was necessary to stop the robber, but went out of your way to make sure you didn't hurt him any worse than you had to."

"Okay."

"I know this is traumatic. But I want you to know that you kept your cool in a situation that would have challenged even a trained law enforcement professional. The robber is a very violent, very dangerous man – a drug addict who is seriously strung out on methamphetamine. So he was capable of anything. One of his victims passed away earlier today, so he's now facing a murder charge along with everything else."

"Oh. I didn't know about that."

"Well, I think I have everything I need. We'll be in touch, of course, as the charges proceed against the suspect."

"Whatever I can do to help."

"Do you need a ride home."

"No, I'm fine. I have a friend waiting for me downstairs. Thank you, detective."

"Thank you, Mr. Ward. I'll walk you out."

***

Howard was waiting in his car in front of the police station when Bill exited the building. Bill slid into the front passenger's seat of the car, and Howard greeted him.

"Good evening, Batman. Sounds like you've had quite a night."

"That's not funny, Howard."

"Oh come on, Bill. It's a little funny."

Bill was quiet for a moment.

"Okay. Maybe a little tiny bit."

"You okay?"

"Yeah, I think so."

"I mean, breaking up an armed robbery by stabbing a guy. That's pretty hard core."

Bill sighed.

"I'm getting kind of tired of this. I don't know why these things keep happening to me."

"Seems to me they're not happening to you. They're happening to other people. You're just there to catch them when they fall."

"What do you mean?"

"Look, you consider yourself a man of faith, right?"

"Yes, I suppose so."

"Well, I don't know if it's God, or fate, or something else intervening. But three times now people have been in some serious trouble, and you've been the instrument of their salvation. When Shannon and her daughter were in that accident, you were there to pull them from the wreck before the car exploded."

"Okay."

"When those boys set your lawn on fire, instead of demanding retribution you offered them compassion, and provided them with an opportunity to get their lives back on the right path."

"Okay."

"And tonight, well, I don't even want to think about what could have happened to that young woman if you weren't there."

"Okay."

"In each case, you were placed in their path to rescue them. You didn't have to help them. You could have turned away. You always say 'anyone would have done what I did,' but the truth is most people wouldn't. They would have turned and run at the first sign of danger, or just stood there doing nothing. But every time, you responded with courage, character and humility. To be honest, I don't know if I even knew what bravery was until I saw the things you've done."

"That's … that's a lot to take in."

“Yeah, it is. It’s a lot of responsibility. And this time, you’re going to have people both praising and criticizing you, because of what you did.”

“What do you mean?”

“Oh, it’s starting already on social media. Trending topics like hashtag ‘assstab,’ and ‘stabass,’ and ‘assstabber.’ About half of them are for you, the other half are against.”

“I don’t understand why? I only tried to help that woman, to stop that ...”

“Well, it’s a world full of armchair quarterbacks, Bill. Everybody’s got an opinion about everything, and with Facebook and Twitter, and such, they all have a pulpit to preach it from. Gonna get worse before it gets better, I’m afraid. By later this morning, the press calls will start coming in.”

“Oh, Howard. I don’t think I can do that again.”

“Don’t worry, I can handle most of it for you. I’ll prepare a brief statement I can give out on your behalf to anyone who calls. I’ll probably cite the ongoing police investigation as the reason for not saying much. The worst of it should blow over in a day or two.”

“Thank you, Howard.”

“But I think you’re going to have to deal with this for a while. Like it or not, you’re kind of a national sensation.”

Bill put his head back and closed his eyes.

“I’m tired.”

They didn’t speak further for the rest of the ride home.

***

Maggie heard the car pull into the driveway and ran downstairs to open the front door for Bill. It was well after midnight. She watched him exit Howard’s car, and walk up the front walkway as Howard backed the car out of the driveway and drove across the street.

As Bill came in the front door, he looked at her, and she gently put her arms around him and pulled him close, giving him a long, deep hug. She loosened her hold and looked into his eyes, putting a hand to his face.

"Are you okay?"

"Yeah. I just want to take a shower and go to bed."

She led him upstairs.

Chapter 23

Wednesday Evening

The local NBC television affiliate's evening newscast returned from a commercial break, and news anchor Bart Gardetto intoned seriously to the camera.

"A string of violent armed robberies at local convenience stores was brought to an end last evening, with a suspect now in police custody."

Co-anchor Liz Ross picked up the narrative.

"But not without some controversy over who stopped the crime spree, and how he did it. WEST Reporter Dave Streader has been following the story all day and has the details. I should warn, some of the scenes we're about to show you could be shocking for sensitive viewers. Dave?"

The broadcast cut to a live remote shot of the reporter standing in front of the Dairy and Energy Mart in Derbeville.

"Thanks, Bart, Liz. For weeks, an armed robber has terrorized local businesses, robbing convenience stores at gunpoint and then beating the store clerks, often severely and in one case eventually to the point of death. But last night that came to an end, when a bystander intervened during a robbery at this store behind me, apprehending the robber and holding him until police arrived.

"In last night's robbery, police said the assailant entered the Dairy and Energy Mart, ordered the clerk to empty the cash register at gunpoint, and the forced her to go with him to the backroom of the store. A local citizen, who had entered the store just before the assailant, was hiding behind some shelves, and jumped the suspect as he passed, overpowered and disarmed him, and held him until police arrived. Police have released this surveillance video from the store, showing the incident as it occurred."

The video footage appeared as the soft-focus, black-and-white video typical of surveillance systems. The camera was positioned above and behind Bill Ward, showing him crouching behind the shelves, the storeroom door visible to his left. Ivory Jones could be seen stumbling into the scene moving toward the storeroom, followed by the robber prodding her along with a large pistol.

As they passed, the video showed Bill quickly step in behind the robber and sharply thrust a knife into the man's right buttock. The robber then collapsed on the floor, as Bill delivered a hard kick to his ribs and then jumped on his back.

Next, Ivory could be seen whirling around at the commotion behind her, staring blankly at the two men on the floor for a second, then quickly bending down to pick up the pistol and point it at the robber. Bill raised his head and could be seen saying something to the clerk, who responded and then lowered the weapon and returned to the front of the store out view of the camera as the video ended.

Dave narrated the video footage as it was shown. The broadcast transitioned to a mug shot of the suspect police had arrested, staring at the camera wild-eyed and disheveled, and Streader continued his monologue.

"Police have charged 37-year-old Darryl Streeb of Watersburg with numerous counts of armed robbery, assault with a deadly weapon and – most seriously – murder. Mr. Streeb has been previously charged and convicted in numerous cases for assault, battery, robbery, drug possession. The murder charge stems from a robbery committed last week at Catonsville, where store owner Elmer Gladish sustained a fractured skull and other injuries when allegedly assaulted by the robber. Authorities report that Mr. Gladish succumbed to his injuries yesterday.

"Police identified the local citizen who intervened as Bill Ward of Derbeville. You may remember that last spring Mr. Ward was credited with saving a young woman and her baby from a burning vehicle after a very serious tractor-trailer accident on the interstate."

The broadcast cut to footage from the Interstate accident, showing Bill Ward sitting by the side of the road with Shannon Gales and her baby while EMTs attended to them.

The video transitioned to a split screen showing the news anchors in the studio and the reporter standing in front of the store. Bart picked up the narrative, addressing the Dave.

“An incredible story, Dave. Can you tell us about some of the controversy surrounding last night’s incident and Mr. Ward?”

“Well, Bart, some people are saying Ward is a legitimate hero both for his actions last spring and for last night, when he stopped a vicious criminal who has terrorized local storekeepers for more than a month. Others are saying he’s an ego-driven vigilante, someone with a superhero complex and a violent streak of his own.”

Liz picked up the questioning.

“Yes, the stabbing we witnessed in the video was quite savage. And didn’t he also use a knife to save that woman and child last spring? Why does he always seem to have a knife and what is the truth about Mr. Ward?”

“It’s complicated, Liz. We know what he did out on that highway last spring, saving that woman and her baby seconds before their car exploded. By many accounts he’s a quiet family man and a solid citizen. But then this summer Mr. Ward and his family were victims of an arson attack on their property, which apparently stemmed from a fistfight involving their 20-year-old son and their teenage daughter’s ex-boyfriend.

“The ex-boyfriend is currently in jail on drug trafficking charges. And now we have the violent events of last evening. It’s difficult to say what the truth is about Mr. Ward, other than that trouble seems to follow him wherever he goes.”

The broadcast cut back to Bart and Liz at the anchor desk, and Bart addressed the camera.

“Thank you, Dave, for that fascinating report. We should note for our viewers that Dave and WEST cameraman Jerry Jones recently received an Emmy Award for their coverage of the interstate accident last spring, and that Dave will be leaving us for a reporting assignment with our network affiliate in New York. Congratulations to both Dave and Jerry, and best wishes to Dave.”

Bart turned to Liz and engaged in some transition banter.

“Incredible story. He brought a knife to a gun fight.”

“He seems to have put that old saying to rest.”

The both chuckled and moved to the next story on the program.

***

Howard Jones turned off the news broadcast and frowned. He’d been monitoring the story all day, as it was picked up by the wire services and major news outlets, which all noted the connection to the earlier incidents involving Bill Ward and his family. Howard also had been following the sentiment in media commentary and on social networks. He called Bill to give him an update.

“Yeah, it made the local 6 o’clock news, pretty balanced story. The local paper had it and there were a couple wire stories that went national. Again mostly balanced and positive.”

“Well, that’s not too bad.”

“Yeah, but public opinion has been pretty polarized. It’s kind of been building for a while, since the accident last spring. A lot of pro and con about the ‘knife’ thing. Now with the robbery, that’s gone into overdrive. Also a lot of talk about your appearance on Fallon with Javier Fernandez from ‘The Gay Bachelor’ bubbling up again.”

“Yeah. He called me today, just to say ‘hi’ and cheer me up. He’s the Scoutmaster now and invited me to go on a camping trip to Mount Marcy in the Adirondacks with his troop next month.”

“You going?”

"Yeah, I want to. Anything else?"

"You were the talk of local rock radio station I-95's morning show with Ethan and Lou today. Callers were split about 50-50, and so were the DJs. Ethan thinks you're a good guy, but Lou kept calling you an 'ass-stabber.'"

"Ouch."

"Yeah, they had a lot people calling in about it. You know a Richard Camerari?"

"Yeah. He's my barber."

"He told them about how you helped him out when he broke his leg, said you never mentioned it again, didn't want anything in return."

"Well, that was nice of him."

"And there was a Judge Schukoth. She talked about how you stood up for those three boys who nearly burned your house down."

"Oh, Judge Schukoth, from court last summer."

"The rest of the callers were the usual idiots you get calling into those shows -- don't know nothin' about nothin'. Some talking you up, the others tearing you down."

"Yeah, I suppose. Anything else?"

"It's worse on social media. On the extreme ends you got liberal social justice warriors calling you a vigilante with a messiah complex, and right-wing militias applauding the way you took down the robber and encouraging others to go after criminals and other 'antisocial elements' in the same way."

"Oh boy."

"In the middle you got a lot of people who don't know what to make of you – some think you're a hero while others think you're a nut. It's also found its way into local politics, with one town council candidate making a big deal of it and calling you a menace to the public."

"Oh man. What should I do?"

“Hang tight for now. I’ve been fending off calls for interviews with the ‘ongoing police investigation’ thing. Conveniently, it’s true and most of them are respecting that.”

“Yeah, I’ve had a few calls here at the house, but I’m just letting them go to voicemail.”

“Well, keep doing that, and I’ll try to hold them off. If there are any calls you think we need to return, send them my way and I’ll handle it. Like I told you this morning, with any luck the big noise will quiet down in a day or two. But I think you can expect this to crop up again from time to time. This is becoming kind of a social phenomenon.”

“Thanks, Howard. I appreciate your help.”

They ended the call, and Howard sat and thought for a minute. He was angry. Most of the negative things being said about Bill were uncalled for and unjustifiable, and even some of the positive stuff was unhelpful. It wasn’t going to be enough to hope that it would just die down on its own. Bill needed a few more people on his side and Howard decided to do something about it.

He thought for another minute, then picked up his phone, selected Mort Mortefolio’s number from his contacts and hit dial. The phone on the other end rang a couple times before someone picked up.

“Hello, Mort? Yeah, this is Howard Jones – Bill Ward’s neighbor.”

“Oh, hey Howard. How are you?

“I’m well, Mort. I hope you are too.”

“I’m just great. Hey! Some big news about our boy Bill, right? Stopping an armed robber by stabbing him in the ass. Who knew?”

“Yeah, that’s actually why I’m calling. I need a favor. For Bill.”

“For Bill? Anything. You know that. How can I help you?”

Howard and Mort finished their conversation, then Howard returned a call he had received earlier from a producer at "The Today Show." He also made a couple more phone calls.

***

Thursday Morning

"The Today Show" returned from commercial break, with Matt Lauer seated across from Ivory Jones and Shannon Gales. The camera cut to a shot of just him, the "Today Show" logo on the wall visible over his shoulder, and he addressed the television audience.

"Big story in the news from earlier this week, as a man stumbled into the middle of an armed robbery at a convenience store and stopped the robber, putting an end to a string of violent attacks that had resulted in one death and numerous injured store clerks. The hero in this case is the same man who saved a woman and her infant child from a burning car wreck last spring.

"But now this man is caught it a crossfire of controversy, as across the nation in the news and on social media some are calling him a Good Samaritan while others say he's a reckless, violent adventurer who takes the law into his own hands."

The camera pulled back to show Matt and the two women, and Matt continued his set-up for the interview.

"The man in question – Bill Ward of Derbeville, Connecticut – declined our invitation to be on the show to discuss what happened. But we have with us today Ivory Jones, the clerk from the store where the incident occurred earlier this week. And joining her is Shannon Gales, who Mr. Ward rescued from a blazing wreck along with her daughter earlier this year. Ms. Jones thanks for being here, Ms. Gales welcome back."

The two young women nodded to Matt and responded.

"Thank you."

"Thank you, Matt."

“Ms. Jones, let me start by asking you to describe what happened Tuesday evening in your store.”

“Well, it was about 10 p.m., just a regular quiet weeknight. I was tending the store and studying for an exam, when Mr. Ward came in.”

“Had you ever seen him before? Did you know him?”

“I didn’t really know him, but I remembered him. He’s a regular customer – probably stops in once a week or so for gas, bread, milk, eggs, stuff like that. He always smiles when he comes, always remembers my name, says ‘please’ and ‘thank you.’ Sometimes he’ll ask me how I’m doing, how my schoolwork is going, and he actually takes the time to listen when I answer. He’s a very nice man.”

“What happened next?”

“After we said ‘hi,’ he walked to the back of the store and I took up studying again. Maybe about a minute later, someone else walks into the store. A tall, skinny man.”

“Did you notice anything unusual about him?”

“Well, mostly I noticed the gun he was pointing at me. He shouted at me to open the register and give him the money. And then he ordered me out from behind the counter and told me to go to the back of the store.”

“Were you frightened?”

“I was very afraid. I knew who he was and what he was about to do.”

“Where was Mr. Ward at that point?”

“To tell you the truth, I wasn’t really thinking about him. I was mostly thinking about how I was going to get out of this without getting hurt.”

“We have the surveillance video from the store that the police released that shows what happened next. Would you mind taking us through it as it happened? What you saw, how you felt? I should warn our viewers that this video could be considered shocking and they may wish to remove small children from the room before viewing it.”

The show switched to the security footage, with Bill hiding behind the shelves, Ivory and the robber walking past, and Bill stepping out to stab and subdue the robber. Ivory narrated the scene.

"Well, that shows the back of the store – you can see the door the storeroom over to the left. That's Mr. Ward crouching behind the shelves. Then you can see me walking to the back of the store, with the robber behind me pushing me along. When I got to the door, I heard a noise behind me. Mr. Ward must have jumped out and gone after the robber. When I turned around, they were both on the floor, and Mr. Ward was on top of him. Then I picked up the robber's gun, and Mr. Ward told me to go call the police."

"It must have been horrifying. When you picked up the gun, you looked like you might shoot the robber. What was going through your mind?"

"I served four years in the military police in the Air Force. I did a tour of Iraq, and was a sergeant when I left the service. And I now I'm studying criminal justice in college, preparing for a career in law enforcement. So I know how to handle a firearm. And yeah, I intended to shoot him if he got up."

"What stopped you?"

"Mr. Ward assured me that he wouldn't let the man get up and hurt me. And I believed him. So I went back to the front counter and called the police. I guess you could say Mr. Ward not only saved my life that night – he also saved the robber's."

"Which brings us to our controversy. Considering this incident and the one Mr. Ward was involved in earlier this year, some people are calling him an out-of-control maniac, with a superhero complex or something. What do you think?"

"To be frank, those people are idiots. I was in that store. I know what happened that night. Mr. Ward could have stayed hidden and run away after the robber took me in the back. That's what most people would have done – like those people who have nothing better to do than criticize him for it. But he didn't. He risked his life to save mine."

"I see."

"And it wasn't just what he did then, but what he did afterward. He stayed with me while the police were taking the robber into custody. He sat with me while I cried, putting his own jacket on my shoulders to keep me from getting cold. The next day, he called me to see how I was doing. He didn't have to do any of that either."

"Let me read a quote to you from Yolo Behine, actor, activist-blogger and co-host of the daytime talk show 'The Blab.' 'Is this what we really need? Men running around pretending to be Rambo, rescuing us from danger, using violence to solve our problems for us instead of using reason and good judgment? First it's a knife, next it's an AK-45 assault gun or something. Do we need to return to such oppressive patriarchal memes that are stereotypical to the point of being cliché? Is this this modern world women want to live in, after all we've done, after we've come so far?' Your response to that?"

Ivory had grown agitated and impatient while Matt read the blog comment, and she was very direct and animated in her response.

"My response is that bitch needs to be slapped, and I'm just the girl do it. After my husband was killed in Afghanistan, I became the sole support for myself and our son, Tiran. I go to college full-time and work nights and weekends to support us and my mom. So I don't need some media dilettante who's never struggled to make a rent payment or tried to start a cold automobile lecturing me on female independence, or anything else for that matter.

"Furthermore, she wasn't there that night – I was. And in this case I DID need to be saved. Thank God that Bill Ward was there and was willing to do what he did. This isn't about phony gender politics – it was about courage, and kindness, and decency."

Matt turned his attention to Shannon.

"Strong words. Ms. Gales, based on your own experience with Mr. Ward, what's your take on this."

Shannon hesitated for a second, and then spoke deliberately.

“Ivory is right. That bitch DOES need to be slapped, and she IS the girl to do it. Unless I get there first.”

Ivory smiled at Shannon and the two women clasped hands in support of one another. Shannon continued.

“Honestly, I just don’t know what’s the matter with people these days. Are they so self-centered, so desperate to draw attention to themselves that they’ll run down anyone at any time, without any thought at all? Is this what we’re becoming as a society? This man has saved the lives of three people – four, to hear Ivory tell it – and people are criticizing him for it.

“Let me tell you, out on that highway, my child and I were alone in that car. I was knocked unconscious. I didn’t see – what’s her name, Yolo, whatever? – or any of those other people running toward the danger to save us. It was Bill Ward.”

Shannon paused, and Matt commented.

“You had your own experience of negative publicity and public opinion after that incident.”

“That’s right. Some media vultures from one of those skanky tabloid shows decided to dig up something from my past and blow it out of proportion, and thousands of people on the Internet piled on with all kinds of nasty comments and criticism. People who know nothing about me, people who couldn’t pick me out of a line up, were judging me.

“But you know what? I learned pretty quickly not to become too concerned about what those people said, because it doesn’t matter. It’s more important to listen to the people whose opinions really do matter. Bill Ward taught me that. He was the first person to call me and offer his support when that all happened.”

“You two seem to be his biggest fans.”

Shannon and Ivory glanced at each other and Ivory responded.

“We’re not his fans. We’re his friends. And you stick up for your friends, especially when people are treating them badly. Look, people can second guess him all they want – saying he should have done this or shouldn’t have done that. But we’re here today – alive – because of the things he did. That’s the truth of it.”

Matt ended the interview there, with a quick segue to the show’s next segment.

“Thank you, ladies. We appreciate you being here. More to come on this topic, I’m sure. Let’s go to the news desk now for the latest headlines. And in the next half hour, we’ll talk with Daniel Snider and John French Segall, producers of the Broadway smash hit – ‘Knight Rider, The Musical.’ Then we’ll get a special preview to the new holiday film opening in theaters this weekend, ‘Elf 2: The Search for Santa,’ with Will Smith reprising the iconic role of Buddy the Elf made famous by Will Ferrell in the original.”

***

Thursday Evening

“The Tonight Show” returned from commercial break, and as The Roots finished performing the bumper, the camera settled on Jimmy Fallon sitting as his desk, with two young women seated at his right.

“Thanks guys, great song. We’re back with our guests tonight, singers Swallow Craft and Shaniquah. What a performance of their hit ‘Respect This,’ just a few minutes ago. Hey ladies, I want to ask you about something. You remember when you were supposed to be on the show last spring, and you couldn’t make it because Swallow was sick?

“Uh huh”

“Yeah.”

“Well the guy we had on that night, guy named Bill Ward. Saved that lady and her baby from an exploding car. Right? Well, he’s back in the news this week – stopped a convenience store robbery, stabbed the robber right in the ass, right? The robber had already killed somebody and stuff. Well turns out people are actually getting down on the guy – Bill Ward – for doing what he did. Saying he thinks he has a hero complex or something, always has to go around saving damsels in distress, or something. Anyway, I wanted to get your take on it.”

Swallow spoke first.

“Yeah, I remember him. Shaniquah and I watched that show together that night.”

“Together?”

“Yeah, she’s really my bud – came over with homemade chicken soup to help me get better. Anyway, we saw the show, he seemed like real good guy.”

“He is a good guy.”

“Anyway, I remember that, and then I saw the news this week, and the crap people are saying about him online and stuff. It makes me sick. What’s the matter with people?”

“Right?”

“He saved the woman and her baby. And now his stops this violent robber and saves the woman working at the store. And people are getting on his case about it. I mean, we’re celebrities, right? We get this kind of stuff all the time from people, talking about what we do and how we look. I don’t like it, but I get it. But THIS guy? He didn’t do anything to deserve this. If anything, we need MORE people like him, and screw anybody who doesn’t like it.”

The audience cheered and applauded. Jimmy turned to Shaniquah.

“Shaniquah, what about you?”

“… Is he married? Because that’s the kind of man I’d like to get to know. We use to call that kind of thing ‘character’.’”

The audience laughed and applauded, and Jimmy responded.

“Yes, I believe he is married. And I think he’s probably too old for you.”

“... well, then, does he have a son?”

The audience laughed and applauded again, and Jimmy responded again.

“Yeah, actually he does. A young man named Bryce Ward, around 20 years old, I think. He actually interned on the show last summer.”

“Well, I would like to meet HIM.”

“I think he has a girlfriend.”

“I’ll tell you what. You give him my number and tell him that if that doesn’t work out to give me a call. Because if he’s half the man his father is, he’s someone worth spending my time with.”

Jimmy laughed, and Swallow added another thought to close the topic.

“Oh, and one more thing.”

She reached in her pocket, pulled out a small pen knife and held it up. Shaniquah did the same thing, and after blinking for a moment Jimmy did too. The three of them sat there holding up their pocketknives while the audience cheered and applauded.

Mort Mortefolio was standing in the wings holding up his mobile phone so he could video chat the segment to Bryce as it was happening. As the show cut to commercial, he turned the phone around and spoke to Bryce.

“So, what did you think?”

“It was great. Thanks, Mort.”

“For what? It’s nothing. Jimmy likes your dad, he was glad to bring it up. Do you think your father will watch it?”

“Maybe. But I hope my girlfriend doesn’t.”

***

Saturday Night

The opening credits and theme music faded on "That Metal Show," and the camera settled on host Eddie Trunk and his co-hosts Don Jamieson and Jim Florentine. Eddie addressed the roaring studio audience.

"Welcome, everyone, to the first episode of our regular season this year. We have a great, great show for you tonight. Our special guest guitarist this evening is Reb Beach, from Winger and Whitesnake."

The audience applauded and the camera cut to the musician sitting on his perch next to the studio seating, where he nodded and smiled before the camera returned to Eddie.

"And tonight, our great friend Alice Cooper returns to the show to talk about his latest album and upcoming tour. And at long last, after years of inviting, and pleading and begging, we finally have here in the studio with us a true heavy metal legend – Gene Simmons from KISS."

The audience roared its approval, and after about 20 seconds Eddie had to wave them back into their seats.

"Calm down. Come on. Big show. And we'll get to that very soon. But first, I want to mention something else real quick. There's a 'That Metal Show' alum in the news this week, and we wanted to give him a quick shout out of support. You probably remember we had a guy on the show this summer named Bill Ward. Not THAT Bill Ward – this is the guy who saved that lady and her baby from a burning car last spring. Turned out to be a big fan of the show, and a rock drummer in his own right."

The audience applauded, and Eddie continued.

"Anyway, earlier this week, this guy finds himself right in the middle of an armed robbery at a gas station, and he takes down the robber. All by himself."

Don Jamieson spoke up.

"I know, right? The way he did it, stabbed the crook in the ass. What a badass move, right?"

The audience cheered, and Eddie picked up the dialogue.

"Anyway, so turns out this robber is a really bad guy. Been running around hurting people, putting them in hospital, killed one guy. And now people are getting on Bill's case for stopping him. I can't believe it!"

Jim Florentine spoke up.

"Listen, you know, some people are saying he's some kind of a nut case with a superhero thing going on or something, or that's a real violent guy and everything. But like you said, we've had him on the show, and he's just a really nice, down-to-earth guy. I think he just got caught in a tough spot, and he did what he had to do. Took balls, ya know?"

Eddie responded.

"Anyway, we just wanted to say, Bill, if you're watching, from everyone here on 'That Metal Show,' and all our fans, we're behind you 100 percent and you're welcome back any time."

The audience cheered and applauded.

Chapter 24

Mid-October, Monday Evening

Paige Cantwell sipped her martini, settled back on the couch in her living room and sighed with satisfaction. As was their custom, Silvina the housekeeper had served her a small silver shaker of the cocktail before leaving for the day.

Paige's contentment stemmed from the realization that she had achieved everything she'd ever wanted. In her late 20s, she had left behind a childhood of rural poverty and an early adult life of bad choices. She'd found a man with money who was eager to marry her, allowing her to live in comfort and style.

That Hal Cantwell was 20 years older than her and had achieved his wealth in the garbage hauling business hadn't bothered her at all. And she couldn't have imagined achieving success the way he had, starting with a single truck and building a successful business with a fleet of 50 vehicles through hard work and personal commitment.

The death of his first wife in a car accident had left him middle-aged, alone and lonely. He'd been immediately attracted to the pretty young woman and she'd won him over quickly and easily by flattering him with her attention.

She hadn't minded him much. He'd been kind enough to her, although she was repulsed by the touch of his rough hands. The heart attack that claimed him five years ago had given her relief from that, and now she sat alone with his spacious home and his wealth all to herself.

Shortly after their marriage, she had grown bored with the lifestyle of a kept woman surprisingly fast and found that she craved not only comfort but also respect. She indulged in the country club life and what passed for high society in their small Connecticut town – garden club, charity work, cultural events.

After her husband's death, she added political power to her list of wants, winning a seat on the town council. It hadn't been difficult. The local voters were rubes, and she was able to carve out a constituency among the local elites in her social circle by telling them what they wanted to hear.

Now, she was up for re-election in less than a month, challenging Derbeville First Selectwoman Tricia Guarino for the top spot on the town board, and capitalizing on a local controversy had given her the attention and support she needed to win. That pesky clod Bill Ward had been stirring things up in town again.

God, she hated his type – a typical do-gooder with an overdeveloped sense of responsibility. Not unlike her deceased husband in many ways. But now he'd given her the pretext she needed to grab some attention in the council race – he'd committed assault with a deadly weapon, presumably to "save" another young woman in trouble. The local police wouldn't prosecute him, of course, but it still made good grist for her campaign rhetoric.

There also were rumors about him making unwanted sexual advances toward at least one woman in town. Nothing proven of course, but rumors were enough to create some buzz in time for the election.

Her Chihuahua, Chaco, who had been dozing comfortably at her side, cocked an ear when the phone on the end table rang. Paige looked it with annoyance, wondering why the maid didn't answer it before remembering that Silvina had gone for the day. Paige reached over and picked it up on the third ring.

"Hello?"

"Hello, Gussy."

Paige gasped. No one had called her that name in a very long time. The voice on the other end of the line continued.

"That is your name, isn't it? Gussy? Gussy Pulver, from Enid, Oklahoma?"

Paige choked with fury as she tried to respond.

"Who …? What …? How do you know …?"

"Oh, I know a lot of things about you, Gussy. Like your two marriages before you met Hal Cantwell. The first one to a drug dealer out of Juarez, looking for a green card. The second to an ex-con who just couldn't stay out of trouble. Looks like they both led you down a pretty bad road -- arrests for drug possession, accessory to armed robbery, and solicitation. I'm not surprised you fled east when you had the opportunity – a fresh start, a second chance, and the good fortune of finding and marrying Hal."

"Who are you?"

"Oh, I'm sorry. My name is Howard Jones. I'm one of your constituents here in town and I'm calling to register a complaint. You've been quite unkind to a good friend of mine in your campaign speeches."

"Who is that?"

"Bill Ward. You called him a 'wild vigilante,' a 'dangerous adventurer' and 'knife-wielding madman running free.' I believe you also threw in 'pervert' for good measure. You said he's causing a major disruption to our tranquility and tarnishing the good image of our town. I think that's a bit unfair, considering the fact that he's saved at least three lives and stopped a major crime spree in this town. You're remarks have taken quite a toll on his reputation around here."

"I didn't mean ..."

"Oh, I know, it's all just politics, what with the election coming up and everything. Got to find something to stump about on the old campaign trail, which is tough to do in a sleepy little town like this one. He was just ... convenient."

"How did you find out ... about me?"

"I do a fair amount of political consulting in my line of work, so I know who to call to find out things like this. The technical term is 'opposition research,' and you became my opposition when you decided to pick on my neighbor."

"What ... what do you want?"

"Oh, not much. I just want you to apologize, recanting everything you've said about Bill – publically, and showing genuine remorse. I've taken the liberty of drafting a prepared statement for you. You'll find a copy of it in your mailbox."

"Is that it?"

"Well, of course you'll have to withdraw from the election and resign your position on the town counsel. You know, to convince everyone that you're truly sincere."

Paige paused and licked her dry lips before responding.

"And if I don't?"

"Then everything I know about you goes to the media. All of it. I'm sure they'll be quite interested. I mean, this is made-for-TV stuff right here – upstanding public servant turns out to have a sordid criminal past. That will be the end of your fine reputation, your good standing in the community and your prospects for first selectwoman. Oh, and I'm guessing law enforcement officials will take notice too. There is the matter of you skipping out on your parole back in Oklahoma all those years ago."

"You … you can't …"

"Actually, I can. And I will. But it doesn't have to come to that. You can continue to live in our community, quietly and comfortably in your fine home. No one ever has to find out. Just do exactly as I say, and everything I know about you can stay hidden."

"Why … why are you doing this?"

"Because Bill Ward is a good man, and he doesn't deserve the treatment he's gotten from you or a lot of other people in this town. You may have money, position and some small degree of power. But he has something you'll never have."

"What's that?"

"He has a friend like me. I'll expect you to issue that statement, word for word, first thing in the morning. Otherwise …"

Gussy heard the line go dead.

***

Tuesday Afternoon

Maggie Ward entered the Pick and Shop Supermarket, skipping the shopping cart queue near the entrance, as she only needed a few things for dinner that evening. Instead she bent down to pick up one of the small plastic hand baskets located near the front of the store, and when she straightened up she saw her neighbor Marguerite Des Barres ahead of her in the produce section.

Maggie began walking toward her and when the two neared each other she saw Marguerite noticeably turn her head away. Maggie took a breath and then addressed the woman directly and clearly, for all around to hear.

"Don't you look away from me!"

Marguerite snapped her head around, eyes wide, and responded.

"What?"

"You heard me. I know what you've been saying around town about my family – about my husband. Let's see if you have the guts to say it to my face."

"I don't know what you mean."

"You know exactly what I mean. You've been telling people that Bill came on to you and that when you wouldn't go along he tried to force you."

"Why … I …"

Marguerite fell silent, and Maggie continued.

"That's what I thought. Like most lying cowards, you're all big talk until confronted. Not that anyone who matters would believe you anyway. First of all, you wouldn't know what to do with a real man like Bill. And second, no guy has ever had to force himself on you. Your legs might as well have an on ramp."

"How … how DARE you talk to me that way?!"

Marguerite stepped around her cart and lunged at Maggie, only to be stopped cold by a hard slap across the face.

"Oh! You … you HIT me!"

"That's right, I did."

"I'll … I'll have you arrested. For assault. I'll sue you!"

"Yeah, I don't think so. Because all these people saw YOU come at me. And so did the security cameras, there and there."

Maggie gestured at the other shoppers and pointed at the surveillance cams, and Marguerite looked at them absently in stunned silence. She held a hand against her stinging face and Maggie continued.

"There's more like that coming if you say anything else about my husband, so I'd suggest you keep your mouth shut. Otherwise, there isn't enough makeup in the world to spackle over what a few more good slaps will do to your face."

It was deathly quiet in the produce department, the other shoppers looking on in stunned silence. The two women just stood silently for a moment, then Marguerite dropped her head, tears welling in her eyes. Maggie broke eye contact and spoke again, in a quieter voice.

"Get out of my sight, Marguerite."

Marguerite abandoned her cart and fled the store, running past an assistant manager and a stock boy who had watched the whole episode from a spot near the front door. Maggie took a deep breath, her cheeks blushing pink from a swelling mixture of emotions -- exhilaration, self-consciousness, surprise, and a little self-satisfaction.

After taking a few seconds to compose herself, she lifted her head and walked past the gaping customers to continue her shopping. The other shoppers resumed their own activities, with a few discussing in hushed tones what they had just witnessed.

A few minutes later, Maggie headed for the cashier stands, paid for her purchases and walked toward the exit. As she left the store she smiled at the two store employees still standing at the front door, their mouths agape as she passed by, and she addressed them pleasantly.

"You gentlemen have a lovely day."

The two stared after her for a moment, before the stock boy broke the silence.

"Well, that was something."

The assistant manager looked the other way and responded.

"I don't know what you're talking about. I didn't see anything."

***

Friday, Early Evening

Howard knocked on the office door of Trevor Powell, one of the founding partners of the public relations firm Howard worked for, Bonham Kramer Powell Communications. He and Trevor rarely spoke, so he was mildly surprised when one of the administrative assistants had dropped by an hour earlier to tell him Trevor wanted to see him at 6:15 that evening.

Normally Howard would have been wrapping up for the week by about 6 on a Friday, but when a managing partner asks to see you, it's generally a good idea to accept the invitation. Trevor didn't look up as he beckoned Howard to enter.

"Come in. Have a seat."

Howard sat in one of the guest chairs in front of the desk, but found it difficult to settle in. He realized that the two front legs of the chair were slightly shorter than the rear ones, making it an awkward perch. Howard knew this was by design, the message being that Trevor preferred visitors were uncomfortable in his presence and that he didn't want anyone sticking around for very long.

Trevor had a reputation for reclusiveness to the point of being antisocial, even with the other senior partners in the firm. He almost never left his office other than for occasional meetings and to depart at the end of the day, usually well into the evening after everyone else had left. He didn't attend social functions the firm sponsored for the staff, and never made small talk with any of the associates.

While the other partners were involved in the day-to-day account activities of the firm's clients, Trevor played a largely administrative role. Some said he hadn't actually spoken to a client in years, and it might have been true. Still, as a founding partner, he held tremendous influence over the decisions of the firm, particularly regarding hiring and promotions, and especially regarding the naming of new partners.

As a senior vice president who had successfully managed several of BKP's largest accounts, Howard knew he was in consideration for partnership. But the appointment of new partners required unanimous approval of the three founding partners, and Howard knew Trevor frequently tendered a veto for those decisions.

Those who were passed over often left the firm for competitors, and occasionally clients followed them out the door. The other founding partners were concerned about the loss of talent and its impact on the firm's accounts, but there was little they could do about it.

Trevor seemed to have a general dislike of people and little regard for the associates of the firm at all levels, particularly the more senior ones like Howard. He was stingy with praise and quick with criticism and cutting remarks, often unwarranted and usually done to embarrass the target of his abuse in front of others.

No one really knew why he was such a sour man, and while most regarded him as an equal-opportunity offender some noted that he seemed especially hard on women and minorities at the firm.

Trevor continued working at his computer while keeping Howard waiting. It was rude, and intended to be so, but Howard restrained himself from interrupting despite his rising annoyance. Finally, Trevor sat back and swung around to face Howard. He spoke first.

"Well ..."

Trevor let the word trail off and didn't continue. Howard was just about out of patience and forced the conversation forward.

"Amy said you wanted me to stop by."

"Yes, I did."

"What can I help you with, Trevor?"

"Well, nothing really. I just wanted to talk about some of the things I've observed over the past few months – your activities outside of the office."

"What are you referring to?"

"Primarily, the extracurricular professional counsel you've been giving to this person from your town. Bill Ward, is it? He's certainly been making quite a name for himself in the news, with his various ... escapades."

"You mean, like saving lives, stopping armed robberies, things like that. What of it?"

"Well, I just wonder if that's the type of thing, the type of person, our agency should be associated with. After all, we have a roster of very prestigious clients and I imagine this might have an effect on how they view us."

Howard was now completely out of patience and his response was measured but sharp.

"For openers, the agency is not associated with this 'type of person,' as you put it. I am. And what I do on my own time is my own business, and none of yours."

"It is if it damages the prospects of this business. And I have to say, it doesn't bode well for your prospects here at BKP."

It was now clear to Howard what this meeting was about. He ignored the implied threat and continued, barely containing his growing anger.

"And second, the principals for the clients I work with are actually quite impressed with how I've helped Bill out. They like the way I've protected the reputation of someone who has become the target of unfair and unwarranted criticism. Several have told me so -- said it gives them confidence that I can do the same for them if they get caught in a bind."

"Is that so?"

"Yes, it is so. You might know that if you ever actually talked to our clients."

"Excuse me?"

"You heard me."

Trevor paused, his own anger rising at Howard's impudence. He continued.

"Promotion decisions will be made in the next several months. I think you should consider what this could mean for your ability to continue rising at this firm."

"Well, if it's a choice between you and my best friend, I don't even need to think about it at all. And I'd suggest YOU better think about what it might mean for this firm if I don't continue to have opportunities for advancement."

"Meaning what?"

"Meaning I manage five of the largest accounts at this firm – three of which I personally brought in since I came here nine years ago. The principals at all of those clients have assured me that their faith in this agency is due largely to my management of their accounts. Several have mentioned that if I left the firm they would follow me, and it's a pretty sure bet the others would too, as well as a number of BKP associates who work on those accounts."

"You are aware that your contract with this agency has a non-compete clause."

“No, actually, it has a non-solicitation clause. That means I can’t actively court the business of our current clients. But doesn’t mean I can’t accept it if they freely choose to bring it to me.”

“I’m not sure our lawyers would see it that way.”

“Well mine does. And in any event, if you decided to take legal action to stop me you’d still lose the business. Clients don’t generally like getting dragged into messy court battles, and if they decided to leave BKP with me it would be because they have no faith in you. Again, you might know that if you ever actually talked to a client.”

Trevor’s face flushed with rage, and his voice was tighter and louder when he responded.

“That’s the second time you … how DARE you talk to me that way, you …”

“Yeah, this is me daring. If there are two things I can’t abide it’s bullies and bad manners. And since you seem so fond of ultimatums, let me give you one.”

“And what is that?”

“When I come in on Monday, I better find an envelope on my desk with one of two things in it. Either a very generous severance package, as stipulated for early termination in my contract, or an offer to immediately make me a full partner.”

Trevor was speechless and Howard let his remarks hang in the air for a moment before continuing.

“We’re done here.”

With that, Howard got up from his chair and walked toward the door. As he left the office he spoke once more.

“Have a lovely weekend, Trevor.”

Trevor somehow managed to get out one last riposte as he grasped to gain some small semblance of control.

“Close the door behind you!”

Howard left the door standing open.

***

Late October

From the Connecticut Business Journal's "On The Move" column:

"Bonham Kramer Powell Communications of Shilton has named Howard Jones as a full partner in the firm. Jones, who joined BKP nine years ago, was a senior vice president, managing clients in the public sector, consumer products and electronics industries. He will continue in those duties and also will be responsible for all new business development at BKP. He is the first new partner named at BKP in six years. BKP also announced the retirement of founding partner Trevor Powell …"

Chapter 25

Early November, Wednesday Evening

Bill Ward and Robert Perkins sat at the kitchen table chatting and having a cold drink of water after Robert's drum lesson. They had been meeting on Wednesday evenings nearly every week since July, and Robert's playing had been improving measurably.

In addition, he had started dropping by on Saturdays to talk and help Bill out with yard work and odd jobs around the house, occasionally staying for lunch or supper. He and Bill had bonded, and the entire family had grown fond of Robert.

Robert had been working for his Uncle Bob's heating and plumbing business and had met the state requirements for his plumbing license. At his uncle's urging, he also had started taking business classes at Saugatuck Community College that fall. His uncle's goal was to groom Robert for a management position and then eventually to take over the business when he retired. Robert didn't know it, but Bill had suggested the classes to his Uncle Bob, and they were splitting the cost of his tuition.

"Yeah, my uncle said if I do well at Saugatuck and get my associate's degree, he might even help pay for me to get my bachelor's degree too."

"That's great, Robert. How do you like it so far?"

"It's okay. I'm doing pretty well in my business management class, but accounting is kicking my butt."

"Well, keep working at it. I'm sure you'll do fine. And how did your audition go?"

Over the weekend, Robert had gone to a tryout for a local band called The Skechers. They played a mixture of pop tunes done in a reggae style, and were very popular on the local club and high school dance scene.

"Oh, I forgot to tell you. I got it! We have rehearsals for the next couple weeks, and then a show coming up at Iggy's Sports Bar the weekend before Thanksgiving."

"That's great, Robert. Your drumming has really come a long way over the past few months. You have real talent, and I can tell you've been working at it. Between work, school and this, I think things are really coming together for you."

Robert paused seriously before responding.

"You know, I … I don't really know how to say this. But I really appreciate all you have done for me. You and your whole family. If you didn't …"

He let the sentence trail off. Bill responded.

"Look, I know you had a tough time of it. Growing up without your father. Like many young men your age, you acted out a little, made some bad choices. But you managed to get yourself back on the right path."

"You can say it. I was a punk, and I nearly screwed up my whole life."

"Well, with some exceptions, no one should be judged solely on the mistakes they make. You had the opportunity to make it right, and you're making good on it. That's all anyone can expect."

"Getting arrested really scared me. It made me realize I'm not a kid anymore. I gotta start acting my age, taking more responsibility. Taking care of my mother and my little sisters. They deserve better than the way I was acting, and they're depending on me. I'm just glad you gave me a second chance – more than a second chance. You've been …"

Again, he let the sentence trail off, unsure how to express what he was thinking. Bill allowed the silence. Robert shook his head and rolled his eyes, as he if were surprised by what he was about to say next.

"I can't believe I'm even going to ask you this. I really don't have the right."

"What is it Robert?"

"Well … since I've been coming around more, Olive – your daughter …"

He let the words trail off.

"Yes, Robert, I know who my daughter is. What is it?"

"Well, we've been talking a lot and she's really ... she's ..."

"Go on."

"Would it be okay ... with you ... and Mrs. Ward ... could I ... ask Olive to go out?"

Robert winced after he finished the sentence, and waited for Bill's response. Bill smiled slightly.

"I have to say, that's a pretty brave request – considering what my son did to her last boyfriend."

Robert responded quite seriously.

"Oh, I would *never* do anything like TJ..."

Bill chuckled.

"I know you wouldn't, Robert. And I'm not entirely surprised you asked. I've seen the way you and Olive look at each other, the way you talk quietly together. Considering how our relationship with you began, I appreciate the respect you're showing to her mother and me by asking this way. It shows real maturity."

"Thank, uh, thank you."

"Of course, it all really depends on whether Olive is willing. This isn't the 1800s. We don't decide who she goes out with. With one recent exception, of course, but there were extenuating circumstances."

Robert let out a deep breath in relief.

"Thank ... thank you."

"And while we don't usually tell Olive who she can see, we do have a few house rules. This may seem a little old fashioned, but there are a couple things I think you need to understand. Olive is only 17, and she has a pretty full schedule with school and field hockey. So no going out during the week while school is in session."

"Okay."

"You're welcome to visit her here at home at any time, provided it doesn't interfere with her studies, but curfew is 10 p.m. on weeknights. And of course you can go see her compete during games whenever you'd like."

"Sure, okay."

"On weekends, we'll want her home by 11 p.m. That can be extended to midnight under special circumstances. But we'll want to know in advance where the two of you are going and what you'll be doing. No nightclubs or bars, no place where there's alcohol at all."

"Of course. That won't be an issue."

"So if you want her to come hear you play at Iggy's, her mother and I will have to come with her. I'm sorry if that's kind of a drag."

"Actually … I was going to ask you if you wanted to come hear me play with the band."

"There's nothing I'd like more. I'm honored that you would ask me. And I'm sure Maggie and Olive will enjoy it too."

Robert was elated and relieved, and he sensed it was time to make his exit.

"Okay. Good. I better go. I have some studying to do tonight, and I've got an early morning on the job site tomorrow. I'll call Olive tomorrow. And, uh, see you again next Wednesday for my lesson?"

"That will be great, Robert. I always look forward to it."

Maggie and Olive were sitting around the corner on the staircase, out of sight, listening to the whole conversation. Olive gave her mother a hug.

***

Mid-November, Monday Morning

Bill was at his desk, making final changes to a PowerPoint presentation on the Simplified Coverage Model project for his boss, Betsey Wetsel. He'd spent most of the fall working on the project, developing a workable plan for the effort to change the way OpenSwitch salespeople were deployed and compensated on the company's client accounts.

It had taken a lot of late nights and weekends, essentially compressing six months' worth of work into about 10 weeks. He had skipped a visit to Bryce's college with Maggie for homecoming weekend, missed more than a few of Olive's field hockey games, and even cut short a family celebration for his and Maggie's wedding anniversary.

But he had been able to guide the project team to an effective solution that would roll out the new compensation plan on time in January, effectively saving the project. All throughout the effort, Betsey had been goading him. To be fair, she probably thought she was helping, but her suggestions and contributions often just got in the way of the work.

He had finished up the final report the previous week, and over the weekend she had sent him additional edits and comments. He made the last few changes, closed the file and emailed it to Betsey. A few seconds later his RightNow instant messaging pinged. It was Betsey.

"Can you come to my office right now?"

He sighed. She probably had more changes. He typed a quick message back.

"Sure. Do I need to bring anything?"

"No."

"OK. BRT."

Bill rose from his desk and reflexively grabbing a pad and pen as he headed for the door. When he arrived at Betsey's office, the door was almost completely closed, so he knocked before entering.

Betsey's voice beckoned him to enter, and when he walked in he saw her seated at her desk, and in one of the guest chairs was Paul Bernard, the human resources director for their department. He and Paul had worked together many times and liked each other. Paul looked uncomfortable and Betsey sat pale and stony-faced as Bill took a seat. He didn't say a word. He knew what was about to happen. Looking down, Betsey began to read from a document on her desk.

"I'm informing you that you've been selected for a workforce reduction through the OpenSwitch Technologies Strategic Capabilities Recalibration Program. Under this program, your position is being eliminated and you will …"

Bill interrupted her.

"Betsey. You can spare me the speech. I know what this is."

Betsey looked at him blankly, and Paul squirmed in his chair. Bill had been hearing the rumors for weeks that another round of job cuts was being planned, although he had received no indications that he was being specifically targeted. He normally didn't pay attention to such things, taking a fatalistic "if it happens, it happens" view about them.

Now, all the pressure from Betsey to finish up the final report on the Simplified Coverage Model project made sense. He was aware of the impending deadline for the project, but her insistence that the report be completed before the end of last week was well ahead of that.

Betsey finally broke the silence awkwardly.

"Fine. I have a packet here that details the terms of your separation – severance pay, outplacement services, options for extending your benefits. You will remain on the payroll for the next 30 days, at which time your employment will be terminated."

Bill reached for the packet and stirred from his chair as if preparing to depart.

"If there is nothing more, I'll just …"

"Actually, I would like to set up some time over the next few weeks to discuss transitioning your work and your team lead responsibilities."

Bill settled back into his chair and responded.

"Excuse me?"

"Well, uh … in order to ensure an orderly transition, I'd like to be able to talk about how to transfer your work to others in the group. There's the final touches for the Simplified Coverage Model report, and …"

Bill cut her off, his voice even but firm.

"Betsey, let me make something perfectly clear. You and OpenSwitch have seen the last lick of work you're ever going to get out of me. You've decided you no longer need my services? Fine. You can start getting used to what that will be like right now."

"But … you're still on the payroll for a month. Just what do you intend to do for the next 30 days?"

Without saying a word, Bill sat back and put his feet up on her desk. Betsey sputtered with outrage, but tried to maintain her composure.

"Well, I … I had hoped we could do this in a way that's appropriate and professional …"

"Don't speak to me about propriety and professionalism, Betsey. There's nothing appropriate or professional about what's happening here, and we all know it. Now, if we're through here, I'll be on my way. Good luck."

Betsey looked at Paul for help, but he just shrugged. She spoke angrily to Bill.

"If you refuse to fulfill your responsibilities, I can take action to have you terminated immediately, for cause. The HR guidelines stipulate …"

Bill stifled a laugh as he responded.

"Oh really? Actually, I know you've been snooping around, trying to find a way to fire me for cause."

"I wasn't … snooping …"

"Please. We both know better than that. Find anything? I guess not, or we wouldn't be having this conversation now, would we? In any event, if you want to terminate me for failing to perform my professional duties that will require two months of documented warnings."

Betsey sat speechless and Paul brightened slightly, enjoying her discomfort as Bill continued.

“Assuming you get all that done, because of my level and length of service, that will trigger a full evaluation of my performance, arbitrated by a review panel of your peer managers. That normally takes two months, and automatically suspends the resource action notice. If the board finds cause for my dismissal for anything other than gross misconduct – stealing, for example – the HR guidelines require that I be put on a six-month Performance Improvement Program.

“And if at the end of that program, the review board still finds cause for my dismissal, I STILL get the one-month notice and full separation package. So basically, it will take you almost a year to get rid of me instead of a month. Don’t quote the rules to me, Betsey. I wrote most of them.”

Betsey glanced over at Paul for help again, and he tried to mask a smirk as he responded.

“Don’t look at me. He’s right.”

Bill let the silence hang in the air before continuing.

“Now, if there’s nothing else ...”

He got up from his chair, nodded to Paul, and left.

***

Betsey was preparing to leave for the day at around 5:30. That was earlier than she normally left, but she was drained. She had not anticipated the confrontation with Bill that morning, and it rattled her. She was startled by his nerve.

And the truth was, with the departure of him and several other key members of his team, she wasn’t sure how she’d be able to deliver on her department’s commitments to the company.

She had offered several of them the opportunity to return as contract employees, at lower pay and without benefits. Several had rejected the offer immediately, while a couple more were considering it. She hadn’t even bothered to make such an offer to Bill. She was sure what his response would be.

The warbling of the phone on her desk roused her from her thoughts. The little display window on the phone indicated that it was someone on the third floor calling, but she didn't recognize the extension. She picked up the handset on the second ring.

"Hello?"

"Have you lost your mind?!"

Betsey recognized the angry voice as Herve Pardon's. She hesitated before responding.

"Herve. I don't … what are you talking about?"

"I'm talking about putting Bill Ward on the resource action list. Are you an idiot?"

Betsey flushed with anger and humiliation, trying to steady her voice as she responded.

"I … I know he's your friend, but the selections were made by a review board consisting of …"

"Don't tell me how it works. I KNOW how it works. The final selections may be approved by a committee, but YOU put HIS name on the list in the first place."

Betsey was silent. The truth was each manager had been given specific targets for layoffs, emphasizing the selection of long-tenure, high-salaried employees. She didn't especially care one way or another about Bill, but he fit the demographic perfectly. And she knew that failing to submit the right number of names that met the criteria was not an option.

Herve continued his rant.

"And this has nothing to do with my friendship with Bill. Do you have any idea what's going to happen when the media gets hold of this? I can see the headline now: 'OpenSwitch Fires Hero.' Did you and the 'review board' think of that?"

"No … no, I guess we didn't."

"Well you better think about it now. It won't be long."

"What do you want me to do?"

"Make it go away. Get him back."

“But if I take him out of the program, we won’t hit our demographic target number.”

“Don’t worry about it. I have another name we can add to the list.”

Betsey heard the phone click.

***

Bill Ward’s office door was slightly ajar and the office itself dark. Betsey tentatively pushed the door open, reached in to flick on the lights and stepped in. The office was bare -- practically empty except the desk and chairs.

Bill’s books, family photos and other personal items were gone. Framed award citations and training certifications that had previously decorated the office were stacked neatly on the floor, leaning against the wall in the left rear corner of the room. Piled one on top of one another in the center of his desk were his laptop, mobile phone and company identification badge.

Betsey blinked at the starkness of the room, turning as she heard a voice behind her.

“He’s gone.”

It was Duane Burns. She responded to him.

“When … when did he leave?”

“This morning. Came back after his meeting in your office, cleaned his things out and was gone within a half hour.”

“I need to talk to him.”

“Well, he doesn’t want to talk to you. And he’s not coming back.”

“That’s unfortunate.”

“What’s really unfortunate is he won’t be around to do all your work for you anymore. Now everybody’s gonna find out real fast what a fraud you are.”

Betsey was shocked by his brazenness, and it took her a second to respond.

“You … you can’t talk to me that way! I’ll file a complaint with your manager about your … insubordination!”

“Go screw yourself, Betsey. I don’t care what you tell my manager. I don’t work here anymore either.”

Betsey stood with her mouth gaping, unable to respond, as she watched Duane walk away down the hall, a backpack slung over his right shoulder and a box tucked under his left arm.

Chapter 26

Tuesday Morning

Bill was in the family room of his home, working on the computer at the desk in the back corner. He'd spent most of the morning putting together his post-OpenSwitch game plan – updating his resume and LinkedIn profile, contacting recruiters, and reaching out to tell friends and associates the news, and enlisting their help in finding new opportunities.

Maggie had left right after breakfast for a Bonsai Bear client meeting, so he had the house to himself. They had spoken the evening before. Maggie was enraged at how Bill had been treated, but completely supportive of anything he wanted to do going forward.

Cushioning the blow was the fact that their finances were in pretty good shape. Maggie's jewelry business had grown dramatically over the past year. She had a talent for selling and a passion for the products, and had used both to create a going venture.

Bonsai Bear operated on a network marketing model, and she had worked her way up to the Lead Creative Artist level, with more than a dozen Bonsai Bear franchisees reporting to her. That meant she got commissions on everything they sold as well as her own sales. Over all, she expected to gross a high five-figure salary that year.

Bill's severance package would provide seven months' pay before taxes, but he knew it would probably take at least that long to find a new job because of his age and salary level. He had passed his 25-year anniversary mark at OpenSwitch, meaning that his retirement fund and equity were vested and secure. He also had some additional income from his endorsement deal with Schraber Knives, which was slated to continue at least through the following year.

So, in general, he was actually in a very good position to make a career change. His plan was to start looking for consulting opportunities in the short term and build up as much business as he could while looking for a regular position. If the consulting business grew enough, he might even consider making it a permanent thing. He'd already received some very positive reactions from former colleagues now working at other companies, and might have new work coming from some of them as early as the next week.

Since receiving the news of his layoff the previous day, he had experienced a range of emotions, including anger, disgust, a bit of sadness. But the overriding sensation had been relief. There were a few people he would miss, but the job itself had become so stifling and the work environment so oppressive he wouldn't miss it at all.

The phone ringing on the table behind him broke the silence, and he reached back to grab the receiver.

"Hello?"

"Hello, Bill. It's Walt Schraber. I tried to reach you at the office and on your cell, but didn't get an answer, so I thought I would leave a message here. I didn't expect to get you at home in the middle of the day. Everything okay?"

"Oh, yeah, sure Walt. Everything's fine, although it's funny because I was going to call you today too."

Bill had planned to fill Walt in on his job news and offer his services as a part-time consultant.

"Oh, funny. What's up?"

"Well, you first."

"I just wanted to tell you that advice you gave us about our manufacturing operations has really worked out well. That idea of synching up our equipment maintenance calendar and our employee training schedules, and mapping them to run opposite our high sales periods is really paying off big time."

"Glad to hear that, Walt."

“Yeah, really. We’ve been able to reduce productivity losses and associated costs by about 50 percent. The integrated schedule ensures that all equipment in the factory is in perfect running condition during peak manufacturing intervals. And while we’re running maintenance and repairs, the operators on that equipment can complete training for safety certifications and new skills that allow them to advance in their careers. They love it.”

“I’m really happy it’s working out for you, Walt. You guys have been great to me, with the endorsement deal and everything. I’m glad I was able to provide some additional value. Frankly, after what happened at the convenience store last month, and all the publicity and everything, I thought maybe you were calling to tell me you wanted to end the endorsement thing.”

“Are you kidding me? First of all, cutting and running on our friends and business associates is not our style. Sure there was some negative publicity, but frankly most of our customers have been highly supportive of you.”

“Really?”

“Yeah, and not only that, but orders for the Bill Ward Signature Tactical Folder are through the roof, particularly with the military, law enforcement and firefighters. We can’t make them fast enough, and we’ve had to divert more production capacity to those.”

“Wow, no kidding.”

“But listen, there’s something else I wanted to talk to you about.”

“Okay.”

“As I told you before, I plan to retire next year. My daughter, Jeanine, will be taking over as president and CEO, and my sons will be in other leadership roles in sales and supply chain. But the help you gave us in manufacturing really got us to thinking. We could really use some assistance in running our day-to-day operations. Someone who can focus on both the details and the big picture.”

“And you thought of me?”

"I can't think of anyone who could do it better. We know you. We like you. You share a lot of the same values and views as us. And you've already shown us what you can do."

"Well, you said Jeanine will be taking over as CEO. What does she think?"

"Actually, it was her idea. She just asked me to call you because you and I have worked the most closely together. Of course, we'll put together a full compensation package for you to consider that will be competitive with what you've been making at OpenSwitch. I've gotten the sense from what you've told me that you're not especially happy there, so I'm hoping you'll be open to the opportunity."

"Walt, this is really unexpected. And I do appreciate it. The only thing I'm concerned about is the location – I'm not really in a position to relocate my family right now."

"Well, we thought about that too. And despite our old-school roots, we're pretty adaptive and used to working in a virtual way. Kind of have to, with half of our executive team traveling the world most of the time and a lot of our manufacturing capacity located overseas."

"I can imagine."

"I think we could work it out so that you could work over here two-to-three days a week, and the rest from home. We'd leave it up to you to manage it however you need to – we trust you to be here when you need to be here, and we have a company apartment here in town that will be at your disposal. I think you mentioned it's under two hours driving time from your home to our site, so the back and forth should be pretty manageable."

"Well, Walt, this is really unexpected. I'm very flattered and very interested. Of course, I need to talk to Maggie about it."

"And we need to get you the full details of the offer. But I wanted to tee it up with you and give you a chance to start thinking about it before we went any further. I know it's a big step for you."

"I certainly will give it my full consideration."

"Great, I'm glad you're interested. Let's plan to talk again in a day or two when Jeanine and I have pulled everything together."

"Okay, great."

"Now, your turn. What was it you wanted to tell me?"

"Funny you should ask ..."

***

Wednesday Evening

The phone rang at the Ward's home and Maggie walked across the kitchen to answer it.

"Hello? Oh, hello Herv. Pardon? ...What? Oh, okay, Her-VAY. What can I do for you? ...Yes, Bill knows you've left a couple messages for him. I'm sure he's been meaning to return your calls. Excuse me? Yes, let me see if he's available."

She put the phone on mute and walked downstairs to the basement where Bill was on his drum set, working on a couple of new songs for an upcoming gig with The Dead Lunchladies. When saw her, he stopped playing and removed his headphones.

"What's up?"

Maggie smiled slightly and held up the phone.

"It's Her-VAY."

He groaned, and she prodded him.

"You going to talk to him?"

"I'd prefer not to."

Bill had been ducking calls from Herve and several other former colleagues since Monday. He was a bit self-conscious about his dismissal and didn't really feel like talking about it with them.

"Well, it's up to you. I can tell him you're busy. But you're going to have to talk to him eventually."

Bill paused for a second, and then responded.

"Okay. I'll take it."

She handed him the cordless receiver, smiled at him and went back upstairs. Bill flicked off the mute button and spoke.

"Hello?"

"Well, you certainly are a tough guy to get ahold of, Bill."

"Only to the extent that I didn't want to be gotten ahold of, Herv. What can I do for you?"

"It's Her-va … never mind. Well, I have something I want to talk to you about regarding OpenSwitch."

"If it's about my dismissal on Monday, there's really not much to discuss."

"Well, there's this – I want you to come to back. Working for me. Director's title. Your own team. What do you think?"

"Well, that's very generous of you, Herv. But I'm not sure I really want to do it."

"Look, there's no question you've gotten a raw deal – for a long time. But we can put that in the past, start over. Like when we first began working here."

"It's not just that. It's the whole place. Over the past several years it's become absolutely toxic, and we all know why. I'm tired of working for so-called leaders who treat people like garbage. There isn't one of them who could spell the word 'leadership' if you spotted them the first 10 letters."

"Well, there's no question our leadership here has been a … challenge."

"Herv, it's a jackass factory."

Bill heard Maggie call down the basement stairs from the kitchen.

"Bill! Your language!"

He chuckled as Herve continued.

"Well, I think things are about to change in that regard. Have you heard the news today?"

"About OpenSwitch? No, I've kind of tuned it all out. What happened?"

"Big shake-up at the top. Sandy is out."

"What? What happened?"

"After our last earnings report, the SEC got a tip that there was some strange stuff going on with our financials. Had to be an insider, because whoever it was really knew where the bodies were buried. The info the whistleblower turned over was detailed and damning. Funny business with the ledger, phantom client accounts and phony deals."

Bill suspected immediately that it was Duane Burns who had called the SEC – he was in a position to know. Bill did not share his suspicion.

"Whoops."

"It gets worse. As the SEC was poking around they discovered that Sandy's husband, Rupert, has a little girlfriend on the side. Turns out their pillow talk included all kinds of inside information Rupert had heard from Sandy – stuff that nobody was supposed to talk about. Big deals the company was about to close with clients, acquisitions and divestitures that were in the works, financial information on merger targets, stuff that could move the stock in a big way."

"Oh my."

"It still gets worse. Turns out this little girlfriend has ANOTHER boyfriend – a bigwig at some Wall Street brokerage firm – and she's been telling HIM everything Rupert told HER, which Sandy wasn't supposed to be telling Rupert in the first place. And now the four of them are in big trouble."

"Oh boy."

"Oh yeah, they're all going to jail. The board voted to remove Sandy as CEO earlier today, and the SEC is holding a press conference in the morning to announce a full investigation. But word's already leaked out."

"Wow."

"Which is why I'm calling tonight. New leadership is coming in, with a mission to clean things up and a big broom to do it. No more shady deals. No more creeping layoffs. No more monkey business with the financial reporting. No more treating people like crap."

"I wish I could believe all that. Who is it?"

"The board appointed Bob O'Reilly."

Bill knew Bob. Earlier in his career, he and Herve had worked for Bob in the Technology Services business unit. He was a good guy, very smart, with a PhD. in applied physics and electrical engineering from MIT. Bob was a real leader who possessed both brilliance and integrity. He had been viewed earlier as a possible CEO candidate, but had been shouldered aside in favor of Sandy.

After she was appointed CEO, Sandy kept him pigeonholed as EVP for the Advanced Science Division. She would have preferred to get rid of him entirely, because he constantly challenged both the soundness and integrity of her management decisions. He was one of the few OpenSwitch executives brave enough to do so.

The problem for her was that he really was brilliant and had a habit of making the right calls on new technologies that would benefit the company. Bob also was articulate, likeable and approachable, making him a favorite of customers, Wall Street analysts and journalists. Consequently, the board of directors liked him, so she was stuck with him.

For his part, Bob could have left at any time. Others had, and had found new and better opportunities elsewhere. But he felt he had too much of himself invested in the company and that someone should continue to be a voice of reason and truth at OpenSwitch. He believe – quite correctly, it turned out – that eventually the other senior leaders and their methods would fail, and he'd be in a position to help turn things around.

Bill responded to the news.

"Good pick. He's a good guy, and I'm sure he'll do good things for the company."

"Yeah, and he's already cleaning things up. No more BS, no more nonsense. He's meeting with all the senior leaders one by one – dismissing the ones who he doesn't think can do what needs to be done and telling the ones remaining exactly what he expects of them. He's building a real leadership team."

"Good for him. I assume this means you're staying."

"Yes, I spoke with him earlier. No more 'Chief Value Officer' – I'm just the EVP of sales and marketing now, with a mission to help rebuild our reputation and confidence in our brand. First thing on the list is for me to set up a series of one-on-one meetings between him and the CEOs of our top 50 clients so he can reassure them. And once the dust settles on the SEC investigation, he wants a conference call with the Wall Street analysts and top business reporters who follow us."

"Well, good, Herv. I'm happy for you."

"And that's where you come in. I can't do this by myself. I need someone with your skills, your discipline, your gift for organization to help me."

"Is that all?"

"No. I also need someone who can keep me honest and tell me when I'm doing the wrong thing."

"So you want me to be your conscience."

"In a sense, I guess. Look Bill, I know people kind of see us as the odd couple – you the Boy Scout and me the playboy. But the truth is, there's no one in this company – no one – I respect more than you. You're about the only one I can really trust, that I can call a real friend."

"Well, thank you, Herv. I think you know I feel the same way about you."

"I can't promise we'll make OpenSwitch what it once was. But we can make it a decent place to work again. But I need you -- we need you – to do that. If you won't do it for me, do it for all the good people still here who need our help."

"You're laying it on a little thick there, Herv."

"I'm just being honest. But if that doesn't convince you, shoot, just do it for me. Save MY bacon."

Bill smiled as he responded.

"That's more like it."

"And I want you to know that when Bob asked me what staffing changes I planned to make, I told him I wanted to bring you over and he said he thinks that's a good idea. So big endorsement right there."

"I'm surprised he remembered me."

"Well, he did – he specifically remembered some of the work you did for him back in the day. Said you'd be a great choice for my team. So, what do you say?"

"Well, I'll think about it. But I'm going to have some conditions."

"Really? I'm kind of surprised."

"Well, the truth is I have another offer I'm considering. It's very attractive, and if the details work out right, I'm pretty inclined to take it."

"I see. Well, what do you want? What will it take to keep you at OpenSwitch? Bigger title? More money?"

"I think you know me better than that. First, those young women in your office – your 'concubines,' as everyone calls them -- they have to go."

"Bill, I assure you, every single one of them is a highly qualified, highly skilled business professional."

"Good, then it should be no problem finding other opportunities for them at the company."

"Honestly, Bill, anything you may have heard, I promise you there's been nothing going on between them and me. Despite my reputation, the truth is since I married Danielle 15 years ago there's been absolutely no extra-curricular activity. I guess you were a better role model for me than you might have guessed."

"Then why surround yourself with beautiful young women like that?"

"Call it my mystique. Call it my ego, if you want. Even though I'm not a player anymore, I sort of liked people thinking I am."

"And that's why they have to go. If we're going to help turn things around at OpenSwitch, appearances matter. You're a marketing guy – you should get that."

Herve sighed, and responded.

"Okay, you win. I'll starting making some calls first thing in the morning about placing them elsewhere. What else?"

"I want this week's layoff cancelled and everyone restored to their former positions."

"That's a tall order, Bill. I don't know if I can swing that."

"Well, if Bob really wants to do the right thing, he shouldn't have a problem with it. It was a stupid, short-sighted move, and we're going to need those people and their experience to help right the ship."

"I'll see what I can do."

"All of them, Herv, or no deal. Jenny Stuart, Duane Burns, Betsey Wetsel, and everyone else."

"You know about Betsey?"

"Yeah, I heard."

"I'm kind of surprised you want to save her too, since she's the one who took you out."

"She can rise or fall at the company on her own merits from here on out. But she should get the same shot as anyone else. You have a problem with her?"

"Not really. Although she's had one with me for a while."

"Yeah, what IS the deal with that?"

"Well, the truth is right after I got married to Danielle, Betsey and I were at a conference and she came on to me. I turned her down. I think that really pissed her off, and she was worried I would tell people about it. But I never did."

"Well, that's her problem then. But like I said, she gets the same shot as anyone else."

"Okay. I can't make any promises, but I'll see what I can do. I'll talk to the EVP of HR about the layoff and we'll walk it down to Bob tomorrow."

"Tell Bob it's a great way for him to immediately demonstrate to the world that he's calling the shots now and isn't afraid to undo some of the bad decisions Sandy made."

"Good point. Anything else?"

"No, I think that covers it."

"Okay, give me until the end of the week to work this all out. Promise me you won't make any decisions until then."

"Okay, Herv."

"Thanks, Bill. Have a good night."

"You too, Herv."

Bill hung up the call, walked upstairs to the kitchen and put the phone back in its cradle. Maggie was there waiting for him?

"So how did that go?"

Bill sat down at the kitchen table.

"Turns out your husband is a pretty hot property right now. Herv just offered me a job."

"And you've got the offer from Schraber too."

"Yup."

"So, what are you going to do?"

"I don't know yet. But we'll figure it out together."

She smiled at him, letting him know that she was with him no matter what.

Chapter 27

Saturday Morning

Bill came into the kitchen from the garage, grabbed his mug from the counter, poured himself a cup of coffee and sat at the kitchen table. He'd been out in the yard cleaning up the fall leaves since right after breakfast almost without a break, and it was now late morning and he was tired.

He glanced over to where Buddy normally would have been waiting by the kitchen door, expecting to see him there, and winced at the realization that the dog was gone. It was the third time he'd done it that morning, and each time it brought a sharp new stab of pain.

Buddy had been such a great companion and was especially a part of Bill's Saturday morning routine. Bill sat back and drank his coffee slowly, letting it soothe the physical soreness from his morning's labor and the mental ache of his loss.

The yard work had taken him a lot longer than usual because he was working by himself. Olive had an away game for field hockey over in Bixby, and Robert had driven over to watch her, so he wasn't available to help. And of course Bryce was back at college for the fall term. Bill smiled at the thought that his son would be home for Thanksgiving break soon.

Maggie came into the kitchen and greeted him cheerfully.

"All done?"

"Yes. Took a while, but it's all done and cleaned up."

"Good. Now you don't have to worry about it for another year. I can make some lunch for you in a little bit if you want."

"That would be nice. I think I'll take a shower first, if that's okay. Where's the ibuprofen?"

"Hall closet at the top of the stairs. There's a new bottle. Oh, and Howard called while you were outside and asked if we could come over. He said he had something he'd like to show you."

“Oh. Okay. Did he say what it is?”

“No.”

“Do *you* know what it is?”

“Yes.”

Maggie gave him that smile that said “Don’t ask me any more questions.” He knew that when it came to anything involving Howard and him, Judy and Maggie shared all secrets.

“Okay. Let me shower first, and then I’ll go over before I eat.”

Maggie smiled again, with a glimmer of mischief in her eyes, and watched him rise slowly from the table and leave the room.

***

Judy answered the door at the Jones house and welcomed Bill and Maggie warmly. She called out to Howard to let him know that the Wards had arrived and Howard met them in the kitchen.

“Hi, Bill. Thanks for coming over. How’s the job thing going? Made a decision yet?”

“Soon. I have the details from Schraber and OpenSwitch now, so we’ll probably decide this weekend. How’re things going for you?”

“Couldn’t be better. The new position is working out real well, and I’ve been able to bring in some new accounts that’ll really help us grow the firm.”

“That’s great.”

“In fact, I just got a call yesterday from a colleague of yours at OpenSwitch – Herve Pardon. Asked if we’d be interested in helping them manage the fallout from last week’s news and develop a plan for rebuilding the company’s reputation. You wouldn’t know anything about that, would you?”

"No, Herv didn't talk to me about that. But he knows I know you, and about what you've done to help me. And he knows about you and your firm, and what you guys do. I guess he figured if I can trust you, he can too."

"Could be. We're meeting this week. Said there will be another fellow there too – Gar Lewis. Know him?

"Yeah, he just got bumped up to senior director of communications. He's a good guy, good at what he does. You'll like him."

"Good to know."

"Is that why you asked me to come over."

"No."

"Okay. What's up?"

"Why don't you come back in the family room with me?"

"Okay."

Maggie and Judy stayed in the kitchen while Bill followed Howard into the next room, where the Jones' daughter Jade was sitting on the couch. Nestled on her lap was small, chocolate lab puppy. Bill's heart leaped when he saw the dog, and he spoke to Jade.

"Well look at this little fella. When did you get him?"

"This morning. It's a girl. I named her Peaches."

"Well, she's a sweetie, isn't she?

Bill instinctively reached out and scratched the puppy behind her ears, and Peaches responded by nuzzling against his hand. Out of the corner of his eye, he saw something move on the floor over to the left. He glanced over and saw another puppy, identical to the first, in the corner worrying a tennis ball.

"You got two?"

Howard responded.

"That one's yours."

"What?"

"He's yours."

Bill didn't know how to respond, so he walked over and squatted by the second puppy to give him a pat. The puppy forgot about the tennis ball and turned his attention to Bill, who picked him up and stood up. The puppy immediately snuggled in against his neck. Howard broke the silence.

"Jade has been begging for a puppy forever. She always loved your dog and has wanted one for as long as we've known you. Judy and I finally broke down, and I found a breeder nearby whose dog just had a litter. When we went to get ours, we decided we should get one for you too."

"Howard … I can't … this is …"

"What's the problem? You need a dog, I got you a dog. End of story."

"I don't know if … I'm ready."

"Dude – Maggie, Judy, the girls, me, we've all seen how much you've been missing Buddy. The best way to fill that dog-shaped hole in your life is with another dog. Trust me. You're ready."

The dog snuggled in closer to Bill and licked his face. Bill spoke to the puppy.

"How you doin', pal? What do you think? You want to come home with me?"

Howard spoke.

"Peaches and Pal – I'd say that's settled."

"But this must have been really expensive. Can I pay you for him?"

"Nope, he's my gift to you. Call it repayment."

"Repayment for what?"

"For being my best friend."

Bill grimaced slightly before responding. Howard queried him.

"What?"

"You know, to be honest, I don't even like you that much."

Howard laughed.

“Funny. You’re a funny man.”

He called out to Judy in the next room.

“Hey Judy, get ready – Bill Ward just told a joke.”

She called back.

“Shut UP! He did not!”

They could hear the women laughing in the kitchen.

***

Epilogue

Bill Ward returned to OpenSwitch, where he worked with Herve on the turnaround of the company. He remained a business consultant for Schraber Knives, advising the new CEO on how to improve operational efficiency.

Maggie Ward continued to grow her jewelry business, becoming the most successful sales executive in the company’s history, with more than 100 creative artists in her network. Her success allowed her and Bill to retire in their late 50s, and spend their time with family and traveling together.

Bryce Ward proposed to Jasmine Jones on Christmas day, with all their parents approving. They got married the week after she graduated from college. Two years later they had twin boys, who they named Howard and William.

Olive Ward and Robert Perkins continued to date through her senior year high school and college, and got married. She became a Kindergarten teacher and he took over the plumbing business after his uncle retired. They had two daughters, named Maggie and May.

Jade Jones corresponded with Tryone Green while he was at Marine boot camp, and they started dating when he returned home on leave. She attended college with Olive, and after graduating she began working as a graphic designer. She and Tryone married when he graduated from Officer Candidate School as a second lieutenant.

Howard Jones continued to help grow BKP Communications until it was purchased by global public relations firm The YYZ Group. His stock options from the purchase allowed him and Judy Jones to retire early like the Wards.

Duane Burns decided not to return to OpenSwitch and on Bill's recommendation was hired as vice president of operations for Schraber Knives. Duanita Aviles calls her "Uncle Duane" every year on her birthday, and he always sends her a present.

Shannon Gales and Ivory Jones became close friends, and started a local non-profit group called Safe Families, providing education and resources on everything from self-defense skills to personal safety.

Howard and Bill remained best friends for the rest of their lives.

###

Author's Note: Thank you for taking the time to read my first novel, "Ordinary Man." Positive reviews are always a big help for first-time authors. So if you enjoyed it, please consider posting a brief review on Amazon and Goodreads. And if you didn't like it, well, forget I mentioned it.

You can follow what's happening with "Ordinary Man" on my Facebook page, Ordinary Man by RJ Cadmus.

Made in the USA
Monee, IL
13 July 2021

73507231R00166